THE
FIREFIGHTER

THE FIREFIGHTER

SUSAN LYONS

P.J. MELLOR

ALYSSA BROOKS

APHRODISIA

KENSINGTON PUBLISHING CORP.
http://www.kensingtonbooks.com

KENSINGTON BOOKS are published by

Kensington Publishing Corp.
850 Third Avenue
New York, NY 10022

All Kensington Titles, Imprints, and Distributed Lines are available at special quantity discounts for bulk purchases for sales promotions, premiums, fund-raising, and educational or institutional use.

Special book excerpts or customized printings can also be created to fit specific needs. For details, write or phone the office of the Kensington special sales manager: Kensington Publishing Corp., 850 Third Avenue, New York, NY 10022, attn: Special Sales Department, Phone: 1-800-221-2647.

ISBN-13: 978-0-7582-1538-3
ISBN-10: 0-7582-1538-X

First Trade Paperback Printing: February 2007

10   9   8   7   6   5   4   3   2   1

Printed in the United States of America

Contents

Hot Down Under

Susan Lyons

Acknowledgments

As always, deep appreciation to my fabulous critique group, Nazima, Betty and Michelle, and to brilliant brainstormers Nancy, Jude and Kate. Thanks to Doug, because if he hadn't wanted to dive the Great Barrier Reef, I probably never would have made it to Australia. What a wonderful country! Thanks to my editor, Hilary Sares, for asking me to write this novella and for saying, "Sure," when I asked if I could set it in Oz.

My appreciation to the firies at Smithfield Fire Station in Queensland for a fun and informative morning. And thanks to firefighters all over the world. You are true heroes.

I invite my readers to visit my website at www.susanlyons.ca, email me at susan@susanlyons.ca or write c/o PO Box 73523, Downtown RPO, Vancouver, BC, Canada V6E 4L9.

1

"Tash, describe your personality with three adjectives," my grandmother says.

"Hmm?" I lift my head from my book on Australia, and turn to her.

She's dressed for travel in navy stretch pants and a cotton sweater, and looks comfy in the business class seat. The champagne glass on her tray is empty and the women's magazine she bought in the airport is folded to an article with the heading *R U In Synch?*

"It's a test to see how compatible you are with your prospective mate," she explains.

"I don't have a prospective mate."

"You should, you're almost thirty."

"I'm twenty-eight." With nary a serious prospect in sight. And no, I'm not thrilled about that. But you see, I'm not the kind of woman who inspires romance in a guy. I'm the perennial girl-next-door type—and the street is definitely not Wisteria Lane.

"We'll do the quiz for the two of us," Nana says. "See how much we have in common, besides our coloring."

I've never been one to waste time on those foolish girly quizzes, yet she has me intrigued. "Three adjectives for you, and three for me?" At her nod, I think hard. There are a million words to describe Nana but I'm analytical and I want the best ones. "Loving, generous and . . ." I want to say flaky or eccentric, but that would be rude, and I do love my grandmother. "Impulsive. What did you say for yourself?"

"Spontaneous, passionate and loving."

So we hit two out of three. Passionate, though? Well, if she means a passion for living and making life fun—without much regard for the consequences—I guess she's right.

"Now you," she says.

"I'd say, rational, analytical and intelligent."

"I said, intelligent, well-intentioned and uptight."

Okay, so much for holding back on being rude. I really should've said flaky, but at least I'm on the higher moral ground here.

Uptight?

Give me a break, Nana. I'm not uptight. I'm . . well, you know. Rational and analytical. I like lists, I like control, I like predictability. I'm the opposite of a flake.

And yes, we *are* blood relatives. She's my dad's mother.

A male flight attendant pauses beside us. "What can I get you, lydies?" He speaks in an accent that combines twang and drawl. Sounds kind of like a cat with laryngitis. Nana says it's a typical Aussie accent. Well, what else would you expect, flying to Sydney on Qantas?

The accent must be contagious, because ever since we boarded the plane Nana's own faint twang, still present after sixty years in Canada, has been intensifying.

"More champagne, please." My grandmother beams as she lifts the glass she emptied far too quickly.

Oh great. I'm supposed to be looking after her and, since I'm an inexperienced traveler, my parents gave me a list of guidelines. Number one: double-check departure gates and times. Number two: stay hydrated.

"But wine dehydrates you," I caution her. Ms. Well-Intentioned. Yeah, she was right about that adjective.

Nana shakes her head, half fondly, half . . . less fondly. "Come on, Tash girl, live a little for once. Besides, I have a toast to make."

And of course two ladies off on an adventure can only toast in champagne. Okay, she's got this one right too. I grin at her and tell the attendant, "I'll have champagne as well. And can we get two bottles of water, please?"

He fills our glasses with bubbly, tips us a wink. " 'Ere ya go. Cheers."

I raise my glass to Nana. "To a safe and successful trip."

She clicks hers against mine. "Right you are." We both sip, then she takes a deep breath and lets it out, almost like she's letting all her stresses escape with it. "And now here's my toast. To home, Tash. The place of your heart."

We're 32,000 feet up in the air and six hours into a day-long trip across the world to the land Down Under. "To home," I agree, touching my glass to hers. Yes, already I miss Vancouver. My beloved Pacific Northwest. Land of blue oceans and green, forested mountains. Cool colors, a temperate climate. The place where Nana and I belong.

No, I refuse to feel homesick. It's only two weeks. The time will fly by. Nana has inherited her sister's estate and I need to meet with the lawyer, handle a million details, sell the house. Not to mention keep an eye on Nana and make sure her impulsive nature doesn't get her into trouble, as has happened more than once in the past.

My mission—and my family gave me no option but to accept it—is to handle the estate and business affairs, and bring Nana home safely. Although we all adore her, with her generous, loving nature, her joy in life, her charming eccentricities, the consensus is she really is a bit of a flake.

Like, when Mom and Dad picked her up to bring her to my law school graduation, and she was wearing a red sweatshirt proclaiming "Proudest Grandma in the World." Nice sentiment, but yes, I'd have been the laughingstock of my class if Mom hadn't made her change.

That was trivial, though, compared to when Granddad died and Nana wanted to sell the family home and give all the proceeds to her favorite botanical gardens.

Her heart's as big as the world, but unfortunately she doesn't have any of those rational, analytical genes the rest of us inherited from Granddad. Hence—yes, I am a lawyer and the jargon pops out from time to time—my Nana-minding role on this trip.

Poor Nana. This whole thing has to be very hard for her. Although she only saw her older sister every ten or so years, Nana always said Auntie Bet was her best friend. What with my aunt's heart problems her death wasn't a huge surprise, but I know Nana's been mourning.

I have two sisters and a brother. We argue a lot, get on each other's nerves—and I can only imagine how devastated I'd feel if something happened to one of them.

I touch her hand sympathetically, but she lifts it away to raise her glass again. Her eyes are as sparkly as the bubbles in the champagne. "Another toast. To finding a bloke. A handsome, charming, *sexy* bloke."

What? "God, no. Tell me you're not planning on matchmaking. This is a work trip. I won't have time to think about men."

"Not for you, dear." Her eyes narrow as she does a quick top-to-bottom appraisal of me, in my own navy pants and tailored shirt. "Though God knows it's a good idea." Then she shakes her head, seeming to dismiss that thought, and beams at me. "A man for *me*."

"A holiday romance?" I raise my eyebrows. At seventy-seven, she's been widowed for five years. She dates, but after more than half a century of marriage seems happy to play the field. God, I should have seen it coming. Of course she wants a holiday fling.

In some ways, the woman's younger than I am.

Which is, of course, why I'm here to look after her. Good old *rational* Tash, looking after her *passionate* Nana. I want her to be happy, but I can't believe a short term, long-distance romance is going to do it for her.

"Well, good luck with it," I tell her, hearing the skepticism in my voice. Surely the odds are slim she'll meet an eligible guy and actually—*No, Tash, don't go there.* I absolutely do not want to think about Nana and some Aussie . . . you know.

Still smiling—it's one of those secretive smiles—she sips her champagne and settles back to read her magazine.

I unbuckle my seatbelt and stand up to stretch and get my briefcase from the overhead compartment. From it, I take the papers sent by the lawyer in Clifton Beach, Queensland, and start reviewing them to ensure I didn't miss anything the previous three times.

Nana's asleep now, snoring softly. I tilt her seat back, drape a blanket over her and send a thank-you winging to Vancouver. The whole family chipped in to fly us business class, so we'd have some hope of being comfortable on the fourteen-hour flight.

I'm less sleepy than bored, so I shove aside the legal papers and pull out the book my older sister gave me. "So you'll see what you've got yourself into," she'd said.

The book is *In a Sunburned Country* by Bill Bryson. I leaf through, reading snippets here and there, sipping diligently from my bottle of water.

I learn about rip tides, sharks, poisonous jellyfish, and all manner of insects, snakes, plants, etc., etc.—each of which can kill me in its own extremely horrible way. Even those cute kangaroos might pummel you like a boxer with their front legs, and slash you with those huge hind ones. Yeah, apparently Australia has *way* more deadly et ceteras than anywhere else in the world. Nana and I are walking into a death trap. Shuddering, I swap the book for the legal papers, vowing never to set foot in the ocean or the Outback.

A little while later, Nana jerks, gives a back-of-the-throat snort, and she's awake.

I reach over and give her arm an affectionate squeeze. "Nice sleep?"

"Nice dream."

"What about?"

"You don't want to know."

"Why not?" I hate being told what I do or don't want to do or know.

Her lips twitch. "A sex dream, if you must know."

A sex dream? She's teasing. I hope.

She glances at the pile of paper on my pull-out table. "No sex dreams for you, I see."

"Everything looks straightforward. Auntie Bet's will, the real estate papers, the house insurance."

"Tash McKendrick, you can't tell me you didn't already go through those papers a dozen times before we left home."

Okay, there's another adjective for me: thorough. And for her: perceptive.

"I researched house prices in Clifton Beach," I say. "Depending on the condition of this place, you could get half a million. Beach front is pricey."

"I don't think so." She pulls the airline magazine from the pocket flap in front of her and flips it open.

"Yes, really. Nana, when you visited Auntie Bet she was in Cairns. Have you even been to Clifton Beach?"

"We went for the day, last time I came home. When she was thinking of buying there. It's beaut." Her eyes now look a little tired and red, but they're still sparkly. "Did I tell you I have mates there?"

"Yes, you said some other old friends moved at the same time your sister did."

Nana nods. "They all wanted to live in a quiet beach town. Bill and Margaret, and Trev and Allison."

"You knew them when you were growing up?"

"Bill, Margaret and Trev, yes. Trev met Allison when he was away at university in England." She glances down at the magazine, flips another page or two. "Allison passed away earlier this year."

"Oh?"

Nana looks up, the eye-sparkle stronger. "Did I mention that Trev was my first beau?"

"What? Before Granddad?" A horrible suspicion begins to dawn. What's my impulsive Nana, the one who describes herself as passionate, up to? "Nana, you aren't thinking the two of you might, uh . . . ?"

"Hook up?" she says calmly. "Stranger things have happened. We're both widowed, and we always did hit it off."

"But you married Granddad."

She shrugs. "I'm not saying I didn't love him, or that we didn't have a happy marriage. But it was a rebound thing."

I'm in shock. This is a bit of family history she's never seen fit to reveal before. "You were on the rebound from this Trev?"

"He was a couple of years older, wanted to be an engineer, and he let his family send him to England to study." She sighs. "If we'd been more mature, maybe we'd both have waited. But I was right pissed at the bloke, and your granddad came along, a fine-looking, intelligent man, and—" She breaks off. "I married him. Then Trev met Allison at university."

"Granddad swept you off your feet."

She laughs, all the fine lines on her face crinkling. "That's one way of putting it."

"And the other?"

"Got me in the family way, as we said in those days, then went back to Canada. When my parents found out—and mind you, this was still the forties—they wrote his parents. Before you could say 'bun in the oven,' I was on a boat and a church was booked for our wedding. But that'll be our secret, young lady. No one else in the family knows. Your Granddad and I lied about our anniversary date."

For a few minutes, all I can do is stare at her. "Why are you telling me this now?"

She shrugs. "So you don't think I'm too daft if, well, things move a little quickly once Trev and I get together."

Poor old dear, I don't want to see her get her heart broken.

"We've been writing, you know. We still hit it off."

"Oh." Again, she's surprised me.

"At our age, there's no time to waste." She gives a chuckle. "Well, that's true at any age. If something's right, grab onto it."

"Maybe. But there are so many things to do, before you know it's right."

"Like, have sex?"

"God, no!" I squeeze my eyes shut. "Okay, yes, but I really don't want to know about your sex life. I mean, things like making sure you're compatible." Damn, now I'm sounding like her stupid magazine.

"Like, in bed?" Her eyes are sparkling with mischief.

"Good God," I say wryly. "Who is this person who's inhabiting my grandmother's body?"

And suddenly—maybe it's the effect of champagne—but I'm not so bothered by this outrageous conversation. I'm feeling less like I'm with my grandmother and more like she's a girlfriend. Someone I might really talk to, joke with, share secrets with.

But that's crazy. She *is* my grandmother, and I'm supposed to be looking after her, not encouraging her dreamy notions.

She's grinning. "The closer I get to Oz, the more *me* I become."

Oz. She's always called it that, and it always makes me think of the yellow brick road. Here we are, Nana and me, off to meet the Wizard. An odd pair we are, because she's delighted and I'm thinking, there's no place like home and I'd rather be there right now.

"Back in Vancouver," she says, "there have always been so many expectations. From your granddad and his folks, your dad and your Aunt Liz, then all you grandkids. Everyone tried to put some label on me, fit me into some role. I never got to be just Delia." She nudges me in the ribs. "Believe you me, Tash, when Delia was a girl, she was a lot of fun."

Delia's still kind of fun, to tell the truth. Now that she's forcing me to start seeing her as a real person, not just a grandmother. It isn't fair, is it, the way we slot labels onto people. Like, if someone is "nana," we don't see past that, don't ask about her hopes and fears. Her dreams.

But . . . "You're thinking you can go back to being that girl with Trev?"

"Or be a whole new Delia. My family's all grown up now, you don't need me. I'm free, for the first time in sixty years. Just like you, Tash."

"I'm free?"

She laughs. "Footloose and fancy free, if you'd only let yourself. You wait and see, you're going to be a different girl in Oz."

But why would I want to be? I like the woman I am.

"You might even stay there with me," she adds.

"You've lost me. Stay where?"

"In Oz."

"But . . . what do you mean? We're selling the house and coming back home."

She shakes her head, her eyes dead serious. "I know that's what the family wants but I'm not a child and I'll make my own decisions. Tash dear, for me *home* is Australia. Always has been, always will be. If you go back to Vancouver, you'll be traveling alone."

I gape at her. My first thought is, she's nuts.

But she's an adult. Maybe a little eccentric but not stupid. It hurts to think she might be happier in Australia than with us in Vancouver, but she's right that the decision is hers to make.

No, of course she won't stay. This whole thing is a fantasy she's built up in her head. Once she sees the reality, she'll realize she belongs back home.

Of course, if by chance she does decide to stay, the family will kill me.

Oh, damn. What have I gotten myself into?

Our friendly flight attendant stops beside me. " 'Ow's it goin'?"

Crappy. Please God, won't someone come along and rescue me from this impossible situation?

Maybe he reads the desperation in my eyes because he leaps to my rescue in the best way he knows how. "Another glass of the bubbly?"

"Oh, why the hell not."

2

Smoke? Do I smell smoke?

I'm only about a tenth awake and my body's saying, *no, let me sleep!* My exhausted brain recalls travel, travel and more travel. Four airports, three flights and a long taxi ride, transporting me across a nineteen-hour time difference. I roll over and bury my face in the pillow.

But still, there's that smoky smell and it irritates the back of my travel-dried nose and throat so I have to cough.

Where am I, anyhow?

I remember. Australia. In the spare room of the house Nana inherited. The pretty cottage across from the ocean, where the air is warm and humid and scented with flowers as well as the sea.

But now the air reeks of smoke. I fumble for the switch on the bedside light but nothing happens. The power must be out.

The smoky odor's getting stronger. Not cigarette smoke. Nor is it pleasant and woodsy like the old-fashioned fireplace at Nana's house in Vancouver. It's more like—

Jesus! I think the house is on fire.

I leap out of bed. From groggy I've gone to so awake my heart's racing triple-time. The air's hot and dense with that horrible smell. And in my ears there's a strange crackling, rushing sound. Weird, and scary.

"Nana! Nana!"

"Tash!" Her call is faint, almost eaten up by that spooky sound.

I grab my cell from the bedside table, praying the battery hasn't run down. I open it, dial 9-1-1. An operator voice says, "Your call could not be connected. Please check the number and try again."

What the hell? Don't they have 9-1-1 here?

Nana calls again and I toss down my useless phone and run across the room. The hallway's dark and full of smoke and—oh my God, there are flames to my left! Not many, just a few licking out a door and across the ceiling. They're the feelers; the animal is behind them, gathering itself to pounce.

Where's Nana's bedroom? I was so tired last night, I wasn't paying attention. All I remember is, it's a one-story house, with the living room at the front and the bedrooms at the back. Please, let her bedroom be to the right, away from the flames. "Nana? Where are you?"

The floor's warm, making me aware I'm barefoot, wearing only a lace camisole and the skimpiest of bikini panties. I have a lot of skin exposed, and the hot air's stinging every centimeter of it. I turn to my right, stumble down the dark hall, squinting against the smoke. "Nana!"

Behind me I hear a crash and a vigorous, "Shit! Damn. Tash?"

Oh, God, she's behind me, where the fire's burning.

I turn to face thicker smoke and that darting border of flames. Terrified, I walk toward the fire. "Where are you? What was that crash?"

"I fell!" She coughs. "Damn it, I'm trying to get up but—" Her voice breaks off and I hear a moan, then more coughing.

"I'm coming." The smoke scratches at my throat and I have to cough too.

Those flames are mesmerizing. Beautiful, in a strange way, as they curl and dance across the ceiling. I move toward them, staring up into their red-gold depths, unable to look away even though my eyes burn from the smoke.

My feet meet an obstacle and I trip and fall. On top of my grandmother.

"Watch where you're going!" she snaps between coughs.

She's sprawled across the doorway, face down, and I'm crossways on top of her. She must've tripped, then I stumbled onto her.

I pull myself off, glancing past her into the room. And freeze.

Yes, it's her bedroom. I remember it now. The old-fashioned four poster, the picture window with lacy curtains.

Except, the window and curtains aren't there anymore. Instead, there's a wall of flame. Not pretty curls of reddish-gold but a fierce conflagration eating the wall, moving across the ceiling and out the door. Over our heads.

I scramble to my knees. Thank God I'm here to save her. "We've got to get out of here! You have to get up!"

"You think I haven't tried? I must've broken my leg."

We're both coughing, I can barely see her—it's dark, smoky, my eyes are burning and watering.

"Oh, Jesus! Okay, then . . ." I try to think. I'm not tiny, but nor is she. Can I lift her?

Do I have a choice? Lift, drag, whatever it takes, I've got to get her out of here before the beast leaps on us.

"Can you roll onto your back? I'll try to lift you and it'll be easier that way."

Through rasping coughs, she says, "You can't lift me."

"This is *not* the time to be negative."

She gives a choked laugh. "Go for it, girl. Prove me wrong." The laugh dies abruptly as she shifts position, struggles to roll onto her side and gives a couple of wrenching groans that make me shudder in sympathy.

I try to assist as she makes it onto her back, and all the time I'm wondering how I can lift her. Scoop her up in my arms, the way a parent carries a child? Or over my shoulder, in a fireman's lift?

And speaking of which, where are the damned firefighters?

Is the whole neighborhood sleeping so soundly no one's noticed this house is on fucking fire?

Anger gives me a needed surge of adrenaline. I squat beside Nana and get one arm around her shoulders and one under her legs, take a deep breath and lift with all my strength.

I get her up a few inches, gasp for air, choke on smoke, and it's all I can do to put her down without dropping her. My body's pouring sweat and my silk lingerie is plastered to my skin.

When I can speak again, I say, "I'll drag you. Hands under your armpits. It'll hurt, I'm sorry, but there's no other way."

"Do it," she says grimly. Is her voice getting weaker, or is it just that the fire's louder?

I squat again, hook my hands behind her shoulders and under her arms, take another deep breath—shit! I can't breathe without coughing.

Giving up on the idea of deep breaths, I take shallow ones and begin to pull her. Yes, I can do this. In tugs and fits and starts, coughing as I gasp for air, but I can pull her.

The only thing is, I'm not moving her fast enough.

We're inching backwards down the hall away from the fire, which means I'm facing it. The flames are doing a crazy dance, sometimes resting, sometimes leaping.

Through almost constant coughs and moans of pain, Nana says, "Sorry, Tash. My fault. Had a candle burning, fell asleep. The wind came up, must've blown it over."

I don't have any spare breath or I'd say it doesn't matter how it happened, we just have to get out. I keep tugging her. Inch by inch. We've reached the living room, it can't be more than twenty feet to the door. But as the fire strengthens, I grow weaker.

"Leave me," she says. "Save yourself. I love you, Tash."

"I am *not* leaving you!" I manage to rasp out, and give her a mighty jerk.

She groans and I try not to imagine what it must feel like to have a broken leg bumped along the floor like this.

Her coughing stops.

"Nana?" I pause one precious moment, heart pounding even faster, and lean close to her face. "Nana?" *You will NOT die on me!* I can't say the words aloud, and she wouldn't hear me if I did.

She's breathing, I can feel puffs of air from her nostrils, but she's passed out. It's probably for the best. She can escape this nightmare.

But I can't. My burning eyes are leaking hot tears, my skin feels like it's frying and I'd give anything for one breath of fresh air. The noise has grown to be huge, immense. A monster's eating up the house.

We're in its path.

And no one's coming to save us.

My nostrils and throat are scorched, the floor's so hot it burns my knees. And I realize, we may not make it.

I'm panting, sobbing, struggling with every ounce of strength to shift Nana's body. I won't give up, I can't leave her.

Can't see a damn thing now, the smoke's so thick, my eyes so swollen. There are crashing sounds too. Walls and ceiling falling, I guess.

Is this how I'm going to die?

Bryson said Australia was a death trap. I'd imagined crocodiles, slashing kangaroos. Not something so damned prosaic as fire.

My arms are so exhausted they drop feebly to my sides.

I'd feared an exotic death. Box jellyfish. Stonefish. Funnel-web spider.

My shoulders sag, my head's drooping, I want to lie down and sleep. Don't want to die here, so far from home.

Taipan—a snake with the most deadly venom in the world. Paralyzes you.

I *am* paralyzed. I've sunk down on my knees, my body curled over Nana. Coughing helplessly.

Something grabs me from behind.

Crocodile. It's going to take me under the water, do a death roll.

Weakly I slap at it but it crams something over my face and yells, "Breathe!" in a male voice that cuts straight through the din of the fire.

I gulp in . . . air. Air that's not full of smoke. It makes me cough again but I suck in more, greedily. An oxygen mask. Someone did come to rescue us.

I rip the mask off. "Nana!" My hoarse scream tears out of my aching throat.

He forces the mask back in place. Then I'm being lifted, as easily as if I were a baby, and I'm jiggling along in my rescuer's arms as he runs through the living room and out. Out, out the door, outside into fresh night air that makes me cry with relief.

I jerk the mask off again. "My grandmother!"

As he puts me down on the grass, all my sore eyes can make out is a tall, broad shape in firefighter gear. "We've got her. Anyone else in there?"

I shake my head. Realize how good the night air smells. Yes, it's smoky, but nothing like inside the house. Am I imagining it, or is there a scent of tropical flowers?

"Her leg's broken," I tell him. "Be careful with her."

A blanket's spread over me, then someone's handing me a bottle of water. Nothing has ever looked so appealing. The top's off and I gulp it down, and it's fresh too, and cool, cutting through the sooty burn at the back of my throat. My skin's on fire, the blanket's too hot and I shrug it off, and drink greedily.

"Okay, that's enough," my rescuer says. "Put the mask back on. You need oxygen."

In the background my aching ears still hear the roar, crackle, smash of the fire, and there's a bunch of male voices barking back and forth, saying things I can't quite catch. My guy's voice cuts through it all, as fresh and crisp as the cold water.

My eyes struggle to bring his face into focus. Nice. Very nice. Strong bones, tanned skin, eyes that are maybe blue, maybe gray. Can't tell in this light, with smoke-blurred vision. Can't see his hair either. Fair or dark, under his helmet? Either would look good with that face.

And I'd thought the water looked appealing!

His mouth quirks up into a grin and then he's reaching out, one hand on the back of my head, gently hooking the oxygen mask over my face again. Oh, right. He'd told me to do that.

Okay, I'm officially losing it. I guess that's what smoke inhalation and a near-death experience can do to a girl.

"Your grandmother's conscious," he reassures me. "I can see that from here. She's talking to the ambos."

Conscious. I breathe a sigh of relief. But what are ambos?

He reads my puzzled frown. "Right, you're a tourist. Should've known from the accent. Ambos are ambulance paramedics."

I nod my understanding.

"You'll both be going to the hospital in Cairns so they can assess your condition." He glances down my body and something changes in his face. From looking concerned, he's gone to looking . . . interested. Man-woman interested. Not that it's a look I have much personal experience with.

I follow his gaze. Oops, maybe I shouldn't have shrugged the blanket off. I forgot I was wearing skimpy lingerie—and it's now plastered to me, leaving nothing to the imagination.

I'd say my body's pretty average. Slim, toned, nothing special. Guys see me as the gal-pal, best-bud type of woman. Good company for a movie, game, chat or some sex, but nothing to inspire lust.

Soot must be flattering. The firefighter's expression has gone hot and intense.

And I feel a whole different kind of heat flood through my body, in response to that hungry gaze. Life and death. Male and female. Can't get any more basic—primitive—than that.

I want him.

Without knowing the color of his eyes or hair, his name, whether he's married with a half dozen kids, I want him.

His head jerks and he shifts his gaze from my nearly nude body to my face.

And there's a moment. One of those moments, but stronger than I've ever experienced before, where gazes lock and the tension zinging back and forth is almost tangible.

Want you, my eyes tell him.

Fuck, yeah, his say back.

Then he jerks his head again, pulls the blanket over me and lurches to his feet. "You'll be okay now. I have a fire to fight."

I pull the mask off and say, "But . . ."

He's walking away, doesn't hear me. So I don't get a chance to embarrass myself by asking, "Will I ever see you again?"

3

Wearily I shuffle down the hospital corridor in a pair of paper slippers, carrying the bounty given to me by a kind nurse. A face cloth, towel, comb, toothbrush and toothpaste. There are no showers for ER patients, but I can sponge off the soot in the toilet.

I've discovered *toilet* is the word the blunt Aussies use for a restroom. Why do you go there? To pee, mostly. So, call it what it is.

Except, right now my dehydrated body is less interested in peeing than in getting clean. I stand at a sink and stare into the mirror. The face staring back makes me wince.

I'd rather not spend my first morning in Australia in the emergency room, but then, I have nowhere else to go. The only person I know here is Nana, who's been admitted and is sleeping peacefully after having her leg set. They'll keep her today and tonight, under observation. The break's no problem, but she breathed more smoke than I did, and she's older. More vulnerable. But everyone's assured me she should be fine, so I'm hugely relieved.

Along with guilty. She was my responsibility. I shouldn't have fallen asleep without checking to see that she was okay.

If I can find some place to go, they'll discharge me now. They tested my carbon monoxide level, and, good girl that I am, I passed that test like I've passed every other test in my life. Even so, I look like crap and feel seriously grubby.

I start the water running, balance hot and cold, fill the basin. Then I dunk my head and use antibacterial liquid soap to wash my hair and face. I towel myself, then comb my hair and fluff it up with my fingers. The color's okay, a ruddy shade of brown that looks like nutmeg. But it's short, fine and limp. Even with my expensive cut, it'll go flat in no time without styling gel.

My gingery lashes cry out for mascara and my eyes, the same Wedgewood blue as Nana's, look like they've had a rough night. Thank God I at least have great bone structure.

I give my reflection a tired smile, then use the face cloth to give myself a sponge bath.

Okay, now I'm ready to tackle my future.

No purse, wallet, credit cards, passport or other ID. No clothes except the revealing hospital gown and silly slippers.

The logical thing would be to wait until offices open and phone the lawyer who's handling Auntie Bet's estate.

Pride overrules logic. I can't let this be his first impression of me. I'm here in my professional capacity as a lawyer, to handle Nana's affairs. I want to meet the Aussie solicitor looking like a businesswoman, not a waif.

That leaves Nana's friends in Clifton Beach.

But she'd hoped to surprise Trev. She hadn't told her "mates" when we were coming, wanting a day to rest up from travel and get herself prettied up. I don't want to spoil her fun. The woman's going to be in a cast for the next few weeks; she deserves every moment of fun she can wring out of life.

So, I'll have to phone home and ask my family to wire money to a bank.

Nana and I had called them yesterday to say we'd arrived safely. Now I'll have to confess that I, the person they'd entrusted with her well-being, almost let her burn to death.

I step into the bustling corridor and head in search of a phone. Just which family member will I select? Doesn't matter, the news will spread like wildfire.

Fire. The very thought makes me shiver.

"Hey, Tash McKendrick. 'Ow ya goin'?" a male voice calls from behind me.

Behind? Quickly I spin around, grabbing the back of my gown with my free hand and pulling the edges together. Too little, too late, I fear.

And how did he recognize me anyway? Not to mention, know my name?

I'd have recognized *him* anywhere. God knows how, since all I'd seen was a few inches of face, but I know this is my firefighter.

His eyes are blue. Brighter and more vivid than mine. Summer sky blue, against tanned skin. And his hair's glossy black, damp, a little longer than I'd guess is typical for a firefighter.

The man is even better looking than I'd first thought. He's the kind of guy who looks equally good in a tux and in casual clothes such as he's wearing now: jeans, a blue T-shirt worn untucked, some kind of rucksack slung over his shoulder. Tooled cowboy boots.

Hmm. Interesting. Cowboy by day, firefighter by night?

"You feelin' all right?" he asks, and on him that Aussie drawl sounds incredibly sexy.

His question makes me realize I've again gone off into a trance, just looking at him. I flush, from head to toe, as I gaze into those eyes and, yes, it happens again.

Another moment, like last night. A spark leaping back and forth, ready to ignite.

Wow, is this what they call chemistry?

I absolutely will not say, "I want you." At least not in words. So I clear my throat and find neutral ones. "Yes, I'm fine, thanks. They're discharging me." Swallowing smoke has made me hoarse, but the effect's not bad. I've got that Dietrich thing going on.

I glance away from the intensity of his eyes and come back to reality. We're in the middle of a busy hospital corridor. A couple of nurses forget their hurry, though, and dawdle by with their gazes fixed on my companion like he's an oasis in a desert.

Or a firefighter, in the middle of a blazing fire.

Which reminds me . . . "You saved my life." I stick out my hand. "Thank you."

He gives an easy smile. "No worries." Takes my hand, holds it, then something's flowing back and forth between our linked hands. Something fizzy as champagne that makes my entire body zing with awareness.

Thank God the hospital gown is baggy because I know my nipples have beaded. Could use a pair of panties though, if he hangs onto my hand any longer. This man definitely makes me hot.

He's grinning a lazy, suggestive smile. "Can't say it was too much hardship, carrying you out of that house." His gaze flicks down, then up again. Nearly naked. That's what he means.

This man actually likes my body. He doesn't even seem put off by my un-madeup face and unflattering gown.

And there's one thing I know for sure. This is a guy who can afford to be picky when it comes to women. I can just imagine the way they must throw themselves at him.

Speaking of which, it's probably time to disengage my hand from his. Which I do, reluctantly. "Not that it's not, uh, nice to see you, but why are you here?"

"C'mon, let's get out of people's way." Clearly he knows his way around the hospital because he's soon found us a curtained-off cubicle that's empty. "I checked at the front desk and they say your grandmother's coming along nicely."

"She is." And how sweet of him to ask about her.

"The house didn't do so well, sorry to say." He drops a shoulder to let the rucksack slide off, and I dart a glance to his left hand. No ring. He pulls something out of the bag.

At first I haven't a clue what it is, this blackened, twisted lump. Then . . . "My purse."

"Your ID didn't make it through the fire. You'll want to replace your credit cards, passport, driver's license."

I don't want to touch the purse. "The house is really bad?" No one at the hospital has been able to answer that question.

His eyes soften with sympathy. "Looks like it'll be a tossup, whether to restore it or tear it down and start over. Sorry, we did all we could."

I realize he must have just come off shift, after fighting to save Nana's house. "Thank you." But God, what a mess.

"Neighbors said you and your grandmother just arrived last night?"

"Yes. She inherited the place from her sister. We were going to . . ." Well, we hadn't resolved what to do with it. Could we sell a burned-out wreck?

"You got a solicitor here?" he asks.

I draw myself up a little straighter. "I *am* a lawyer."

His eyes crinkle in a quick smile. "No offense. Just meant, if a solicitor was handling the estate, there'd be adequate insurance coverage."

"There is. I've seen the policy."

"So you shouldn't suffer any financial loss." He grimaces. "Just lots and lots of inconvenience."

"Yeah," I agree gloomily.

"You don't want this?" He holds up the purse again.

It had been navy, like a lawyer's purse should be. But the

leather had been the softest, finest imaginable. I'd paid a lot for it. One of those feminine indulgences like my silk lingerie that reminds me I'm a woman.

It can be replaced. Like the house. Like my passport and credit cards. My clothes, jewelry, everything I'd brought with me that I loved. The important thing is, Nana and I will be okay.

I can't tear my eyes away from my purse. If the man who held it in his big, long-fingered hands hadn't come along when he did, Nana and I would be in much the same shape as it was.

For the first time, it really sinks in that we could have died.

The trembling begins in my hands, moves up my arms, then my whole body's shaking and my eyes are filling and overflowing.

"Hey, now." He sounds alarmed, but the next thing I know, he's reached out and gathered me in.

My shaking arms wrap around him and cling. Tears pour down my cheeks.

"It's okay," he says. "Everything's going to be okay."

He's right. We could have died, and the fact that we didn't makes everything else—the losses, the inconvenience and hassles—trivial. Unable to speak, I nod, the movement brushing my nose against his soft T-shirt. Making me aware of the warm, hard muscles underneath.

"I d-don't do this," I manage to gulp out between sobs. "I'm n-not the emotional type."

"Can see that," he says dryly. Then, "It's shock. Everyone reacts differently."

The tears are easing. Emotion spent, relaxing against him, I become aware of the way my senses drink him in. A tangy soapy scent that tells me he showered recently, those fantastic muscles against my cheek. Cautiously my hands move on his back, exploring, finding another set of impressive muscles.

His body stiffens for a moment, then relaxes and now his hands begin to roam. Down my back. One slips inside the opening of the gown and touches—no, caresses—my bare skin just above my waist.

I suck in a breath. Let myself move a little deeper into his arms.

Bring my belly up against the front of his jeans and press, feel him respond.

So's my pussy, not to mention my tits and pretty much every other square centimeter of skin. God knows how I moved so quickly from tears to super-arousal. Maybe it's that life-and-death thing.

But he's feeling it too. His cock's rigid against me and under my cheek his chest is heaving. He lets out a soft groan.

I turn *him* on?

This really is an upside-down land, where a man like this reacts to a girl like me as if he's been on a desert island for the last ten years, and I'm the first woman he sees when he gets off.

Not that I'm complaining. My ego is loving it.

"You don't mean this," he mutters. "It's not me, it's just reaction. From the fire."

"And what are you reacting to? The fire as well?" I raise my head so I can see his face. He's a firefighter, so maybe fire's a turn-on.

His dark cheeks are flushed, his eyes blazing. "God no. You. Just you. But I shouldn't. You're vulnerable."

Vulnerable? The fire, my tears, of course he'd think that. But he's also the hottest man I've ever seen, and the only one who's looked at me this way. Yes, I could have died last night. And that means, if there was ever a time for *carpe diem*, this is it. I'm going to seize the day.

And the man.

"Not vulnerable," I tell him. "Horny. For you."

He gives another groan, then as if he can't help himself reaches down, cups my bottom in both hands through the gown and pulls me up even harder against his erection. I wriggle against it, wishing we were both naked.

Want you. My whole body is saying it, and his is answering back.

"You're not going to turn me down," I tell him.

He gives a choked laugh. "Nope. Be a fool to do that." He starts to bend down for a kiss, then suddenly straightens. "Crap, we can't do this here."

Oh God, we're still in the hospital. I'd lost all sense of my surroundings but now I hear voices on the other side of the screen. Did they hear us too? Hear me proclaim my horniness?

I flush. "No, not here."

We both loosen our grip until we're holding each other lightly, bodies barely touching. Staring into each other's eyes. This is a dream, it must be, for him to look at me with this hunger.

"But we're definitely gonna do it," he says, and it's not a question.

"Oh, yeah, we're gonna do it." A shiver of pure lust ripples through me.

"Then let's get out of here."

"Yes!" Then reality sets in. "Oh no, there's paperwork to sign, and I need to check on Nana, leave a phone number." I bury my face in my hands. "God, I don't have a phone. Or clothes, or any money."

He grabs one of my hands and tugs it away from my face. "No worries. Let's go do it."

"Do . . . *it?*"

A wicked grin, a slanting wink. "I like the way your mind works, Tash McKendrick, but I meant the paperwork."

With a start, I realize something. "I don't even know your name."

"I'm Mick Donovan." He grins widely, squeezes my hand. "G'day, Tash, and welcome to Oz. How'dya like it so far?"

His smile is infectious so I give him one back. "It's been an adventure."

"You ain't seen nothing yet."

His words prove truer than I'd anticipated. I hadn't figured that, half an hour later, I'd be roaring down the wrong side of the road on the back of a silver Ducati motorbike, my arms wrapped tightly around Mick's lean waist.

Wearing pajamas, a bathrobe, hospital slippers and a motorcycle helmet.

This is definitely not my Vancouver lawyer image.

On the other hand, I'm in the land Down Under, where not a soul knows me. The thought is amazingly liberating. So's the rush of wind. And the knowledge that Mick Donovan wants me.

It's like I came out of that fire a new woman. A sexy, attractive one.

A gutsy, probably insane, one.

The old Tash would never take off with a man she didn't know. Wear PJs in public. She'd never prioritize sex ahead of arranging for replacement credit cards.

The fire must've fried a few brain cells because at the moment I don't give a damn about where I'll sleep tonight and how I'll acquire a decent set of clothes. Once I'd reassured myself that if anything happened with Nana the hospital would phone Mick's cell phone—or mobile, as they call them here—I had only one thought in my head. To get naked with Mick.

From everything I've seen and felt, I know he's going to have an amazing body. I wrap my arms tighter around him, snuggle closer against his T-shirted back, feel his muscles flex in response. My nipples perk up under the cotton pajama top, and the throbbing of the bike between my thighs is giving my pussy ideas.

To distract myself, I concentrate on the scenery. Where is he taking me?

From the hospital in Cairns he's headed into a residential neighborhood. Older homes sit side by side with modern apartments, and there are enough exotic flowering trees and shrubs to tell me I'm in the tropics. Not that the warmth of the October sunshine wouldn't have been enough clue.

Mick pulls up in front of a red brick building that looks like it might be a fourplex, with two units up and two down.

Awkward in the clothes the hospital gave me, I scramble off the bike. My body's definitely achy and my skin feels as dry as I imagine the Outback must be. Any chance Mick stocks body lotion?

"Come down with cold feet?" He looks concerned. Disappointed.

Have I? No, I just got distracted by the strange scenery and my aches and pains. Now that those blue eyes are focused on me, I know perfectly well why I'm here. And it has nothing to do with *cold* anything!

I shake my head. "D'you realize this is my first morning in Australia? I've been here less than a day."

"Then let one of the locals make you welcome." He reaches for my hand.

I take it eagerly, my aches dying away as a transfusion of Mick vitality surges into me.

Or is that lust?

He takes me around the outside of the building to the back, where I get a quick glimpse of a courtyard garden with flowering plants and a water feature with a nude cherub, then he points to a flight of steps to the second story. "You live here?" I ask, wondering about that cherub.

"Rent the flat above the landlady," he says. "She's a sweet old duck." He winks. "Pretty much deaf, too."

And why would I care if she was deaf? Does he think I'm a screamer?

If so, he's going to be disappointed. I'm a good enough

lover—I know all the moves—but I'm not one for raking my nails down a man's back and screeching like a banshee.

The stairs are narrow and he starts up ahead of me, with an animal-like grace. He thrusts open the door, grabs one of my hands, pulls me inside and then we're kissing.

For a first kiss it's—OH MY GOD.

Usually there's some fumbling, testing, trying to find the right angle. Wondering how soon to open. Figuring out if the other person's a sucker, nibbler, slobberer.

Mick is—I have to say it again. OH MY GOD. Perfection.

He has the best lips imaginable. Soft but firm. Gentle but utterly masculine. He teases, sucks one corner of my mouth. Lazily, like he has all day. But he pulls me close, very close, and his erection is talking a whole different, more urgent, story. My pussy's an eager audience.

His seductive lips flirt across my top lip, suck the bottom one, then his tongue licks the seam between them.

I'm so lost in the sensations, I don't even know if I'm responding or just standing there in a state of bliss, letting myself be kissed.

4

My state of bliss ends abruptly when I realize I probably stink of smoke, despite my sponge bath. I ease away an inch. Mick shows no signs of being turned off—the indicators definitely point in the opposite direction—but my feminine pride makes me say, "I need a shower."

"No you don't." He pulls me back, nuzzles my neck below my ear.

"Why don't you join me?" Hoarseness makes my voice sexy and suggestive.

"Shower together?" I feel his smile against my skin.

"You could help me get clean." I envision his soapy hands running over my breasts, down my tummy, between my legs. Nerve endings ignite, the heat of arousal rushes through me.

He lifts his head and gives me a cocky smile. "I could help you do lots of things."

And hopefully one of them is achieve orgasm. "Prove it to me in the shower."

He undoes my sash and tugs the bathrobe off my shoulders. Suddenly I'm nervous about getting naked. I have small, high tits and an ass to match, with only a gentle curve of hip. If Mick's into voluptuous . . .

Wait a minute, he's already seen my body. Next to naked, in my skimpy lingerie. And he was turned on.

Mick starts to undo the buttons of my pajama top and I really wish I had some of my secret indulgence lingerie now, not this plain-Jane outfit.

I bat his hands away. "Where's the bathroom?" Every woman looks beautiful in the shower, with water streaming down her body. Right?

"Over here." He leads me across his living room.

I'm guessing the apartment—flat, as he calls it—came furnished. The antiques and chintz patterns don't look like Mick. They're attractive, but not masculine.

And he is most definitely both.

I step into the bathroom and see it's similar to the one in Auntie Bet's house. A ceramic tile floor with a drain in the centre. A combination tub/shower where there's no shower rod or curtain, just a half-door at the shower end. No drain in the tub. Nana told me, if the tub overflows, the water goes down the drain in the floor. Weird, how different countries have these small, distinct variations in how they handle the basics of everyday life.

Sure, Tash, think about the plumbing rather than whether he'll find you sexy.

Nervously I scramble out of the pajamas, step into the tub and get the shower going—not too hot because my skin's so sensitive from the fire—then turn to face Mick.

The expression on his face, the erection under his fly, tell me he does find me sexy.

I breathe a sigh of relief. "Lonely in here." I dip my head under the spray to give him the hopefully irresistible image of water cascading over a naked female.

When I emerge from the water he bends down to take off his

boots. Then he straightens and in one quick move yanks the T-shirt over his head.

My breath catches. Wow! He's broad-shouldered and powerful, but leaner than most of the body-builders at the club, his muscles long rather than bunchy. Tanned a rich, uniform brown, he looks like a guy who swims, surfs, spends a lot of time being active outside. The opposite of me, who's usually in an office, and gets my exercise at a fitness club.

This is definitely not a man who's bought into the trend to get rid of body hair, and I thoroughly approve. Dark curls spread across his pecs and a trail V's down to his waist.

I'm happy to stand back and enjoy this striptease. And a tease it definitely is. Who ever said women didn't get off on looking? I'm here to prove they're wrong, in the way my nipples bud, my pussy swells and melts.

I'm too turned on, too curious to feel nervous anymore.

He unfastens the button at his waist. My gaze is on his distended fly as he lowers the zipper. He shoves his hands into the sides of his jeans, and begins to pull them down, along with his underwear.

His skin's a shade or two lighter here, but still tanned. Then his cock springs free. He gives a sigh of relief.

My sigh is admiration. Oh, yes! Now, that's exactly the way a cock is supposed to look.

He gives it a quick stroke from bottom to top. Like he's greeting an old friend.

Normally I'm kind of inhibited, especially with a new guy, but that's not how I feel with Mick. I want to touch him. All of him, but mostly that thick brown shaft with the bulging veins and dark, swollen head. I realize I've opened my mouth, am running my tongue around my lips. Tasting innocuous shower water, when what I want is his musky flavor in my mouth.

He has me so hot and bothered, I have to find a way of retaliating. I pick up the bar of clear green soap by the shower and get my hands nice and sudsy, then run them over my breasts in slow, sensual circles, pausing to fondle the beaded nipples.

His cock jerks and he grasps it again, holding it as he watches me.

I let my head fall back, run my tongue around my lips again, as suggestively as I know how. The arch in my back has thrust my breasts out, and I continue to soap round and round, teasing the nipples.

A part of me is saying, *who is this woman?* Where did I get this self-confidence?

Well, that's easy. Mick gave it to me, in the hungry way he watches me. As if the woman he sees is utterly sexy. And so he makes me believe it.

He releases his cock and steps into the tub. "I'm glad you came to Oz."

"Me too." On the plane, I'd wished myself back in Vancouver. Now I'm Dorothy, in a magical world.

He moves forward, takes my head between both of his strong hands and angles it just the way he wants, then leans down and kisses me. He thrusts both our heads under the center of the shower and I close my eyes against the streaming water.

Delight. In this land, kisses come under waterfalls, in rainbow colors and showers of stars behind my closed eyelids.

But I can't breathe. Gasping, I tear my lips from his, thrust my head out of the spray and gulp in air. Then I pull him close and this time initiate the kiss.

His body's hotter than the water cascading over my shoulders. He brands my front from chest to thighs, his rigid cock trapped between our bellies.

My hands roam, exploring his powerful shoulders, moving down his back as it tapers to his waist, dipping into that special spot at the base of his spine. Then down to curve around his muscular ass.

So much sensation, I'm overwhelmed.

His lips soft yet demanding, his tongue flirting its way into my mouth, tasting faintly of coffee and mint. Mint, kind of like the green herbal smell from his soap that permeates the damp air. The flex of his butt muscles under my fingers, the hot water pounding my back and splashing over my shoulders to wet Mick's chest, slicking the curly black chest hair against his body.

The pouring-rain sound of water almost covering the smaller sounds, the little gasps and moans we both make.

And in the center of it all, that bold thrust of cock.

I wriggle against it, wishing I were taller, wanting that firm pressure between my legs.

He eases his mouth from mine and then he's bending, touching his lips to my nipple. Sucking and playing with it like he did with my lips. Water slips and slides across my skin, but his mouth centers, focuses, draws all my concentration to my breast.

No, not *all* my concentration. What he's doing to my nipple creates an immediate response further down, where I'm already throbbing with need.

I'm tempted to tug on his hair, pull him up, tell him I'm ready. Yes, usually I love foreplay—need it, to be honest, to get me in the mood—but the woman in the shower isn't the usual Tash. She's a creature forged by fire, and she's inflamed and hungry and wants this man inside her. *Now.*

Mick raises his head and I think, *yes, now!* but then he begins to suck my other nipple and the sensation is so exquisite I moan, "Oh, yes," and throw back my head.

My gaze catches the shadow of a movement. Across the room there's a mirror above the sink. And in it, my own reflection.

Wow. I look like a woman in an erotic movie. The water's darkened my hair and it clings to my head, otter-smooth, calling attention to my dramatic bone structure.

The mirror reflects the back of Mick's head against my breast.

He tugs my nipple gently with his teeth and I gasp. Watching my own reaction in the mirror, seeing the flush on my cheeks, doubles my arousal.

His head moves and now he's tracking kisses down the center of my body. I can guess—hope—where he's going.

When he reaches my navel he does something I can't even describe, kind of like puffing air into it but better. His lips hover on my skin and they and his tongue vibrate, like he's humming or playing the harmonica.

Then, in the mirror, his head disappears from sight. Trickles of water run from my shoulders down to small, firm breasts with rosy budded nipples. My rib cage and flat stomach are shiny with water.

Mick kneels. A gentle hand urges my legs further apart. His tongue slides between them, separates the swollen folds. The woman in the mirror arches, eyes widening, mouth open as she lets out a sound that's half moan, half whimper.

He does that throbbing vibration thing again and my body hums along with him. He licks along me, into me, then there's a finger beside his tongue, then two, and I stretch for him.

I gaze down. All I can see is the top of his head, the back of his shoulders. Water's splashing onto him like he's kneeling under a waterfall. Worshipping the goddess of the waterfall.

I stare back into the mirror. The goddess is me, all flushed and wild and passionate, breasts literally heaving as I suck air in and out through my open mouth. Oh God, his tongue's on my clit. And now his lips, and he's doing that humming thing around it and my clit's dancing to his tune.

I forget about the mirror and focus on what Mick's doing with his incredible mouth and fingers. Inside me, everything tightens, draws together, my body's rushing toward orgasm. My muscles clamp down on his fingers and he vibrates air all around my nub, tongues it gently and the waves crash through me. My knees go so weak I have to grab his shoulders or I'll collapse.

He stays with me, gentling my body through the aftershocks. Then he rises slowly, hands on my hips to hold me steady.

"Incredible," I murmur, reaching for his head to pull him close for a kiss. Suddenly I realize I've had almost no sleep for the last two days, and my body's just enjoyed the best orgasm of my life. All I want to do is get dry and fall asleep with this man.

His kiss is too quick. Impatient. When I snuggle close, of course he's still hard. And that quickly, with just the feel of that rigid organ, I'm wide awake.

My body's never managed multiple orgasms, but I want to feel him climax. Except, we're naked in this shower and something else I don't do, is unprotected sex.

But he's had the same thought. He pulls away from me, steps dripping from the tub and I see we've already soaked the bathroom floor with our splashing. He reaches into a cabinet and in a moment he's back, ripping open the square package, sliding on a condom.

Then he lifts me. My legs wrap around him, my arms circle his neck. He grips me under the butt, holding me so that finally my pussy, swollen and still sensitive from orgasm, is in direct contact with his cock.

I ease up and down in his arms, sliding against his length.

He groans and kisses me, hot and demanding. Urgent.

The urgency's contagious, and now I need to feel him inside me. I tear my mouth from his. "Yes, Mick. Now."

We shift, adjust positions, then he's moving into me, sliding the thick head of his cock between my slick, swollen lips. He's big, but my body stretches to swallow him up.

Friction, hot wet delicious friction as he eases all the way in until the base of his cock rubs my clit. He rests there a moment, my nerve endings scream *move!* The he slides out, almost all the way, then thrusts back and my clit waits eagerly for that tight press when he's fully inside.

He sets a rhythm. The pound and splash of the shower is a background counterpoint to the steady in-out thrust of his cock, the rising beat of our panting breaths.

Each movement teases my nub, and it's craving hard, firm pressure. Mick knows it, I'm sure, and he's deliberately drawing this out. He gives me a little pressure, and when my body's tightened and my breathing gone so shallow I'm almost not breathing at all, he changes the angle, eases off, and the tension relaxes.

And then it dawns on me. For the first time in my life, I might have a second orgasm.

Now it's within reach, I want it so badly. I deserve it, after all I've been through.

And if he doesn't give it to me, I'm going to kill the guy!

I capture his mouth, pour everything I've got into the kiss. Every ounce of that sex goddess I saw in the mirror.

And it works, his movements change, stop being rhythmic and start going wild and uneven. Even so, he manages to find the exact angle to stimulate me, inside and out.

We break the kiss, both panting for air.

All my nerves are wound tight, screaming for release, and he thrusts hard and I'm almost there and then he's sliding out and rushing back in again, grinding his pelvis into mine and yes, that's it—and OH MY GOD!—that's exactly it, and he yells out his release as I climax in spasms all around him.

It seems like we cling together for hours in that pulsing orgasm.

Gradually, sexual satiation fades pleasantly into tiredness. My head's on his shoulder and I could close my eyes and go to sleep.

"Hey, Tash." He jiggles my body. "Don't go to sleep."

HOT DOWN UNDER / 41

I struggle to raise my head. "You're mean."

His whole body shakes with laughter. "Better not insult the guy who's holding you up."

Oh yeah, right. I'd almost forgotten, it's so comfortable here in his arms. But the poor man is hoisting well over a hundred pounds.

Reluctantly I let him ease out and set me down. "Sorry, I'm just so tired." My body illustrates the point with a jaw-wrenching yawn.

"One of those women who falls asleep right after sex?"

"I was tired at the hospital," I protest, "but you made me forget. D'you know I was traveling for more than twenty-four hours, then only got a couple of hours sleep before the fire, and there's the jet lag factor too, and—"

"Tash?" he breaks in. "I was teasing."

"God," I groan. "Sorry. My brain's not functioning." I yawn again.

"Let's get you to bed."

"Have to wash my hair." I gaze around, bleary-eyed and fuzzy-headed, looking for shampoo.

He sighs. "Girls. Course you do."

Girl? "I'm a woman," I grumble.

He chuckles. "Yeah, I'd noticed. Sorry. You some kind of feminist?"

"You some kind of chauvinist?" I retaliate, knowing Aussie men are reputed to be. Damn it, he may give amazing sex, but a woman deserves respect too.

He laughs. He also takes me gently by the shoulders and tips my head back, into the shower spray, careful the water doesn't run down my face. "Not so's I've noticed."

"Good." I think about his work, and how it must attract alpha males. "Are there many female firefighters here?"

"Sure. Not as many, because the physical tests involve things like lugging a lot more pounds than you even weigh."

"If they make it, are they treated as equals?"

He picks up a bottle and squeezes some of the contents into his hands. "A few of the guys give them a rough time. But the women bring a lot to the team and the other firies are learning to respect and trust them."

"Uh, firies?" I try to replicate his Aussie twang, not sure if he said "fairies," or what.

He turns me so my back is to him, and begins to shampoo my hair. Oh, bliss!

"We call firefighters firies here," he says. His fingers stroke through my hair, massaging my scalp, making it hard to concentrate on anything else. "You know," he adds. "Oz is the place where we add 'ie' to everything. Barbecue's a barbie, can of beer's a tinnie."

"Firefighters are firies?" I giggle.

He pauses in his scalp massage. "Yeah. What's so funny?"

"Sounds like fairy. Which in Canada's a word for gay. And I'm guessing that's not how most of you alpha male *firies* want to be thought of."

He chuckles. "Too right. Course we do have a few gays, including a couple of the female firies, but yeah, there's lots of testosterone at the fire station."

Testosterone. Mick has it, in plentiful supply. But he isn't above shampooing a woman's hair, and making a fine job of it. His hands are like his lips. Soft but strong, gentle but deft.

I sigh with pure enjoyment.

When he eases my head back and rinses the suds out, I regret the end of the massage. "I always shampoo twice," I tell him. It's only the truth, after all.

"I can arrange that." He lathers up again, and repeats the shampoo massage. I let him support most of the weight of my tired head and think blissfully that I could handle hours and hours of this. Day after day. I yawn again and close my eyes.

Somehow I manage to stay on my feet as he rinses my hair

again, then soaps my body. I'm grateful he doesn't linger too long on my erogenous zones. I don't have the energy for more sex, no matter how wonderful it might be.

Dimly I'm aware of him saying, "You're asleep on your feet." And of turning off the shower and drying me with a big towel. Then he hoists me into his arms and next thing I know I'm sinking down between navy cotton sheets, rolling over, feeling his warmth spoon against my back and . . . I'm gone.

When I wake, it happens slowly. I'm aware of a sense of well-being, comfort. Smugness, like I've done something wonderful.

Gradually, awareness seeps in, like a movie being rewound in slow motion. The sleeping man beside me. Amazing sex in the shower. The motorbike ride. The hospital—oh God, Nana!

5

I jerk up in bed. Is Nana okay? What time is it? Light streams through the window, so at least it's still daytime. Mick's bedside table holds a clutter of newspapers and books, a coffee mug, a beer can, but I don't see a clock.

Grabbing his shoulder none too gently I shake him. "Mick, wake up."

He grunts, yawns, stretches, gives me a happy grin. "Hey, Tash."

"I have to phone the hospital. What time is it?"

His gaze sharpens and he nods. "Yeah, course you do. But don't worry, they'd have called if there was a problem." He sits up, scans the messy table. "Where's my mobile?"

"Mobile?"

"Mobile phone. Oh yeah, right. Jeans pocket."

Then he's out of bed, walking in a long-strided saunter to the bathroom.

Good God, he looks fantastic. I pinch my arm. Wince. Yes, it's really me. I actually had sex—double orgasmic sex—with this beautiful man. And he woke up seeming happy I was there.

He leans out the bathroom door. "It's one o'clock. Heads up."

"What?"

"Catch?" He holds up his cell—mobile—phone. Then he tosses it straight to me. "Gotta take a piss." He retreats into the bathroom.

Okay, he may be beautiful, but he's definitely a guy.

I open the phone and realize I have no clue of the number or even the name of the hospital. From the bathroom I hear the toilet flush, water running, then he saunters out in all his glorious nakedness. This time I try hard not to notice. "Phone number?"

"Sorry, wasn't thinking." He takes the phone from me, calls directory assistance, then dials a number and hands the phone back.

As I take it, he stretches lazily, then sinks down and starts doing push-ups. Still naked.

When a woman answers I explain who I am and ask how Nana's doing.

"I'll check for you, dear," she says with cozy informality. Waiting, I enjoy the scenery.

Then she comes back. "She had a nice lunch, we have her medicated for the pain in her leg and she's having an afternoon nap. Everything's looking beaut."

I'm relieved but feel guilty. Poor Nana woke alone, hurting, in a foreign hospital. While I was sleeping off fantastic sex. First I almost get her killed, then I abandon her. Did I leave all sense of responsibility back home in Vancouver? "When she wakes, would you tell her I called? I'll be in as soon as I take care of a few things."

I hang up. God, there's so much to do. I have to make a list. I have a terrible memory, and I'm paranoid about forgetting things, so I'm addicted to lists.

Besides, every time I look at Mick I lose my train of thought.

He stops with the push-ups and rises easily to his feet. " 'Ow's she goin?"

"Good. But I can't believe I left her to wake up alone."

"The nurses will've been good to her." He sits on the bed and touches my arm. " 'Sides, you needed rest."

True, and I'd love nothing better than to go straight back to sleep. Except, maybe, to see if sex with Mick is as great out of the shower as in. But neither's in the cards right now.

"I need to see Nana, but first I need clothes," I tell him, a bit panicky. "And I have to deal with my credit cards, get some money, figure out where I'm going to stay tonight."

"Can stay here," he says.

Not being a girl who takes things for granted in relationships, I'm pleased he's not tired of me yet. "That's, uh, generous of you."

"Selfish." He strokes my arm so lightly his fingers just skim the surface, and all the fine hairs stand up to greet his caress. Amazing how erotic this can be, a simple touch on the arm.

For him, too. His cock's rising and I want to touch, fondle, lick, explore every inch of it.

"Oh, Mick, I can't relax until I see Nana and get my life under control."

One corner of his mouth turns up. "Got a bit of a thing about control, do you?"

"I guess." I'm not a control *freak*, but I do like being organized, having my list, feeling like I control my life rather than vice versa.

Since I first smelled smoke, life's thrust me onto a rollercoaster and I need to slow down, assert myself. Not give in to the temptation of this naked man with the sexy blue eyes, the seductive smile, the swelling penis.

The stroking fingers. I groan and wrench my arm away. "Stop doing that."

He laughs. "Okay, okay. No worries." He walks over to a

dresser. "We'll get you *organized*, then to the hospital. But after that, I'm having my way with you."

Good-natured. Especially for an alpha male. The lawyers I know would've turned this into a power struggle. Tried to manipulate me into bed, where they'd have had an orgasm and I'd have lain stressed out, making my list in my head. How did I have the great good luck to be rescued by a firie who's gorgeous, a great lover *and* considerate?

He turns, his expression serious. "Something I need to say."

Our gazes meet. "Okay," I respond warily.

"Should've said earlier," his voice is apologetic, "that I'm not into anything serious. But I like you, Tash. It'd be fun to spend some time together."

I have to smile. "How can you like me? You barely know me."

"Know you're brave enough to risk your life to save your nana. Know you're sexy and passionate."

Three adjectives again, but different ones this time. Brave, sexy, passionate. No, the man doesn't know me at all. But I like the way he views me. "I like you too," I say. "I like how you make me feel. And no, Mick, I'm not into serious. I'm only here for two weeks, to help Nana."

He studies my face carefully and I know he'll see I mean it. Suddenly I remember my grandmother's and my conversation on the plane, and laugh. "Nana's going to be thrilled. Seems she's a great believer in holiday flings." And I'd thought the notion impractical and foolish, but the fire and Mick have made me a convert. My analytical brain can even rationalize that it'll be good for me to have great sex, as well as the ego boost of having Mick find me attractive.

He chuckles. "Your nana sounds like a bonza lady." He tosses me a T-shirt and a pair of shorts. "See how these go."

"Thanks." Men's clothes. Better than PJs, but I'm still going to look like a clown.

For the first time since I woke up, I think about my appearance. Gingerly I touch my hair, then wrinkle up my nose. Bedhead. "You don't have any hair gel, I suppose?"

"No way."

Nah. Macho guys don't use that stuff.

In the bathroom I study my reflection. Hmm. Not as bad as I'd expected. My hair's kind of spiky, but it's got body, for once. My eyelashes cry out for mascara, and I add to my mental list. Thank God Mick does have some heavy-duty, guy-type hand lotion, and it's just what my parched body needs.

When I put on his clothes, the only good thing is the T-shirt's so big it hangs down to cover the baggy shorts.

When I come out of the bathroom he's wearing a similar outfit, but his T-shirt hugs lean muscles and the shorts reveal gorgeous legs. Not fair. He studies me, lips curving.

"Yeah, I know," I say, trying to be a good sport. I've always done well at that; it's part of the reason I'm good best-bud material. "Pretty funny, eh?"

"You wearin' anything under that shirt?"

I pull it up to show him the shorts. "Of course."

"Nothing like a sheila in a bloke's shirt," he says. "Makes a man think of sex."

Well . . . okay then!

Before we leave, I borrow paper and a pen and start my list. Then he helps me order a replacement charge card to pick up later, and in the meantime loans me some cash. I call the lawyer and insurer to set up appointments for tomorrow. Hurray, three ticks on my list.

Then we head out for shopping and lunch.

"First stop, a shoe store," I tell him as we climb onto his Ducati. I've almost worn through the paper slippers.

It's a short ride to an area filled with funky shops and cute restaurants. The first shoe store has fun casual wear, not what

I'd normally choose at home, but this isn't the time to be picky so I buy a flirty pair of green flip-flops.

Hand in hand, Mick and I wander down the block. I enjoy the sunshine, peer in windows. After a couple of bumps from other pedestrians, I realize Aussies walk on the wrong side of the sidewalk. They're also doing a lot of staring at me, and nudging each other.

"What's up with all the wink-wink, nudge-nudge?" I ask Mick.

"Looking like that, they figure you just rolled out of my bed," he says smugly.

"Really?" If I was walking Georgia Street in Vancouver, among businesspeople and shoppers, I'd be too embarrassed for words. Here, where no one knows me, where I'm strolling with the hottest guy in all of Cairns, I feel pretty darned smug myself.

I bump my hip against his. "Perceptive, aren't they?"

He bumps me back. "What next? Food or clothes? Or wanna go to my place and roll back into bed?"

I bump him a little harder. "Food." A minute ago, my female vanity would have voted for clothes. But now I'm reveling in this people-know-we-just-had-sex feeling. Besides, I'm starving and all these neighborhood restaurants are sending out delicious aromas. "Something quick. I still have so much to do."

He points kitty-corner across the street. "That pub has good basic food, and it's fast."

Although I'm tempted by Thai, Indian and Italian, fast basic food fits today's bill. "Sold."

Inside, it's dark after the sun. The place has an English pub feel with heavy wood and a dartboard. The menu's on a blackboard behind the bar, and we step up to order. Mick opts for a burger and fries and I, aiming for healthy, say, "A tuna sandwich on multigrain, with salad."

He orders draft beer, I choose a glass of Australian sauvignon blanc and we settle at a window table to wait for our meals. Across the table, he takes my hand, and I feel a quick zip of sexual energy. But right now, my list is more important.

I give his hand a squeeze then pull out my list. He gives a resigned sigh and raises his beer.

"Tomorrow I'll have to cancel my other charge cards, arrange a new passport. Driver's license—God knows how I deal with that. Find a hotel for Nana and me. Talk to the lawyer about the prospects of selling, now that the house . . ." I shake my head sadly. "It was a pretty house, Mick. Auntie Bet had a great garden, and a bunch of knickknacks she obviously loved."

"Prime location, right across from the beach. Your nana selling?"

"I hope so." Surely she would now. The fire had to be a bad omen, a message there was nothing here for her.

"So, Tash." He sprawls back in his chair, one hand on his beer glass. "You got all this stuff to deal with, but what else you have planned for this holiday?"

"It's not a holiday. Just doing what we need to do, then going back home."

"Wonder when your nana's going to be up to traveling?"

"Oh, damn, I hadn't thought of that." Even if I can persuade her to come back where she belongs, she may not be able to travel. I bury my face in my hands.

"No worries." He reaches over to touch my forearm. "Things'll sort out."

"Easy for you to say."

Our meals arrive and I salivate at the sight of his French fries before noticing I didn't get my salad. "I ordered a sandwich with salad," I tell the young server.

"Yeah?" she says, seeming not to see a problem.

Mick gives a quick laugh. He lifts off the top of my sandwich and I see lettuce, tomato and beet. Sliced beets? Odd.

"Salad," he says. "It means veggies in a sandwich. Did you want a separate salad?"

I shake my head. "Forget it, I don't care." Suddenly it's all too much. Salad doesn't mean salad? And beets, in a tuna sandwich?

"'Ere," Mick says, shoving my wine glass toward me. "Bottoms up, then have another. And let's talk about your holiday."

"It's not—"

"Yeah, yeah, I heard you. But you can't come all this way and not see Oz. Look, I'm off for three days, I can rearrange some things, free myself up. We can go sailing, snorkeling, hot-air ballooning—"

"Ballooning?" Despite my better judgment—what keeps those balloons in the air anyhow?—I'm intrigued. "They do hot air ballooning here?"

His grin's a bit sly but all he says is, "Sure do."

God, he's tempting. A gorgeous, sexy man volunteering to tour me around. And from the sparkle in his eye, tour guide isn't the only service he's offering. My blood heats in response.

Reluctantly I shake my head. I have responsibilities. "I doubt I'll have time for tourist stuff." I flush, embarrassed. "Um, sex is great, though. I hope we can, uh, see each other sometimes."

He chuckles. "Figure we can work that out. And some holiday stuff too. Now eat your lunch, drink your wine, we'll start getting things sorted."

Despite his easygoing ways, he's surprisingly efficient. After I make another call to confirm Nana's all right, he guides me around the shops. I buy a couple of brightly colored tank tops, a light cardigan, shorts, a broomstick skirt in blues and greens, a turquoise bikini that for now serves as undies. My choices are brighter and more casual than what I typically wear at home, where I have that lawyer reputation to maintain, but they suit the sun and the extravagant tropical flowers.

Mick's persuading me into a holiday mood, as he pulls clothes off the racks for me to try, teases me about my choices, drapes an arm over my shoulder while I study shop windows. Each glance, each touch, sends a little zing through me, making me think of and crave sex with him.

I try to keep my focus. Next on my list, clothes for Nana. Easy here, because she's always enjoyed vivid colors. Then I say, "Now I need a suit and proper shoes, to see the lawyer."

"Don't need to be stuffy, to get business done."

Hmm. Maybe I don't, in the village of Clifton Beach. Can I actually go in the broomstick skirt and green flip-flops? I laugh, loud and free. "Why not?"

He pulls me close for a kiss that has me tingling from head to toe. And mostly in between.

"What's that for?"

"Felt like it. You're so pretty, so sexy, such a good sport about all this crap that's been happening to you. Just makes me want to kiss you. And by the way, when I kiss you . . ." He presses his groin against me suggestively.

My body heats and I ease away. "Me too. And *you're* the good sport. Spending your day off helping me get my life back in order."

He laughs. "Yeah, major hardship, spending time with you."

God, but he's sweet.

"You're saying you actually enjoy shopping with a woman?"

He shrugs. "Maybe wouldn't be my first pick. But a person can turn anything into fun, right?"

Well, Mick sure can.

Next on the list is a drugstore, which he calls a chemist's. He waits outside for that one, but when I stop at a lingerie store he's through the door ahead of me.

"Here, this'll suit you." He holds out a black silk and lace camisole with matching tap pants.

They're the kind of thing I'd have picked for myself. My

taste in undies has always bordered on risqué. Have to do something to balance that sedate lawyer exterior.

Mick's hand brushes the side of my breast. "Try them on. I'll find you some other stuff."

The salesclerk, an older woman, is occupied with two giggling girls who are picking out items for one's honeymoon. She waves me toward the back of the store.

There, I find a decent-sized fitting room. When I change into the black lingerie, the mirror gives me back a reflection that makes me grin. Just wait until Mick sees me like this. If he liked me in baggy PJs, he'll love me in black lace.

The fitting room door begins to open and I let out a squeak, then see it's Mick, carrying slinky and lacy clothes in all shades. His eyes widen. "Knew you'd look good in that." He drops the other clothes on the chair. "Gives a bloke ideas."

Then he locks the door and pulls me into his arms, leaning down, slanting his mouth across mine, beginning a kiss that's soft and seductive. He doesn't give me a chance to respond; his lips are on the prowl—across my cheek, over to my ear. He sucks the lobe, darts his tongue inside. I imagine that sexy mouth on my pussy and feel my tap pants growing damp.

"Oh yeah," he whispers, "lots of ideas." He pulls me up against him, so I can't avoid knowing what kind of ideas. His cock's hard and all my female parts quicken in response.

I groan. "Mick, we can't."

"Can too. Just have to be quick. And quiet."

This is insane. We'll be caught. Arrested, or at the very least, embarrassed and tossed out on the street.

Me in a cami and tap pants, Mick with his shorts and boxer briefs down around his ankles, which is where he's shoved them while I've been making a list of the "cons" of doing this. There's one very big "pro," though. His hungry erection, staring up at me.

And another. The hunger in my own body, that's been building since we woke up.

He brushes the pile of lingerie off the chair, finds a condom in his shorts pocket, sits down. "Come here," he murmurs, sheathing himself.

My aching pussy won't let me say no. Hurriedly I step out of the tap pants then I'm climbing onto his lap, facing him. He reaches between us, eases himself inside me as I lower and stretch to encompass him. His arms go around my shoulders and then he's kissing me, not soft and teasing any more but demanding, urgent.

I kiss him back the same way, my body lifting and falling in a rhythm that's beyond thought, beyond control. Purely physical, building the friction, the tension, driving toward climax.

I whimper and his kiss swallows the sound.

There's a light tap on the door and we both freeze.

"Yes?" I call, voice strained.

Mick shifts position and I can barely stifle a moan.

"Everything all right in there?" the woman calls.

"Fine. Good."

His eyes meet mine, full of laughter.

"Got the right sizes?" she asks.

Now it's a giggle I'm stifling. "Perfect fit so far."

"Sorry I've been so tied up with those other girls."

I borrow one of Mick's expressions. "No worries. I'm doing fine on my own."

He rocks his hips to remind me—as if I needed any reminding—that I'm definitely not doing this on my own. My muscles contract involuntarily, gripping him, and the laughter fades from his eyes as the blue deepens and his expression goes steamy. *Want you*, it says. *Now.*

"I'll leave you to it then," she calls. "Let me know if you need anything."

"I'm all set."

Mick and I hold still as footsteps retreat, then I hear three female voices begin to chatter in the distance.

"Got all you need?" Mick whispers in my ear, thrusting his cock high into me and making me gasp.

"Oh, yeah!"

We pick up where we left off, in a fast, driving rhythm that quickly brings us both to the brink of orgasm. I press myself hard against him as he thrusts up, and my body surges into a shuddering climax that triggers his.

We don't have the luxury of enjoying the post-orgasmic glow. Hurriedly he adjusts his clothes, I wipe myself with tissues and step into the tap pants. "Guess I'm taking this outfit."

"And all the rest." He gestures to the pile on the floor. "Don't try them on, or we'll get busted for sure."

I imagine trying on each outfit, having sex in each. He eases the fitting room door open and peeks out. "Coast's clear. You go first. I'll slip out while the clerk's wrapping that stuff."

It doesn't take us long to finish the rest of the chores on my do-today list. We drop parcels off at his place, I freshen up, then we roar off to the hospital.

I love the feel of Mick's body as I slide close and wrap my arms around him. It's funny, this chemistry thing between us. It's there all the time, and I feel sexier and more sexually aware than I ever have with a guy, but it's like glowing embers. When there's time and privacy, we'll blow on them and they'll burst into flame, but for now we'll enjoy the warm glow.

When he parks the bike at the hospital, Mick says, "Want me to wait or come with you?"

I like it that he offers. How many men would want to spend time with a girl's grandmother? And I'm pretty sure Nana—the Delia I got to know on the plane—would enjoy meeting a hot firie.

We get her room number and I hurry down the hall, eager to

reassure myself she's okay. I step into the room, Mick behind me, then stop in surprise.

My beloved grandmother, leg in a cast, is sitting propped up on pillows, her face glowing as she chats with a man who's seated in the chair by the bed. His face, handsome behind a silver beard, is glowing too. And he's holding her hand.

6

"Nana?"

She glances up. "Tash! It's so good to see you, dear. Come let me look at you."

I obey, hugging her tightly. "I'm fine, Nana." I stand straight for her inspection.

"I can see that. In fact, I'd say fire agrees with you. I've never seen you so vibrant." Then she glances past me. Her eyes widen then twinkle. "Or maybe it's not the fire, but your friend?"

"This is Mick Donovan. He's one of the firefighters who rescued us last night."

"Come over here, young man."

When he reaches out his hand to shake hers, she pulls him down for a big hug. "Thanks, Mick. And call me Delia, will you?"

"You're welcome, Delia."

"Speaking of friends, Nana," I say pointedly. "Are you going to introduce me?"

Her companion stands. "Trev Monaghan, Tash. Delia's been

telling me about you." He grins. "You're a looker too, just like her."

I shake his hand, doing a quick appraisal. He's medium height, medium build and distinguished, in a healthy, out-doorsy way. Silver hair, hardly thinning at all, tanned skin and a firm grip. A casual short-sleeved shirt, beige pants, leather belt, leather sandals.

He strikes me as poised. Confident but not pushy.

My granddad was taller, more forceful, yet Trev has as much presence in a quieter way.

"Did Nana call you?" I ask him.

"I certainly did *not*," my grandmother breaks in. "I'd never have let him see me like this if I'd had a choice."

Trev rolls his eyes. "You look great."

Nana flushes. "No," she goes on, "he showed up a couple of hours ago, as I was waking from a nap. He brought those." She gestures toward a huge bouquet of exotic flowers, most of which I can't even name. "Pretty, aren't they?"

"Lovely." Back home, if anyone thinks to bring Nana flow-ers, it's old lady stuff like a pot of African violets or chrysan-themums. But Trev's remembering Delia, the fun girl he once knew. And I'm guessing the woman in the hospital bed is thrilled.

"News travels quickly in Clifton Beach," Trev says. "But I'm not sure I'll forgive Delia for not telling me when the two of you were coming, so I could pick you up at the airport."

"Oh, you'll forgive me," Nana says, and the two of them ex-change a glance that makes me look away. A glance that says there are embers glowing here too.

Well . . . hot damn! Looks like she's going to get her ro-mance after all.

And suddenly I'm blushing, because I beat her to it. And be-cause she's always been just my nana and now she's this inter-esting new woman named Delia. And we're alone together in

Oz, me having had and her apparently contemplating having hot sex.

I sit carefully on the edge of her bed. My body promptly tells me how tired and sore it is. I could happily lie down beside Nana and catch a few hours sleep.

"How are you?" I ask. "Have the doctors got any test results?"

Mick quietly finds another chair and sits beside me.

Nana looks rather like a queen, propped on her pillows with her subjects gathered around her. Quite happy to hold court, she fills us in on the details, ending with, "So they want to play it safe and keep me overnight, but I'll be discharged in the morning."

She focuses on me. "Tash, have you been to Bet's house? Trev says it was pretty much destroyed. All our things are gone?"

I hand her the bag of new clothes. She takes a quick peek, then smiles.

"I haven't been by yet," I say, "but Mick says the same thing. I'm so sorry, Nana. Your sister's house, all her things."

"Me too." An expression of sadness crosses her face, then it's gone. Briskly she says, "But it *is* just things. The two of us are hale and hearty. That's what counts."

We share a smile. "I know what you mean. Puts things in perspective, doesn't it?"

She flicks her gaze past me, to Mick. "Apparently so."

I glance at him. He winks. I clear my throat. "I'm seeing the lawyer and insurers tomorrow. And I'll find a hotel for us."

Mick's foot nudges mine as Nana, cheeks pink, says, "No need. Bet's old friends will put us up."

"That's so kind." I glance at Trevor. "So, what's the plan?"

He darts a glance at Nana, like he's passing the ball to her. Mick bumps my foot again, and all the embers in the room glow brighter, heating the air.

Nana clears her throat. "Margaret and Bill have a spare room and would be happy to put you up. And I'll, uh, stay with Trev."

I raise my eyebrows. She's really planning on shacking up with a guy she hasn't seen in over half a century?

Wait a minute, she's in a cast, on painkillers. How much can happen?

But they're both blushing.

The family back home would hate this, but suddenly I'm rooting for Nana. She survived a fire, and if she wants to check out her feelings for Trev, then she should damned well go for it.

In that moment I realize that, while she'll always be my grandmother, she's turning into a girlfriend too. We'll both have our little holiday flings and who knows, hers might even turn into something more. I wonder how Trev might feel about moving to Vancouver.

I lean forward to hug her. Then I whisper in her ear, "He's hot. A definite silver fox."

She splutters a surprised laugh. Then, a spark of mischief in her eyes, she says, "Trev will give you Margaret and Bill's address. I'm sure Mick will have no trouble finding it."

"Um . . ."

The air behind me stirs, my nape tingles, warm breath tickles my ear. Mick whispers, "Tell her you got a better offer."

"I, uh, Mick already said—and he's offered to give me a ride to the lawyer's, and . . ." I stumble then trail off.

Now her eyes are dancing. "I may be gray but I have sharp hearing, young man. Tash, if you have a better offer, just say so."

I shoot Mick a scowl and catch him and Nana exchanging winks. "Okay, okay." I throw back my spiky-haired head, stare her in the eyes, and say, "I have a better offer."

"Good going, girl." She nods approvingly.

Then her eyes narrow. "Have you phoned home?"

"Uh, no, not since last night." Somehow I keep forgetting to put that item on the list. "Have you?"

She shakes her head. "Why worry them?"

Those three words encompass so much. Because, in fact, there's so much they'd worry about.

And yet, I have it all under control. Maybe not in my usual fashion, but in a green flip-flop way. Nana'll be fine, I'll sort out the house and the estate, and as for Trev and Mick—

I meet my grandmother's level blue gaze and in that look we enter into a conspiracy of silence. We have two weeks. Two weeks away from the family's eyes. Loving eyes, yes, but eyes full of expectation and judgment. Two weeks away from real life. "Yeah," I agree. "No need to worry them."

I reach into my new purse, this one not fine navy leather but a colorful woven tote with a drawstring top, and pull out two brand-new phones. "Ours were destroyed in the fire. I'll call home and give them our new cell—mobile—numbers." I hand her one. "I'll just say, oh, that our cells don't work properly here."

She nods. "Will I see you tomorrow, dear?"

"Of course. I'll phone the hospital in the morning and find out when they're discharging you. I'll be in Clifton Beach anyhow, seeing the lawyer, so maybe I can come over to Trev's house?" I shoot him a questioning look.

"Please do." He finds a scrap of paper and scribbles on it.

As Mick and I leave the hospital, he puts his arm around my shoulders and I wrap mine around his waist. I like it, how easily touch comes to him. In fact I like pretty much everything about him. Why doesn't Vancouver make men like this?

"Your nana's a real sweetie," he says, further endearing himself to me.

"She likes you too."

"What d'you feel like now?" We're walking toward the Ducati and he stops and pulls me in for another long, hot kiss. "Maybe some of this?"

I wriggle my pelvis closer, feel his response. My tired, aching body perks up. Reluctantly I say, "I should go to Clifton Beach and check the house."

"It's a good twenty-minute ride north. The house'll still be there in the morning."

"True." Maybe I can let go my sense of duty for the rest of the day. "Tomorrow I'll have more energy to deal with it."

"Speaking of energy, feel like dinner?"

I remember the wonderful aromas from the restaurants we walked past at lunch time. Food is exactly what I need, to revitalize me for sex. "Oh, yes. Something that smells exotic."

"How about Thai?"

"Perfect." Thai restaurants are popular in Vancouver, too, and I love the cuisine. So, maybe there are a few things the same, on opposite sides of the world.

He hands me a helmet and soon we're roaring away, on roads that are starting to look familiar. And I'm almost getting used to people driving on the left.

The Thai restaurant is small and busy. The outside walls are really doors, and they're open so that tables spill onto the sidewalk. We're lucky enough to get a table in the fresh air and I relax into a rattan chair, enjoying the touch of warm air on my shoulders. October, and bare skin. I'm not particularly outdoorsy, but I've always enjoyed those few summer nights in Vancouver when you can linger outside late into the evening. I'd expected Queensland to be too hot for me, but so far I love the temperature.

I lean back, sigh contentedly. Mick and I discuss the menu, agree on selections. Easy, compatible.

Food arrives, we chat about this and that. How can I feel so relaxed with a man who also makes me feel so sexy? A man who's utterly out of my league?

The evening light makes his tanned skin look even darker against the white of his T-shirt. His hair's messy, I don't think it's seen a comb all day, and it suits him. Even lounging in shorts, he has a natural grace. I'd bet he's a great athlete. Just like he's a fantastic lover.

Normally a wine drinker, tonight I'm drinking beer at Mick's suggestion. He's right, the slight bitterness is a perfect complement to the coconut milk curry and the ginger stir fry.

One beer, exhaustion and great food, a balmy night, a stunning man, and by the time a waitress clears the table I'm feeling no pain. "You're right, this seems like a holiday. I wish I didn't have to see the lawyer tomorrow. You're spoiling me for work."

"Good. Know what they say about all work, no play." He reaches across the table and begins to caress my fingers. One at a time. Sliding two of his own fingers up and down one of mine. Kind of like sex.

Heat surges through me. No play? Is that me? No, it's not even Vancouver Tash. I'm always up for a movie, a drink, dinner with a friend. But yet I've never played like this before. "You said you have some time off work?"

"I'm on for two eight-hour days, then two fourteen-hour nights. Last night was the second. Now it's four days off, starting today."

It almost sounds as if he's planning to spend those days with me.

Wow. As my teenage cousins would say, just, like, wow! He's willing to give up whatever else he had planned. Surely I can be super-efficient with my chores and free up some play time.

"Four days off, every eight? What do you do?"

"This 'n' that." He shrugs. "Go ballooning, diving, sailing. Hang out with my brother."

Nice, that he is close to his brother. "Is he older or younger?"

"Uh, yeah." He releases my hand, sits back, begins to play with his second bottle of beer.

"Excuse me?" I must be really tired, because I'm not following.

"Older." He says it softly, with a hint of reservation that makes me curious. It wasn't that tough a question.

"What kind of things do the two of you do?"

"Usually go camping in the bush. I have a four-wheel drive that'll go anywhere. We take sleeping bags, lie out under the stars."

"Sounds nice." Except for the poisonous snakes, the deadly kangaroos, but I guess those wouldn't bother a guy like Mick. "Is he your only sibling?"

"Yup."

I think of my sisters and brother. Superficially we're different, but beneath the skin we have a lot in common. We're all responsible, cautious, practical. I was the only one who showed signs, as a kid, of being kind of wild, but my parents disciplined it out of me. With a start, I remember what they told me. "You don't want to end up like your nana."

Not fair, I realize now. Sure, sometimes she acts on impulse when she shouldn't, but Nana has more going for her than we've ever given her credit for.

"Are you and your brother a lot alike?" I ask.

"In some ways. Both like the bush, chocolate cake, Harry Potter." He takes a swig of beer. Reflectively, he says, "Funny, 'cause when we were kids, I tried to be as different as I could. He was the bright one, the superachiever. You know how it is? You move up a grade and everyone compares you to your brother, and you can't measure up so you go a different route?"

I love how this fantastic guy is opening up to me. "I had a sister to measure up to." And I'd followed in her clever, responsible footsteps rather than choose a different path. "What route did you go?"

He gives a soft chuckle. "Rabble-rouser." He laughs again. "Okay. Asshole."

"Really?" And the asshole became a firefighter, and saves lives?

"Oh, yeah. I wasn't stupid, or a bad kid at heart, but I did like raising hell."

"Your basic bad boy. Bet the girls loved you."

"Pretty much." He says it with a reminiscent smile.

"But you ended up with a responsible job. What turned you around?"

He studies my face. While we've been talking, night has fallen. Street lights and the candle on our table cast light/shadow patterns across his face, making him look older than before. More serious.

He's still quiet, and I reach across the table to rest my hand on his. "Mick? If you'd rather not talk about it . . ." Maybe he got arrested, maybe realized what a dangerous path he was walking.

He turns his hand up and intertwines our fingers. "Davy— my brother—had an accident."

"I'm sorry." I'm guessing this is the fine edge of a complicated story.

"He was in graduate school, studying physics. Set for a brilliant career. There was a car accident, not his fault, just bad weather, faulty brakes." He pauses and his gaze is unfocused, like he's looking at a movie reel inside his head.

"He survived, though."

"Yes. But he came out of it a different person. Brain injury. He has a mental age of around ten."

"Oh, Jesus." My fingers tighten on his. I'm shocked, can't

imagine how I'd feel if something like that happened to someone in my family. And now I understand why Mick couldn't answer the simple question, whether his brother was older or younger.

"He's a bright, inquisitive, self-centered ten year old," Mick said. "Sometimes he's generous, sometimes he's selfish. He can do simple jobs like stocking shelves at the grocery store, but he's not capable of independent living. He's at home with my folks. He will be, so long as they can care for him."

The poor family. What a trauma, for all of them. "And then?"

His gaze flicks to my face. "With me."

Wow. And I thought I was a responsible person.

"How old were you, when he had the accident?"

"Sixteen. He was twenty-three." He heaves a sigh. "Davy could've made a contribution to the world. Maybe even won the Nobel Peace Prize. It's such a fucking waste."

"I can't imagine what it was like for your family."

"At least he didn't die. He's different, but we still have him. And he's happy."

I love it that he thinks this way.

"You'd really take him in, after your parents?"

His blue gaze is steady. "Too right. He's family."

I've learned more about Mick Donovan in the last five minutes than I've ever known about any other man I've dated. And I've discovered he's a better man than any of them. Damn. A holiday fling's one thing, but did I have to pick a man who was so damned . . . lovable?

"Life's not fair," he says softly, distracting me from my thoughts. "Should've been me."

I frown. "What?"

"I was the fuckup. He never did anything wrong. And he was the one who counted. Who could've been something, made a difference."

This amazing man has an inferiority complex? Once I've digested that notion, his words sink in deeper and anger rises in me. I pull my hand from his, then reach over to whack his shoulder. "Thanks a lot. You saved my life. You're saying that counts for nothing?"

He closes his eyes, squeezes them together. "No, course not. Sorry."

I breathe deeply, let the anger cool. "You're saying that saving lives one by one counts for less than doing something that affects the whole world."

He shrugs.

"Hmm." I take another couple of breaths. "So, why did you choose firefighting?"

"It was firies saved Davy's life."

"Ah ha." I lean forward. "They saved your brother, and his life counts even if he'll never win a Nobel Prize. What they did was so worthwhile, it inspired you to follow in their footsteps."

He laughs, one short, genuine laugh. "Yeah, you're right. Jesus, Tash, you're good. I can believe you're a lawyer. A great one, too." His face softens. "Thanks."

I duck my head. "You're welcome."

"We've been talking about me." His voice makes me look up. "What about you? What kind of law do you practice?"

"General practice, in a small firm with a couple of people I went to school with. It's a nice environment. Not so high pressure as the big firms." Still, it's a stress-filled job. And not what I want to think about right now. Normally I'm thrilled when a guy asks about my job, and isn't intimidated that I'm a lawyer. But not tonight. "It's a responsible, demanding job," I tell him. "Like yours is, though not so dramatic. And you know what? Tomorrow I'm going to have to pull my lawyer hat on. That's soon enough. Okay?"

"Sure. No worries." He smiles across the table.

No worries. There's that expression—that philosophy—again. I'm starting to understand it. Sure, Mick has worries, like his brother and his own insecurities. I have them too. Not least, whether I'll be able to drag Nana home again, and whether I'll even want to. But that doesn't mean we have to obsess over our problems every minute of the day.

I hope I gave Mick a boost to his sense of self worth—because he's given me so much.

I tug his hand across the table and lean forward. Touch my lips to the tip of his index finger, then draw it into my mouth. Suck a little, then slide my lips down his length, swirling my tongue around him as I go.

He moans. "God, you're making me hard."

"That was my intention." Only thing is, I'm turning myself on too, imagining my tongue repeating this maneuver with his cock.

"Time to go home." He pulls out his wallet and slaps bills on the table.

"Can you ride the Ducati with a hard-on?"

"Let's find out."

He can, and I rest one hand atop his fly and he stays hard for me. I squirm against the leather seat, pussy sensitive and aching under those skimpy tap pants. The embers that have been glowing all evening are getting brighter and hotter.

When we climb the stairs to his flat and rush through the door, he's still hard.

And when I yank down his zipper, the embers burst into flame.

7

Mick's erection springs into my hands, then I'm down on my knees and he's in my mouth, and I do to his cock what ten minutes ago I did to his finger. My whole body throbs with need but I don't let go of him.

My hands grip the taut muscles of his butt and he gasps, "God, Tash, you gotta stop. I'm gonna explode."

And I want—need—him inside me when that happens. He pulls me to my feet then we're ripping each other's clothes off as we head for the bedroom.

He tosses me on the bed and follows, kissing me like he can't get enough, and I kiss back the same way. Then he pauses and it's like he takes a deep breath and makes a conscious decision to slow down. His kisses soften, turn teasing and seductive rather than demanding. It's not that I wasn't ready for him before, but I can sink into these kisses, enjoy the sensuality of his touch and the echoing ripples through my body.

His lips drift down my neck, explore my shoulders, head toward my breasts. He does that vibrating air thing around my nipples and wow, do they like it. My body arches off the bed. "Where did you learn to do that? It's fantastic."

He chuckles against my areola. Says something that sounds like "didge."

"What?"

"Didgeridoo. You know, the long phallic musical instrument?"

I giggle. "Thought it was called a penis. And I really want to play it some more."

His lips drift over my stomach. "My turn first." Then we stop talking as he makes a lazy, sensual exploration. Everywhere he touches, my body springs to life. I'm more responsive than ever before. Is it that life-death thing, or Mick Donovan's magic?

I don't care, not with the pressure building between my legs and Mick finally approaching my needy clit. He sucks it into his mouth. Applies just the right amount of pressure. Inside my body a wave is building higher and higher, then it reaches a crest and—OH GOD YES—it crashes in a huge, long swoop through me.

Followed by smaller waves, then smaller again, around his lapping tongue. I sigh in relief and pleasure.

But he's still hard, and it's my turn on top. I sit up, then press him down on the bed, on his back.

"Oh-oh." He grins up at me. "I'm in for it now." He stacks his hands behind his head, spreads his legs slightly and I spend a few seconds admiring how perfect he is. From the glossy black hair to the strong, well-shaped feet, and everything in between.

Especially what's in between. That is definitely the best looking cock I've ever seen. They come in so many sizes and shapes, but this one is perfect. Brown and thick, symmetrical, the head full and velvety. A bold, confident cock. He could make a living as a model for a sex toy company.

But right now, he's my own private sex toy, and I intend to make use of him. To the hilt.

I straddle his body, his erection trapped firmly under my slick heat. Then I lean forward to stroke lightly over his shoulders, down his chest, to play with his nipples. With each touch, I shift position, wriggle against his erection, stimulating both of us.

He moves his hips, starts a forward-back slide of flesh against flesh, and with each back and forth pass he rubs against my nub.

"Oh God, Mick, that feels good." I press down harder, feeling my body build again, unbelievably, toward climax. "Don't stop."

"No fear." His voice is hoarse, his face taut, eyes dark with passion.

He reaches up and plays with my nipples, squeezing them gently, and the pressure between my legs mounts higher.

I look down, see his tanned hands against my pale breasts, his black pubic hair mingling with my reddish curls, the dark head of his penis between my thighs. So erotic, to watch us making love this way.

I slide forward, so his firm velvet head rubs my clit, grind myself down on him as he thrusts upward, and then I'm coming again, our bodies locked together.

He grabs a condom from the bedside table and lifts me enough to sheath himself, then he raises me higher, takes his cock in one hand and I'm not even finished climaxing when he's inside me.

"Jesus, Tash," he pants, "I can't hold off, I have to come."

"Then, come."

His hips lift us both off the bed as he pumps into me, and his rhythm's so frantic and compelling I have to rise and fall on him, clench and release around that perfect cock, and suddenly I feel it start again. The building wave of orgasm.

"Mick, oh, God!"

He reaches between us, finds my clit and rubs it as he thrusts even harder, deeper, wilder and then his head goes back and he lets out a yell, and I scream as a shattering orgasm rips through my body.

Thank God his landlady doesn't hear so well.

Bonelessly I sink down beside him. Three orgasms? Wow!

Is it just that he's sexier than any other man I've been with? Or that he makes me feel so sexy? Or that I could've died, and he saved my life? Or the way he cares about his brother?

Mick's a lovable guy.

No! Can't let myself think that way. This is a holiday romance. Stupid to set myself up to get hurt in the end. It's okay to like him, to have great sex, but I won't let it go any further.

He slips out of bed, makes a trip to the bathroom. When he comes back, he scoops an arm around me and kisses my cheek with those soft, firm lips.

"You really play the didgeridoo?"

"Davy and I took it up. We're an eighth aborigine, thought we'd explore our heritage. We sound awful, but it's fun. A challenge, but relaxing too."

"You're a firefighter. I thought you'd be all about risk, not relaxation."

He laughs softly. "I like excitement. There's still some hell-raiser in me. The job's good for that. But the risks are calculated ones. My family can't afford for me to get seriously hurt."

I nod, understanding all about family responsibilities.

"But sometimes I like just hanging out. Stargazing, playing the didge." He squeezes my shoulder. "Watching a pretty lady pick out clothes."

"You really think I'm pretty?"

"Maybe that's the wrong word."

Damn, I should have taken the compliment and not pushed. But he's going on. "It's too, uh, Barbie-doll. You're striking.

Gonna be even more striking when you've had a few more days in our sun, browned up some more."

Striking. That's even better than pretty.

Some people think it's odd I have reddish hair but don't burn. Nana, who has the same coloring, says it's her Aussie blood. We don't tan as dark as Mick—if he's part aborigine he has a head start—but we do turn a nice golden brown.

"You really learned that vibrating air thing from playing the didgeridoo?"

"Yeah, that's how you blow. Soft lips, vibrating lips and tongue. The guy who sold us the didges said think of blowing raspberries."

He's blowing raspberries against my erogenous zones. I giggle.

Mick laughs too. "Davy loved it. Went around blowing raspberries until we convinced him it was rude."

We're quiet a few minutes, then he says, "Tash? You really mean it, about this being a holiday thing?"

"Of course," I say quickly. "You're my holiday treat, but it can't be anything more."

"Got a guy back home?"

"No one special." And the couple of men I've been dating casually are going to look *so* not special, after Mick.

"What're you looking for, long-term? Marriage and kids?"

"I hope so, one day. But only if I meet the right person." I've dated a lot of perfectly okay guys, but I'm only saying "until death do us part" when it sounds like a blessing, not a curse.

I rest my head on his chest. "How about you?"

"I like women, we have a good time, but nothing serious."

"Ever see yourself getting married?"

He sighs. "Dunno. Not sure it's in the cards, what with Davy. That's not your normal 'get married, have kids' situation."

"No. But then, what's a normal family nowadays? There are

so many blended families, single parent families, gay couples with kids."

"True." His lips brush my hair. "You close to your own family?"

"Yeah. Too close sometimes. They expect a lot from me." If they knew what was happening with Nana and me in Australia, they'd be shocked. And disappointed.

In the morning I wake to find Mick spooned behind me, kissing my shoulders and slipping his erection between my legs. I reach for him, squeeze and fondle as he slides against my nub, each stroke making me wetter.

He opens the drawer in the bedside table. "Damn. Out of condoms."

I borrow his favorite expression. "No worries." Then I flip over, slide down in the bed, and he's in my mouth, with my hand circling his shaft. I let his reactions guide me as I learn how he likes to be touched. How tight to squeeze, how fast to pump my hand. Where to flick my tongue, where to swirl it. How hard to suck.

I'm glad he lies back and enjoys rather than shifting around to do 69 sex. I want to concentrate on his body, his reaction. By now I know Mick well enough to be sure my turn will come.

Come being the operative word.

And he is now, with a groan of release.

When he's lain back, spent, and I've sucked every last drop from him, I focus on my own body. The flushed, swollen feel of my breasts and pussy. What will he do with me this time?

He sits up against the pillows and says, "Touch yourself."

I can't.

Yet I did, in the shower. My breasts, anyhow. Sitting in the middle of the bed, I touch my nipples tentatively, fingers circling then teasing them to hard buds.

"Lower," he says, voice husky.

Cautiously I slide one hand between my legs, where I'm already wet. I make a few tentative strokes but I'm too self-conscious to enjoy this.

Until Mick reaches down and grips his flaccid cock and strokes up and down. As I watch, fascinated, he begins to grow.

I slide my finger between my labia. I've never done this in front of anyone. It's sexy, though, as I relax into it. My fingers are so small and delicate compared to Mick's. But I do know where to stroke, how fast to glide, where to press.

And all the time, my gaze is on his hand, pumping his engorged penis. I dart a glance to his face, see the flush on his cheeks, his parted lips as he watches me pleasure myself. Then I look back at his cock and imagine it inside me. My body tightens around my fingers. I move faster, fingers dipping into my wet sheath, sliding out again, while my other hand teases my clit.

The room is ripe with the smell of sex, full of our soft, panting breaths, but neither of us says a word. An illicit feeling adds an edge of excitement that's not there in intercourse, and I'm peaking quickly. Will he come too, when I do? And how could he grow hard again, so quickly?

Is it that arousing for him, to watch me masturbate?

It's definitely that arousing for me, watching him. So arousing I could come now, but I don't, I remove my hand for a couple of seconds, let my body cool a little, then I touch again.

I often fantasize about a man when I masturbate, but this is the first time there's been a real guy present. A real one, with a real cock, a perfect cock, hot and urgent in his own hand.

Oh God, I want to come, my body doesn't want to hold back. So I touch myself again, two quick strokes, a little more pressure, and then I close my eyes, throw back my head as the climax surges through me.

I leave my fingers in place, warm and gentle as my body slowly unwinds. Then I dare to look at Mick's face.

The blue of his eyes is intense, his whole face telegraphs urgency. He grabs my shoulders, spreads me out on the bed, straddles my hips so his cock's between my breasts. He presses them together, trapping himself between them. Staring down, he pumps back and forth, breathing in harsh pants.

I lift my head higher on a pillow so I can watch too. I've never had a man do this before, never imagined my breasts were big enough, but Mick doesn't seem to have any problem.

"Jesus, Tash!" And then he's coming, body jerking, jets of creamy semen ribboning my chest and the tops of my breasts.

Mick offers me the choice of riding to Clifton Beach on the Duc, as he calls his bike, or in his vehicle, a Toyota 4Runner. With reluctance I choose the 4Runner. I have papers to take to the lawyer, and no doubt will collect more, plus I'll likely do some shopping.

We drive by Auntie Bet's house and I could weep at seeing the blackened ruins, then Mick drops me at the lawyer's office and goes off in his shorts and bare feet to walk the long stretch of white sand beach. It's noon when, my chores for the day complete, we join up again to find Trev's place.

Nana's ensconced in the back garden on a lounge chair. With a hot-pink hibiscus blossom in her hair and a glass of white wine beside her, she looks happy and healthy despite the cast on her leg.

Trev and Mick head off to do guy things with the barbecue, leaving us alone.

"We should call home," Nana says. "While we're together."

"You're right." I'm not looking forward to deceiving my family, but if we don't phone they'll worry. I pull my mobile out of my bag. "You go first."

I listen to her end of the conversation.

"Bet's house?" Nana says. "Oh, it has the most beautiful location, right across from a lovely beach." A pause, then, "Tash has been with the lawyer all morning. I'll let her tell you what he said." She hands the phone over.

"Hi, Mom. As I thought, the paperwork's in order. The lawyer seems very competent."

"You don't think there'll be a problem selling the house?"

Feeling guilty as hell, I say, "Well, like Nana said, the location is terrific. That'll count in our favor." Something has to, what with the fire, and Nana's apparent determination to live out the rest of her days in Oz.

"Have you met her old friends yet?"

"We're having lunch with one of them right now."

"And Bill and Margaret have invited us for dinner tonight," Nana says, loudly enough so Mom can hear. Then she whispers to me, "But you don't have to go."

I am looking forward to meeting them, but tonight I'd rather be alone with Mick.

"Is it unbearably hot there?" Mom asks. "It must be such a shock to your system, since you're used to a temperate climate."

Temperate climate, temperate personality. That's what I'd thought. "I was afraid I'd be uncomfortable, but I'm finding I can take the heat very nicely."

"Not to mention the firefighter," Nana whispers, and I wave an admonishing hand at her.

After a few more minutes chat, I hang up, feeling like shit.

Nana and I stare at each other. "It's better they don't know," she says, sounding like she's trying to convince herself.

"I know. We don't want to upset them." But we can only maintain this conspiracy for so long. Ultimately, I'll go home, with or without Nana, and I'll have to account for myself.

"We have two weeks," she says.

"True. So we might as well enjoy them."

Brightening, she gestures around the garden. "Don't you love the flowers? Remember how I kept trying to grow hibiscus and bougainvillea in Vancouver, and they never took?"

She really never had forgotten her love for Australia. Why hadn't I realized that, each time she reminisced about "home"? Jesus, I can be blind. The whole family can. We see exactly what it suits us to see.

"You do love it here in Oz, don't you?" I ask her.

"Dear heart, haven't I been saying so all my life?"

"We weren't listening. You lived with us, in Vancouver. It's our home, so of course it was yours."

"How often have you heard the expression, 'home's where the heart is'? I love you all, but my heart's always been here."

"If you stay . . ." Two days ago I wouldn't have admitted the possibility, but now I have to explore it. "Nana, we'd miss you so much. Wouldn't you miss us?"

"Oh, Tash." She blinks, and tears cling to her eyelashes. "I'd miss everyone so much. But I *belong* here. It's in my blood. This air, the scent of flowers, the climate. *This* ocean and these white sand beaches, not the Pacific coast ones. My blood got thinned down, year after year, until I was barely alive."

Today she looks vibrantly alive. My eyes are misting too as I get up to hug her. "I understand. If you do decide to stay, I'll support you. I'll try to explain to everyone back home." They'll be so disappointed in me, but Nana deserves her happiness. I take her by the shoulders and stare into her eyes. "You will come visit, right? If we pay your way?"

"Of course. And you have to come here. Everyone, but you especially, Tash. Of all the children and grandchildren, I've always thought you're the one most like me."

I go back to my chair and pick up my wine. "Yeah, right. Remember that three-adjective exercise we did on the plane? Your words for me were completely different than the ones you chose for yourself."

She tilts her head to one side, smiling. "I said I was loving, passionate and spontaneous. Well, look at *you* now."

"Hmm?"

"You've always been loving, I see how you are with the family. As for spontaneous and passionate—well, you've taken up with a total stranger and gone to live with him."

"I'm not—"

She holds up a hand to stop me. "He's a darling, and I approve. Don't tell me you'll ever be sleeping in that spare room at Margaret and Bill's. You're living with him."

"He hasn't asked." But I think he will, and can't stop a grin. "Maybe. For the holiday. If it works out, between us."

"It will. You two have chemistry." She winks. "And passion."

"Yes," I say slowly. Mick described me as passionate too. "But this isn't the real me. This is I-could-have-died-in-a-fire Tash."

"It's not the old Tash, but I'd say it's the real one."

She can't be right. This is Tash-in-Oz. "When I'm home, I'll go back to my old self."

"Why?" Nana waves a hand. "Not that your old self was unhappy or boring, or anything awful, just . . ." She pauses, and I wait, curious, until she continues. "She was like me. Her blood was thin, and that's not a good state for a hot-blooded girl. You really want to go back to being her?"

Why isn't it easy to just say, "yes"?

She sips wine. "I've been thinking about defining incidents."

Where's she heading now? "Defining incidents?"

"It's something I read in one of my magazines. For many of us, there's a defining incident that shapes the rest of our life."

"Such as?"

"For me, getting pregnant. If I hadn't, I might've waited for Trev. When he went off to England to university, I felt rejected, hurt, mad. Scared he'd meet someone prettier and smarter. I took up with your granddad as a rebound thing, to salve my injured ego and get back at Trev. If I hadn't got pregnant, Trev and I might've ended up married, all those years ago."

I frown. "Then my dad wouldn't exist, I wouldn't exist."

She shakes her head gently. "I don't regret my choices, and I certainly don't regret any of you. I'm just saying, some incidents have more consequences than we think at the time."

"I can see that." Like Mick's brother's accident, and its impact on his family. The way Mick reacted, growing up and becoming responsible rather than continuing on a path that could have led him into serious trouble.

"The fire," she says. "Maybe that's yours. You already see how you've changed."

Okay, I admit I like some things about the new me. But I'm not convinced they'll transport well back home. No matter how relaxed my firm might be, I can't imagine wearing a broomstick skirt to the office. Nor wearing green flip-flops to Sunday night dinner with my parents.

Nor can I imagine finding a man who measures up to Mick Donovan.

But yet, Vancouver is where I belong. I can understand Nana, who was born in Australia, never losing her love of her homeland. For me, that homeland's Canada.

Trev hurries over to us and triumphantly flourishes a platter in front of Nana. "Here's a treat for you, Delia. Bugs, fresh off the barbie."

The things on the plate look kind of like crabs without legs. I know from Mick that a barbie is a barbecue, but did Trev say "bugs"?

"Bugs!" Nana exclaims. "You grilled Moreton Bay bugs for me?" She sounds delighted.

I turn to Mick, who's followed Trev, and find him grinning.

He bends down, one hand on my shoulder, drops a kiss on my ear. "They're shellfish. Named for their appearance, not their taste. The flavor's like lobster."

"You'll love them," Nana assures me.

She's right. I do.

8

After lunch, Mick and I meet with the insurance man at Auntie Bet's house. Mick fields questions as we walk through the burned-out ruin. He and the insurer discuss construction details, the cause of the fire, what it would take to rebuild. Much as I like being in charge, I have to admit I'm glad Mick's here.

For more than one reason. He's not a guy who holds back. When he's near me, he touches. A kiss, a squeeze on the butt, an arm hugging me. I can't be with him and not be aware of his physicality, his appeal, the way he arouses me.

He takes my mind off the desolation of Auntie Bet's house and gives me something much more pleasant to focus on.

By the time the insurance guy leaves, I've folded my arms across my chest to hide my pearled nipples. Here, where Mick saved my life, I'm so hungry for him I could climb the walls. Apparently he feels the same. Part of the living room still stands untouched and he herds me into a corner, lifts my skirt and cups the damp crotch of my sky-blue thong.

"Mick, stop it," I tell him, even as I squirm against his hand. "Anyone could walk around the house and see us."

"We'll be quick." He puts my hand on his fly so I can feel how hard he is.

"We haven't got condoms."

"I went shopping."

"Oh God, this is crazy." But I can't resist, I have to unzip him.

He hoists me up. My back's against the wall, my legs wrap around him and our lips meet in a searing kiss. I'm throbbing and swollen, and the moment he's inside me I start to come and come, and I'm still coming as he gives a final thrust and lets out a groan of satisfaction.

After we make ourselves presentable, he suggests we walk north along the beach a kilometer or so, and explore the neighboring town, Palm Cove.

The beach is fine white sand and the ocean's a tropical blue-green. We splash along the edge and it's refreshing but not too cold. My broomstick skirt—the same colors as the water—tosses in the breeze, my lightly sunscreened skin is tanning in front of my eyes and best of all, I'm holding hands with Mick. He's pulled off his shirt so he's clad only in shorts, and I see the hungry looks other women give him.

When we get to Palm Cove I find that, where Clifton Beach is mainly residential, this is a small but busy tourist town with hotels, shops and restaurants. The window of a clothing store draws me in. This place has two attentive salesclerks, so it's just me and my selections in the fitting room. The mirror tells me my skin's glowing, the light tan sets off my blue eyes, and my limp hair has found new vitality. Whether it's the climate or the sex, something in Oz suits me.

I pirouette for Mick, wearing a skimpy orange top and a gauzy skirt striped in orange and brown, and his expression tells me the mirror didn't lie. I look hot.

We decide on Italian for dinner, and eat outside under a spreading tree with silvery bark. He says it's a paperpark, or ti tree. Flocks of birds, vivid in shades of green, orange and blue, swoop and chatter. "Parrots?" I ask, but he says they're rainbow lorikeets.

After the meal, we walk back along the beach, the moon lighting our way. Mick dares me to skinnydip and I accept the challenge. The water's cool enough to raise goosebumps, then I'm in Mick's arms and my skin rapidly heats. We splash, play and make love on the beach.

Next morning, Mick wakes me in the dark and I groan.

He drops a kiss on my mouth. "Hot air ballooning. Champagne. Maybe even sex."

I'm a person who wakes slowly, but now he has my attention. "Sex?"

"In the clouds."

"What?"

But he's gone, into the bathroom. Did he really say sex in the clouds? Last night it was sex on the beach. I yawn. I must have misheard. After all, I'm not really awake.

It's fun to zoom on the Duc through the sleeping streets of Cairns. Soon we're on the highway, then on a narrow road that twists and twines uphill through a forest. It's still dark when Mick pulls the bike to the side of the road.

"We're going into the Atherton Tablelands," he says. "You'll see termite mounds—big heaps that look like sand piles. They grow kiwi and lychee up here, and coffee. If you see bags in the trees, those are bananas."

"What are the bags for?"

"So the bunch of bananas ripens at the same time."

Bananas come in grocery stores. I've never thought about how they grow.

When we're riding his bike, we can't really talk, so I'm glad he stopped to give me a travelogue. He makes a call on his mobile, then tells me, "Today we're launching from a coffee plantation with its own small airstrip."

"There's no fixed launch site?"

"Have to check the winds each morning. The ballooning companies have an arrangement with some of the farmers, to use their property to launch or land, and pay afterward."

Then we're riding again. As the sky lightens a bit, the sights of the Tablelands emerge from the darkness. It's dry country but scenic.

Mick turns off the main road and soon we're in a field of short, stubbly grass where trucks, giant uninflated balloons and people are collecting in the dim predawn light.

When we climb off the bike he gives me a big hug and kiss. I feel his excitement. Mine, too, is growing, along with trepidation. I've never done anything like this before. Is it really safe?

But it's obviously an established tourist business. Mick exchanges greetings with a number of people, and fills me in as we walk down the field. I learn that ground crews will inflate the balloons, which he calls envelopes. Passengers and pilots are carried in wicker baskets that dangle below. In space.

"How many do they hold?" I watch tourists head for the balloons and cluster around to watch them being inflated. Across the field, dawn is approaching in streaks of soft coral against a smoky purple sky.

"Big ones take a dozen passengers plus the pilot. We have a couple small ones that usually carry four."

"We?"

He stops and turns to me, and there's a huge grin on his face. "It's my other job. I'm a one-third owner of this operation, with two other firefighters. We call it Firie Air."

"You own a ballooning company?" I stare at him in amazement.

"With our shifts at the fire station, there's lots of time off. Many firies have other jobs, like construction or in the tourist industry. Too tame for me. Three years ago me and a couple of the guys put together Firie Air. Got ourselves qualified to pilot, hired a bunch of staff—ground crew and other pilots—and one guy's wife runs the business end. We do the standard tourist flights other companies do, and also high-priced luxury flights. Fewer people, fancier champagne, fresh croissants."

"You actually fly a balloon?" He fights fires, rides a motorbike, deep sea dives. Of course he flies a balloon.

The surprises don't end there. I expect to be with a group of tourists, but Mick's arranged a private flight, just the two of us. I'm not sure whether this makes me more or less nervous. Now I wish I'd had a chance to do some reading and analyze just how safe ballooning really is.

The crew who are inflating our envelope tease Mick and he jokes back and introduces me. I try to smile, but my tummy's doing somersaults. Mick takes risks, he admitted that to me. Calculated risks, he said, but risks all the same. Firie versus lawyer—clearly our personalities are very different.

I glance down the field and see the balloons are all puffing up with air. They have different patterns, but each design's in red, yellow and orange, with a flame logo saying Firie Air. The woven wicker baskets are tiny and flimsy. Especially ours.

Mick helps me clamber in. Oh great, I'm standing inside a picnic basket with sides that don't even come up to my shoulders.

And speaking of picnic baskets, one of the crew is handing Mick one now, and it looks more substantial than the contraption I'm standing in.

To distract myself, I speculate whether there's champagne and croissants inside, and, despite my nerves, my tummy rumbles. A reminder I've been up for two hours and haven't eaten.

The sun's really rising now, and the sky's turning blue. Lovely, if I wasn't too tense to enjoy it.

"Propane tanks," Mick says, gesturing to two metal canisters at his feet. Then he turns a valve in a contraption above his head. "And this is the burner. Hot air rises, right?" A flame shoots up, into the center of the envelope. The air fills with heat and a rushing, scorching sound.

Fiery air indeed. Now I understand the cleverness of his company's name.

But fire's a force I've learned to be extremely wary of. I eye the flimsy fabric of the envelope. "What if you burn a hole in it?"

"Not gonna happen."

The envelope's lifting, our basket drags across the ground then breaks free. The crew let go the lines that tether us. Mick and I are in the air and my heart's in my throat.

Down the field, other balloons are almost inflated, but we're the first to lift off. We're rising quickly too, and the basket feels surprisingly stable. Cautiously I move to the edge and grip the flimsy wicker, all that stands between me and the sky. I glance down, then, fascinated, scan the ground that's moving away from me. I see farmland, houses, a swimming pool, the shadow of our balloon. Dogs bark, though I can barely hear them over the noise of the flame, and a flock of birds takes wing. An early riser peers up and waves. I wave back, then turn to Mick, smiling.

"Like it?" He grins back.

"It's amazing."

It would be peaceful, but the flame roars and burns. Even though I'm three or four feet from it, my shoulders feel the heat. Not my favorite sensation, after having barely survived a fire. "How can you stand right by the flame?"

"Firie's got to be able to take the heat."

He shuts off the flame and suddenly it's quiet. Now I hear noises from below. Dogs, birds, farm equipment. But we're up high, and it's peaceful. Not so scary after all.

Mick moves closer, putting his arm around my shoulder and

peering over the side of the basket. He points. "See that field? Something moving? That's a roo."

I watch, intrigued, as a kangaroo bounds across the field. Then, as my eyes adjust, I start picking them out too. Mick names the birds, and the different trees, tells me about the farms, houses, their occupants. He varies altitude, letting the balloon drift lower so I can see details, then applying bursts of flame to take us up where the view stretches out for miles and miles.

"How do you steer this thing?"

"Different altitudes have different wind currents, so height determines direction. Right now, if I take us down fifty feet, we'll head over there, where the others are going."

He points, and I realize the other fire-colored balloons are drifting away from us.

"But I'm taking us up," he says, firing the burner. "Figure we can use some privacy."

"Privacy?" When he said sex in the clouds, he wasn't really thinking . . . ?

"Open the picnic basket," he says.

Oh, privacy to eat. No, of course I'm not disappointed. And particularly when, tucked into checked napkins, I find flaky croissants, a box of strawberries, Australian champagne and two glass flutes.

"On the tourist flights the champagne's non-alcoholic," he says. "When we get down we give them a full breakfast with the real stuff, but it's illegal to serve alcohol up here."

"So we're breaking the rules." I'm not a rule-breaker. If he'd told me earlier, I'd never have climbed into the balloon basket. But now that I'm here, experiencing the magic of floating above the countryside, the idea gives me a thrill. And I know Mick won't drink enough to impair his judgment.

He eases the cork out and pours two glasses of fizzy bubbles. We toast the beautiful morning, my holiday, Nana and Trev, and each other. Periodically, Mick flames the balloon but mostly he lets it drift with the winds, and joins me in breakfast. The strawberries are sweet and lush, especially when teamed up with Mick's kisses. The croissants are buttery and light as air.

And speaking of air, we're standing in it.

I'm standing in the sunny sky, looking out over Queensland, as far as my eye can see in any direction. Mick's shirt is off, so the view in the basket rivals that outside. The air has a fresh, morning smell, Mick's kisses taste of strawberries and champagne, and I'm in heaven. My body's so aware, so alive to all the sensations.

"Life doesn't get any better than this," I tell him.

"You ain't seen nothing yet," he teases, a gleam in his eye.

"You didn't really say sex in the clouds, did you?" I ask skeptically.

"What's the matter? Not in the mood?"

He knows I am, my nipples are poking their way through my bra and T-shirt. I know he is too, because I've rubbed against his erection enough times.

"What kind of sex?" I ask, sure he must be kidding. We're a thousand feet in the air, in a wicker basket.

"What kind do you want?" He kisses my ear, trails his tongue around the lobe. "Just don't say slow and lingering. If I take the balloon up high enough, catch the right wind, we should have ten, fifteen minutes."

He flames the balloon higher than we've gone before. I see a few small puffy clouds above us and then, oh my God, we're inside a cloud. The air's cooler, damper, it clings to my skin, and then we're rising out of it and the sun's back. I beam at him. "When Nana's better, you have to take her up. She'd love this."

"I'll take her and Trev. Promise."

And I won't be with them. I'll be home in Vancouver.

There's ballooning there, out in the Fraser Valley, but I know I'll never go up in a balloon again, unless I'm with Mick Donovan.

Okay, so if this is it, enjoy every moment and stop feeling melancholy.

"Tash, you okay?"

I step closer and hug him. "I'm so okay there aren't words for it."

He takes me by the shoulders, holds me away and looks me up and down. Then he pulls me close again. "Yup, I have to agree."

Then we're kissing, and between kisses struggling to get each other's clothes off. He turns off the flame and the world is silent and we're standing naked above the clouds.

His erection thrusts boldly up his belly. I splash a few drops of champagne on it and squat down to suck. Champagne and Mick beats even champagne and strawberries, and I can feel dampness slide down my inner thighs.

He groans, then pulls me up. "Great idea. Some day we'll pour champagne all over each other and lick it off. But right now, we don't have time."

I imagine his tongue all over my body and say, "Then take me, Mick." Our eyes lock, telegraph that *want you* message we've been exchanging since he rescued me from the fire.

Then we're kissing, tongues dueling in our urgency. He sheaths himself, lifts me and I wrap my body around him and cling tight. He spreads my folds with his cock and now he's inside me, thrusting high and deep.

My muscles contract and cling to him, then release as he eases back, stimulating every cell as he goes. Friction, delicious friction as he slips in and out. Slowly, being careful, maintaining our tenuous balance in the flimsy basket.

Our movements may be cautious, but they're intensely focused. We make each one count, finding just the right place to touch, the exact angle, the perfect degree of pressure. Sun and the gentlest of breezes caress our skin. Sex tastes like strawberries, and feels like champagne: celebratory, special and perfect.

"God, Tash," he gasps in my ear, "this is so good."

I squirm lower, adjust the angle so my needy clit gets even more stimulation. He's so beautifully male and he makes me feel so incredibly female. I'd never known my body was capable of all these sensations. Or capable of turning a man on, the way I do Mick.

I know I'm going to come, just another couple of strokes will do it, and I want him with me. I reach down, stretch until his balls are in my hand, caress them and feel them draw up. "Mick, come now."

And he does. And so do I.

9

And that's pretty much how the next week goes. When Mick's off work, we spend time together—which means giving in to the powerful chemistry between us. One day he borrows a friend's sailboat and we dart across the ocean, snorkel in azure waters among hordes of colorful fish, anchor at a secluded beach and have a picnic. With champagne. Which we lick from each other's bodies.

We ride his bike to Port Douglas and explore the shops, then head north into the Daintree Forest, all the way to the long stretch of beach at Cape Trib. Another day we head inland, me-ander west then south through the Tablelands, where I fall in love with the huge, spreading jacarandas with their millions of purple blossoms.

We make love on beaches, by waterfalls and once, even, sit-ting on the Duc. At night we curl up in his bed, pleasantly weary but never too tired for sex. In the morning we sometimes stop by his landlady's for fresh-baked scones, served with Devonshire cream and strawberry jam.

When Mick's working, I try not to think about the dangers of his job. *Calculated* risks, he said. And, knowing how much his brother means to him, I believe it.

Together with Auntie Bet's lawyer and the insurers, I tidy up the details of the estate. And in spare moments, I visit with Nana, Trev and their friends, learn about Aussie dialect and dietary eccentricities, poke through tourist shops.

One morning I'm sitting with Nana in Trev's garden, while he's gone up to the shopping centre for groceries. "You're staying, aren't you?" I ask her.

She pours more tea. "Only just figured that out?"

"I'm happy for you, but not looking forward to telling the family."

"Not your job, dear. It's time you all gave me credit for having a brain in my head, and an ounce or two of reason. It's my decision, and I'll explain."

"Thanks." And I'll try to make everyone understand that we underestimated her wisdom. "What about the house?"

She sighs. "We'll live here in Trev's. I won't need Bet's house, but it was *hers*. I hate to sell it."

"You could rent it, but that's a lot of work."

"Or you could have it."

I don't pretend to be surprised. She's been hinting she'd like me to stay. "Nana, it's lovely here. But I belong back in Vancouver. I'm a Pacific Northwest girl."

"No, I don't think so." She spreads her hands out toward me. "Look at you. You're like bougainvillea. You flourish in this climate. I've never seen you so alive, so happy."

Is it the climate, or Mick? Or both?

"You could practice law here, Tash."

In fact, the solicitor, a sweet older man, has said he's ready to slow down, take a partner.

If I told my lawyer friends back home that I was practicing

in a converted cottage across the road from one of the most gorgeous beaches I've ever seen, they might think I'd gone nuts, but mostly they'd be out of their minds with jealousy.

It would be like an idyllic dream. And, despite the way I've relaxed on this holiday, I'm a realist. "The family," I say. "I belong with them. My practice, my friends. I can't pack up and move my entire life to the other side of the world. Vancouver's my home."

She raises one eyebrow and gives me a gentle smile. "If that's where your heart is, dear."

My heart. She means Mick. But I haven't given him my heart. I won't. "He's a holiday romance, Nana." If I stayed here, we probably wouldn't even keep seeing each other. He slotted me in for a two-week fling, and he'd soon be on to the next girl.

He'd be having sex in the clouds with someone else.

Amazing, how deeply that thought hurts.

"Don't be too hasty to throw away something special," Nana tells me.

The next day, Sunday, Mick takes me to his folks' place for a dinner barbie. His dad's of Irish extraction and his mom's a mix of aborigine, Chinese and English. They're attractive, intelligent, good-natured people who clearly adore Mick and his brother.

Davy looks like Mick though he's softer, his face almost childish in its roundness and expressions. And he's a sweetie. Once I get over how big he is—almost as tall as Mick and outweighing him by a good twenty or thirty pounds—he reminds me of my younger brother Terry, when he was a boy. It's great fun when he and Mick pull out their didges and create bizarre sounds that make the rest of us laugh.

Dinner's simple: delicious hamburgers and potato salad, followed by tropical fruit salad and chocolate cake. When Davy throws a tantrum over wanting seconds of cake, I remember how Terry'd do that too. If Mom gave in, the sugar would keep him awake past his bedtime.

"Come on, Davy," Mick says, "let's have a read." He turns to me. "We always have a book we read back and forth. Right now we're into Harry Potter."

"Come read with us, Tash." Davy grabs my hand and gives me a tug that almost pulls me off my feet.

"I'd love to. I've never read Harry Potter. Can you fill me in on what's happened so far?"

Davy does, in a rush of words, as Mick finds the book. The three of us settle in lounge chairs on the lighted patio and pass the book, taking turns reading a couple of pages. The garden's dusky and the fragrance of frangipani lingers in the balmy air. But then the garden fades away entirely and I'm caught up in the mystical world of Harry and Hermione and Dumbledore.

Mick's reading when a small movement catches my eye. Mrs. Donovan has come to stand in the doorway. She's watching Davy and Mick, an expression of pure love on her face. She glances my way and we share a smile.

There's something in that smile. Suddenly I'm no longer at Hogwarts but in the middle of a cozy family scene. A scene where I fit too well for comfort.

If this was Vancouver, if I'd found a man like Mick . . . yes, I'd be thinking about the future. A terrific man, a family like this, kids of our own coming along. What more could I ask?

But we're not in Vancouver, and the very closeness of this scene tells me Mick would never leave Australia. I was stupid to meet his family. Mick and I should stick to sex; I can't be drawn into his life.

Damn, but he'd be an easy man to love.

Maybe I should break it off now, before I get in any deeper. I go home in a few days anyhow.

Mrs. Donovan's voice cuts into my thoughts. "That's enough for now. It's bedtime, Davy."

Of course he begs for "just a little longer" but she doesn't let him get away with it. He and Mick have a mock struggle over who's getting custody of the book, but she resolves it by whipping it away. She rolls her eyes at me. "Kids. What can you do?"

I try to respond, but the truth is I'm unsettled and unhappy.

We all go inside, and I say, "It's been nice meeting you, Davy. Thanks for letting me share Harry Potter."

He gives me an exuberant hug that swallows me up. "You're welcome, Tash. I like you."

I squeeze him back. "I like you too."

He starts down the hallway then turns around. "Come back and see me again. We'll read some more."

He's so sweet. I'd love to spend more evenings like this, and it hurts to think I'll never see Davy again. If that hurts, what's it going to be like to say good-bye forever to Mick?

Suddenly my throat's swollen with unshed tears and I have to swallow hard. "I don't think I can do that," I gently tell Davy. "Remember, how I said I live in Vancouver, and we looked it up on the map? Well, I have to go home."

"You shouldn't go. Stay here, Tash."

"My family's there, Davy."

"We could be your family too."

And again I have to swallow down tears.

Davy heads off to bed and Mick and I say our good-byes to his parents. When I thank them, his mom gives me a quick hug. "I'm sorry you're not staying in Oz, Tash."

I walk toward the bike and notice she's held Mick back, is whispering to him.

He's quiet after that, and I sure don't feel like talking. Back at his place our lovemaking is different too. Softer, yet more intense. He's in me forever, as we move gently together, change position, rest then resume. The shared orgasm, when we finally let it come, seems to explode through every cell in my body. And again, tears are close.

After, as he holds me in bed, Mick says, "Davy'd like you to stay."

"He's a dear." I try to keep my tone light. "Reminds me of my brother, when he was that age."

"But your brother grew up, and Davy never will."

"True. But he's happy."

"If you stayed a while longer, if things worked out with us, could you see a life that included Davy?"

"Mick!" I pop up in bed and his arm falls away from my shoulder. What's he talking about? "Stay?" I take a couple of breaths. "You want me to stay because Davy likes me?"

He chuckles and sits up beside me, thrusting a pillow behind his back. "Sure, and because my mom says I'd be a fool to let you get away, and Delia's been lobbying me since I met her."

Then he reaches out and takes my hand. "Tash, I want you to stay because *I* like you. This time with you has been great. I don't want it to end."

"B-but we always knew it was short-term."

"Yeah, but I've fallen for you in a big way. Stay, so we can see where it goes."

He's fallen for me? This amazing man has fallen for plain old Tash? No, I can't believe it.

And yet, when I look back at the things we did, the way we talked and touched each other, the intimacy in our love-making . . . With him I'm not plain old Tash, I'm someone new. And this has been much more than a holiday fling.

Oh my God, he actually cares for me. The way I care for him—a fact I've been trying to deny for the last few days.

But wait, what am I thinking? "You know I have to go home."

He stiffens and when he speaks his voice is tight. "I don't know that. Oz could be your home. Why not?"

"Why not?" My heart's racing, and now it's partly anger. "You're asking me to give up my life! Yes, Mick, I have feelings for you. But think about it. Would you pack up and move to Vancouver, to be with me? Leave your parents and Davy?"

"I can't leave Davy," he snaps. "I told you that, the first day we met. Damn, this is why I never get into relationships."

"Yes, you told me and I understand. And Mick, I never asked for a relationship. We've known from the beginning the two of us had no future."

"We sure as hell have no future if that's how you think."

Men. I'm about to tell him I don't *want* a future but that would just prolong this childish argument. Besides, I remember how I'd been daydreaming earlier, watching him with Davy.

"I'm going to sleep." I roll over and turn away.

He huffs and thrashes and heaves pillows around, then is finally still.

I wonder if he gets any sleep.

I sure don't. I'm busy beating myself up for being so damned spontaneous and abandoning my rational, analytical side. This whole affair was a mistake and I could've saved myself a lot of pain if I'd thought with my head instead of my damned pussy. Then, I could've gone home with my heart intact.

I refuse to cry. Not with him lying there beside me.

Maybe in the morning we can find a way of working things out.

At the crack of dawn Mick rolls out of bed without speaking and goes to take a shower. When he comes out of the bathroom, he says, "I'm going to Brizzie for a couple days. Feel free to borrow the 4Runner, but you might be more comfortable staying with Delia's friends."

"Of course I won't stay in your apartment when you're not here." Not to mention, when we're barely speaking to each other. I stalk to the bathroom, wishing I had a robe to cover my nakedness. I grab a towel, wrap it around me and lean out the doorway to ask casually, "Brizzie is Brisbane? Why do you have to go there?"

He's moving about the room, dressing quickly. "There's an event. I was gonna pull out, but I really should do it."

Translation: he'd been going to dump it for me, and now he's looking for an excuse to dump me instead. I'm damned if I'll ask what the event is. Probably a voluptuous blonde. After me, that would definitely be an event.

He's tossing clothes in a duffel. "Keys for the 4Runner are on the dresser. I'll catch a cab to the airport."

The logical thing would be for me to drive him, but it's clear he can't wait to ditch me. If he feels that way, the last thing I want is to borrow his vehicle and have to return it. "Nonsense. You take the 4Runner. I'll catch the bus to Clifton Beach."

Across the room, his gaze meets mine in a long, unreadable look. I sense he's asking a question. *Are you sure?* And I think, *what other choice have you given me?*

I go into the bathroom and close the door. If he cares about me, he'll still be there when I emerge. Somehow, we can work this out.

But the room is empty. He told me he'd fallen for me, and now he's buggered off.

Okay, fine. Last night, at his family's, I'd feared I was getting too close. Thought it might be time to break up. So, this is a good thing.

The ache in my heart confirms it. I was definitely getting in too deep. So, great, now I have a couple days' head start on getting over the arrogant jerk. After all, it's not likely I'll see him again. He said he'd be in Brisbane two days, and my plane leaves in three.

At the thought of never seeing Mick again, tears fill my eyes.

I force them back and bustle around, muttering under my breath as I gather up all the things I've accumulated and load them into plastic bags.

As I walk to the bus stop, I figure I must look like a bag lady.

My brain says a clean break is better. All the same, as I gaze through bleary eyes at the scenery passing by outside the bus window—scenery I'm used to viewing from the back of Mick's Ducati—I feel like my magical holiday in Oz has been tarnished. The memories will never shine as bright in my mind.

I'm so glad Nana's here. She's always offered comfort and sanctuary for us grandkids, and right now that's exactly what I need.

10

It's mid-morning when I show up on Trev's doorstep. He takes one look at me, and the plastic bags clustered at my feet, and says, "You'll be wanting Delia."

"Yeah. Thanks," I say, feeling like shit.

"I'll go for a walk." He steps past me out the door then pauses. "Don't know what happened, but Mick's a good man. And he really cares about you."

Jesus. I've been holding back tears since last night, and now those few words make them overflow.

Trev stares, horrified, at my face. "Sorry, I—"

"It's not you," I gulp, brushing my hands under my eyes.

"Delia's in the kitchen. I'll leave you two alone."

Not capable of speech, I nod and go through to the kitchen where Nana's sitting on one chair with her bad leg up on another. When she sees me, she opens her arms to me. "Oh my dear, what happened?"

I hurry into her embrace, then settle down with a cup of tea and tell the story.

"So," she says, "you're upset he asked you to stay?"

"He tried to turn this into something it wasn't supposed to be."

She shakes her head. "Relationships rarely know what they're supposed to be. You just have to, you know, *do* them. Get in there and expend some energy, and see what results. It's been so clear the two of you have been falling in love."

"But I can't fall in love with Mick. He's tied here." I explain about Davy.

"So, what about this Davy? Would you mind having him live with you, when their parents can't care for him anymore?"

I think of Davy—from temper tantrum to sweet hug—and shake my head. "He's a sweet boy, man, whatever. Old enough to be relatively self-sufficient, to understand things when you explain to him."

"Nice to know your Mick doesn't reject someone if they're no longer perfect. He's a man you can count on, he'll stand by you no matter what."

"He's not standing by me now," I grumble.

"You sent him away."

"He said he was going. It's not like I had a choice." But I remember that moment when his gaze met mine, with an unspoken question.

"You'd rejected him. His pride was hurt. His heart was broken."

"I couldn't—" Do I really have the power to break Mick's heart? My own heart feels plenty battered and bruised, but he's this big, tough, sexy firie. On the other hand, if I could look past my own insecurities, truly believe he'd fallen for me, then . . . "You're right. I hurt him." And now I feel even worse.

"Drink your tea. And examine your heart. How do you really feel about him? If you both lived in the same place, if there were no family issues, if it was just about your feelings."

I do as she instructed, and finally my heart and mind

come together and I see the truth I've been avoiding. "I love him."

"Have you told him?"

I shake my head. "I only just figured it out."

"This reminds me of Trev and me, when we were young. He left, and I gave up on him. Too easily."

"It's complicated. There are issues we'd never work out, like where to live."

"Tash, dear, forgive me for saying this, but that's an excuse. I moved to Canada to be with your granddad, and I was only seventeen. Back then it was days of travel at a horrendous cost. It meant cutting myself off from my family, but for letters that took forever to go back and forth. My sister was my best friend in the world, and I didn't see her for twenty years."

"You did all that for Granddad," I muse.

"Sort of. But more for your father. I loved that little bun in my oven. I wanted him to be legitimate, have two parents, a loving home."

Hmm. If she's right and I've been making excuses, setting up an artificial barrier, what is it I'm afraid of? Don't I trust in Mick's or my feelings?

I've known him less than two weeks. Trusting our feelings wouldn't be rational.

"If the two of you love each other," Nana says, "you'll sort this out. Just remember, home's not a place, it's where your heart is." She raises an eyebrow in a question.

"My heart's with him," I admit softly. "Not Vancouver, not Australia. Just Mick Donovan."

"Then tell him. He's held out his hand. Take it."

"I don't know where he is. All he said was, some event in Brizzie. Could even be a girl."

She shakes her head. "That boy may have been a player

once, but he isn't anymore. When that kind settles, they settle for life. Phone his mother, she'll know where he is."

Nana's right. It's time to stop stalling, making excuses.

Mick's Mom says, "Tash, I thought you'd have gone with him."

"We had a spat," I confess.

"And now you want to make up. Good girl. He's at the fire-fighter auction."

"The what?"

"The firies do this big charity fundraiser. Auction them-selves off, and the proceeds go to good causes."

"Auction themselves off?" To perform what services?

She chuckles. "No, dear, it's pretty innocent. Though they might have to escort a woman to the symphony, or be a guest at a bachelorette party."

"Do you know where he's staying?"

"No, but why not call him on his mobile?"

I've just this minute made up my mind—my God, I'm being spontaneous!—but I know what I'm going to do. "I need to see him. I'm flying to Brisbane. And I want it to be a surprise."

When I hang up, Nana's grinning approvingly. "I'm not above offering bribes," she says. "I'll give you Bet's house as a wed-ding present."

No surprise, the audience at the auction is mostly female. They've spent hours putting on makeup and fancy clothes, and I'm fresh off the plane in a broomstick skirt and flip-flops. I'm late enough that it's standing room only, and the curtain's going up.

Mick's not among the first few men, so I have a chance to figure out how the auction works. It seems to me, from the way the spotlights are set up, that the firies can't really see the audi-ence. Chances are, a guy won't know who's bought him until she comes to claim her prize.

And now the man walking on stage is Mick. In a tux. Used

to seeing him in shorts with his hair messed from swimming or a motorcycle helmet, I'm blown away by this elegant guy.

I barely recognize him. Was I wrong to come here? Wrong about us?

But then the gushing female announcer reads his bio and talks about Firie Air, deep sea diving, sailing, his Ducati. His face crinkles into that familiar smile. And my heart expands in my chest because yes, this is the man I know. The man who wants me. The man I love.

I'm determined to win him. Price doesn't matter. I'm being irrational, which is so *not* the old Tash. This isn't my last chance, there are lots of ways I could meet up with him. But somehow, this auction has become symbolic of the woman who deserves Mick Donovan.

Thank heavens I have lots of credit on my new MasterCard, because the bidding's going high. I hang back, watching, until only two women are left. When one drops out, I put my hand up and join the battle. The poor woman who was sure she'd won shoots me a nasty look, mutters to the girlfriend beside her and throws in the towel.

He's mine.

Heart pounding in my throat, I make my way backstage to where the winners and firies are being matched up. "Mick Donovan," I say clearly to the woman who's collecting money.

"Donovan," she calls out as she processes my credit card.

I sign my name, glance up and there he is. Looking stunned. "Tash?"

I step toward him, more nervous than I've ever been in my life.

"Did you buy me?"

"Yes."

His face is tight, his eyes don't give anything away, but there's an edge to his voice when he says, "Need a ride to the airport?"

The edge doesn't stop me. If I'm right, he's feeling wary, hurt, and wondering why the hell I've come all the way to Brisbane. "I'm not going back to Vancouver for a while."

Hope lights his eyes, but his voice is neutral when he asks, "Problems with the estate?"

I shake my head. "Problems with me. Like stupidity. For almost throwing away the best thing that's ever happened to me."

Now his eyes are glowing and the corners of his mouth lift. "And that would be?"

I'm smiling too. "You, you idiot."

I take a step toward him. Then I'm in his arms and he's pulling me close, so close, like he never intends to let me go. "Damn, Tash, you had me scared. I've never felt like this before. And you just blew me off."

"I'm sorry. That was the old Tash. You don't want to know her. I don't want to know her either. The new Tash is . . ." I smile, remembering Nana's three words. "Spontaneous, passionate. And loving. Mick, I love you."

"You do?"

I capture his mouth with mine and we both sink deep into the kiss.

When we come up, he says smugly, "Well, damn. You really do."

"And?"

"I love you too, Tash."

I'm about to tell him about my talk with Nana, and how she's inspired me to look for solutions to our issues, but he speaks first. "I've been thinking. I was self-centered, expecting you to pack up your whole life and move here."

My heart leaps. "You mean you'd consider Vancouver?"

He clasps both my hands in his. "In the long-term, I have to be with Davy when our folks die. Whether it's here or Vancouver, we're a pair, him and me. You okay with that?"

"I am. But what about right now?"

"I love Oz." He sighs. "And you love Vancouver, I get that. And I'll probably like it too, the way you like Oz. So, I was thinking. A couple years ago, one of the firies worked out a swap with a firefighter in Alberta. They traded places. Maybe a fire station in Vancouver would go for that. Davy and I could talk by email and on the phone, and I'd come back and visit."

"And I'd want to visit Nana." In the last two weeks we've grown so close. She's my best friend. I can't lose that now.

"Course you would. The two of you are like two peas in a pod."

Or two vibrant bougainvilleas, thriving in the sunshine. "I *am* like her, in so many ways. Maybe I belong here too, in Oz."

Oz. Suddenly I remember the last line of *The Wizard of Oz*. There's no place like home.

I lean into Mick's embrace, feeling how absolutely right we are together.

"There's one thing I know for sure," I tell him. "My home is with you."

All Fired Up

P.J. Mellor

Special thanks to Judythe Hixson for her Dumpster expertise.

1

Nick Howard cast aside the useless respirator, doused himself with water and headed back into the burning building. Somewhere amid the smoldering rubble and flames was his old friend. Nick would be damned if he'd leave his last Houston fire without Dave.

Bending low, squinting against the smoke, ignoring the burning in his throat and lungs, he slowly backtracked into the old warehouse, taking shallow breaths into the wet bandana covering his mouth.

Despite his protective eyewear, his eyes stung and teared, blurring his already limited vision.

"Dave!" he yelled. "C'mon! Where are you?"

Behind him, a beam fell with a roar, its heat warming his back through the layers of clothing. The cement floor vibrated beneath his booted feet.

A slash of color to his left caught his attention. It moved.

Crouching lower, he made his way to the lump.

"Dave!" He dropped to his knees, gripping his friend's shoulder.

Dave smiled beneath the soot covering his face, and removed his respirator. "About damn time." He handed his mask to Nick. "Caught my foot." He motioned to a section of downed wall. "It's broken. I think my leg's busted up too."

Nick nodded, a lump of relief in his throat, and probed his friend's leg, wincing at the feel of protruding bone beneath the leggings. He handed the mask back to Dave. "Nothing more we can do. Let's get you out of here."

Sharing the respirator, they made slow progress to the entrance. The EMT checked them out, then loaded Dave into the ambulance. Nick climbed in to ride along to the hospital.

Dave pushed the oxygen from his face and grinned over at Nick. "You're gonna miss this."

Nick leaned back and clasped his hands behind his head, the feel of scorched hair cementing his belief that transferring to the little Texas town of Harper's Grove, population 1,285, was the right thing to do. "Yeah, like I'd miss a heart attack."

His friend took a few more deep breaths, pain etched on his face. "Yeah, well, maybe I'll join you after my leg heals."

"Right. You do that." Nick laughed. Dave was a third generation Houston firefighter. The only way he'd leave would be feet first. "I'll put in a good word for you."

Dave raked a hand through his sooty red hair. "I thought you were the guy to put a good word in with."

"I am. The chief is retiring. Who else would hire your lazy ass?"

"Mmm." Dave opened his unfocused green eyes. "The pain meds are kicking in. See you on the other side?"

Nick drove his red Dodge Ram pickup around the town square of Harper's Grove, the next week, feeling like he'd stepped back in time.

In the middle of the square was the old red brick courthouse, its thick white columns glistening in the midmorning sunshine. Trees with vivid pink and white blossoms perfumed the air. A smattering of vehicles were parked in between the pristine white lined spaces surrounding the courthouse. People were arriving to patronize the shops lining the square.

He noticed the trucks he'd seen bore farm plates, while his simply read truck. The little house he'd rented just off the square was quaint, by city standards, but suited him. Maybe once he was settled, though, he'd think about a small farm so he could boast farm license plates on his truck. The thought made him grin.

Through his open window, he took a deep breath of unpolluted air and smiled.

He was finally home.

Home. She was home. Emotion clogged her chest, constricted her breathing. Blinking back tears, Tricia Lundsford reminded her sappy self she was right back where she started, at emotional ground zero.

Still, she couldn't help but smile at the familiar sights and sounds of Harper's Grove when she parked her Tahoe in front of her grandmother's tea room, Cup Half Full.

The bell above the door tinkled merrily when she walked in. The sweet smell of her grandmother's famous cinnamon rolls filled the air. As usual, the lingering midmorning patrons turned as one to see who had walked in. Conversation ceased.

She wiggled her fingers at them in a meek wave. "Hi, y'all." She shrugged. "I'm back."

Voices erupted in greeting, several people asking where she'd been and why she'd stayed away so long. She side-stepped their questions, intent on getting to her grandmother. Besides, how would one tactfully tell the group of well-meaning busybodies out front that she'd left because of them. Because she wanted to go where nobody knew her name, where she could be herself without having every mistake she'd ever made drawn out to be compared to her latest failure. Anonymity had its advantages.

"Welcome home, Patricia," Mrs. Swift, her first grade teacher, said, peppermint-scented breath fanning Tricia's face as she was drawn into a brief hug. "I know Hannah's missed you something awful."

Tricia nodded, her throat tight as she walked toward the kitchen door.

Her grandmother bent over the oven door, sliding out an industrial size baking sheet of fluffy cinnamon rolls. Flour floated in the air, lit by the sunshine streaming into the big kitchen, giving the room a surreal haze.

"Hi, Gram," Tricia said, once her grandmother had placed the rolls on the cooling rack.

Hannah Collins turned as she wiped her hands on her full-length apron, pale blue eyes widening, then narrowing with her delighted smile. "Tricia! Give me some sugar!"

Tricia found herself immediately enveloped in a smothering hug. Face pressed against her grandmother's ample bosom, she tried to drag in a breath to her oxygen deprived lungs, inhaling the ever-present scent of cinnamon and vanilla she had forever associated with her grandmother. "Gram!" She tapped the older woman's shoulder. "I can't breathe!"

"Oh, horse feathers, don't give me that." Gram released her and stepped back after planting a smacking kiss on her forehead. "You always did overreact." She shook her head of white hair, which always stood out from her scalp like she'd stuck her finger in a light socket. Micro specks of flour floated through the air. "Must've inherited your dramatic flair from your daddy." Her mouth puckered as though even speaking of the man who'd abandoned his wife and infant daughter left a bad taste.

Gram pulled her into another bone crushing hug, then held her at arm's length. "You've lost more weight. You're too thin."

"Gram, I'm the same as I was at Christmas. And that was about twenty pounds overweight."

"I still think you're too skinny. Men like to have something to hold on to," Gram said, arching a brow, "if you get my drift."

"Your *drift* has the subtlety of a sledgehammer."

In response, Gram reached out and unbuttoned the second and third buttons on Tricia's blue henley knit shirt. "Never hurts to advertise a little, Missy. You know, give a little sample of the goods." She winked.

"Gram!"

"Oh, loosen up. Your generation didn't invent sex, you know. All I'm saying is you need to flaunt what you have while you still have it. You make all those sexy clothes and I bet a nickel to a hole in a donut you never wear any yourself."

"I'm trying to make a living by selling what I make." Besides the fact her creations left little to the imagination—no one would want to see that much of her expansive body. "If I kept it, don't you think that would kind of defeat the purpose?"

"You never heard of free advertising?" Gram countered.

The bell dinged in the tea room. Gram stretched to look over the pass through. "Go see who's here, Tricia. Rose went to stay with her daughter and the new baby for a spell, so I'm shorthanded. I need to frost these before they get too cool."

Tricia spotted the stranger right away. He stood out like a purebred race horse among a pack of mules. Tall, he towered over any other man in the room, even while seated. His close-cropped dark hair shone in the morning sunshine, the hard line of his tanned jaw uncompromising. Straight nose, little white squint lines around the outer edges of deep blue eyes, framed by what looked like a double row of sooty black eyelashes.

Wow. What a hunk. Her hand flew to nervously re-button her shirt as she walked to the end of the counter to take his order.

"Don't do that," he said with a grin, nodding toward her buttons, "on my account." He flashed a dazzling white, lazy grin no doubt guaranteed to reduce the female population to mush.

Too bad. She was immune. But two could play that game. Shoring up her bravado, she approached him.

She flicked open another button and leaned low over the counter, willing the Her Highness push-up bra to not fail her now. Her tongue did an exaggerated sweep of her lower lip, while she ignored the jolt of excitement when his eyes followed the movement. "What'll it be?" she asked in an uncharacteristic sex-kitten voice.

His blue-blue gaze dropped to her cleavage, then ever-so-slowly tracked up her chest until he was seeing eye-to-eye with Tricia. A slow grin split his face. "Darlin' you don't really want to know." He sat back on the counter stool and put down the menu. "I'll just have a cup of coffee. Black." He sniffed the air. "Is that cinnamon rolls I smell?"

She nodded.

"I'll take one of those. Make that two."

Re-buttoning her shirt, avoiding eye contact with the other patrons, she asked, "What kind of coffee?" At his blank stare, she rolled her eyes and elaborated. "Regular, dark roast, espresso, decaf or fu-fu."

"What's fu-fu?"

"You know." She shrugged. "Flavored. We have amaretto, hazelnut—"

"Stop." He held up his hand. "I'll just take regular, fully caffeinated, black." His eyes met hers, his voice a low, intimate rumble. "And I want it hot."

Oh, baby. Pictures flared through her mind of them naked, having the hottest sex of her life right there on her grandmother's counter. Sweat popped out on her forehead, while further south moisture of a different kind occurred.

She managed a tight smile. "Don't we all?" Cheeks flaming, but thrilled she'd thought of a fairly quick come-back, she turned and walked toward the coffeemaker, snagging a big white ceramic mug on the way.

Walk smooth, glide, so you don't slosh the coffee, Gram's words from long ago echoed in Tricia's mind.

Her boot heel caught in the little circles of the non-skid runner behind the counter, jerking her progress to a halt.

Horrified, she watched the coffee rise in slow motion out of the cup, hover in the space above the rim for a moment, then splash down to scald her hand and chest.

Before her scream left her throat, the stranger was by her side. He grabbed the cup and set it aside, then pulled her to the sink and ran cold water over her now purple hand.

Tears stung her eyes. Despite her struggling, his iron grip kept her hand under the frigid stream of water. In the distance, she heard the other patrons asking what happened and if she was all right.

Water pressure slacked. Cold water from the spray showered her steaming chest, relieving her aching nipples. She gasped and the spray ceased.

They stood staring at her chest. Her wet, coffee stained shirt clung like shrink-wrap to her breasts, heaving against the Her Highness push-up bra.

"Does that feel better?" he asked in a deep, intimate sounding voice.

Define better. "Ah, I guess." She glanced down again. "I know it's spring break in some places, but did I enter a wet T-shirt contest without knowing it?"

White teeth flashed in his tan face. Up close, his eyes were even bluer. "Yep. And you won."

Was he flirting? Should she flirt back? Why not? "Cool. What did I win?"

"The booby prize—dinner with me."

2

Smooth, real smooth. Did he actually just say booby? Her breasts, which had him salivating the moment she walked toward him, were at the forefront of his thoughts, but he still couldn't believe he said the word. He chanced a glance at her face. She hadn't run screaming, so he took it as a good sign. "Actually, I'm new here and would appreciate the company. You're not married or anything, are you?"

The way she'd looked at him, he'd bet she was unattached but you never know. Relief, totally disproportionate to the situation, rolled through him when she shook her head with a smile.

He turned his gaze away from her mouth before he did something really stupid like kiss her. Unfortunately, his eyes were drawn to her wet shirt and the generous curves beneath. Lordy, what he wouldn't give for her bra to be lace instead of the industrial looking thing she wore. Were her nipples puckered? Would they be small or large, brown or that cherry cola color that drove him wild?

"Hello?" She waved her hand in front of his eyes. "I'm up here."

He hadn't blushed since junior high, but the heat streaking through his face to his hairline felt suspiciously like he'd just revisited puberty.

Her green eyes sparkled with humor. Whew. Pissing off someone you wanted to date had to be right up there with the original sins.

"Let's start over." He took a deep breath and extended his hand. "I'm Nick Howard. Just transferred here from Houston."

"Tricia Lundsford. I grew up here and can't imagine why anyone in their right mind would relocate here." She shook his hand briefly. Too briefly. He found he missed the touch.

Oh, yeah, the town just got more interesting. "Then why did you stay?"

"I didn't. I've been gone for ten years. In fact, I just moved back today. My grandmother owns this place and she needs my help occasionally. Since the lease was up on my shop, I decided to rent the place next door so I could do double duty here when I'm needed." She rocked back on the heels of her cowboy boots, almost toppling into the stack of cups by the sink.

He reached out to catch her, his hand brushing the edge of the cup tower, sending it crashing to the tiled floor.

Around them, laughter erupted.

"Welcome home, Tricia!" someone yelled.

Another called out, "Seems like old times, huh?"

Nick dropped to his knees to help her pick up the pieces of broken cups.

"Tricia!" Gram's voice echoed against the steel appliances. She bumped open the swinging door from the kitchen and charged into the tea room. "What in tarnation are you doing down there? Was that—oh, no, those were new cups!" She grabbed a broom on her way to the couple. "Are you okay?" Her eyes narrowed. "What happened to your shirt?"

Her gaze swung to Nick, now standing with his hands full of broken pottery. "I'm sorry, customers aren't allowed behind the counter."

"Gram! He was helping me." Tricia held out her hand, red and puffy-looking clear up to her elbow. "I sloshed coffee on my hand and I—"

Her grandmother harrumphed. "Wouldn't have happened if you'd been wearing proper footwear."

"I didn't know I was going to be put to work the second I stepped back inside."

Gram fished in her apron pocket. "Here. There's first aid ointment in the medicine cabinet in the apartment. Take the key and get settled. I had the place cleaned and aired out. Even put in smoke detectors and fire alarms." She cast a knowing glance at Tricia, then pressed the key into Tricia's uninjured palm. She glanced over at Nick then back to Tricia. "I've got plans tonight, so I won't be around to help. If you're up to it, though, I could use you tomorrow for the breakfast crowd."

"Where are you moving? I don't have to be to work for two more days. Since I'm already settled, I wouldn't mind helping." He couldn't believe the words that just fell out of his mouth. He'd just met the woman and he was already offering to help her move.

He watched her shapely bottom while she finished sweeping the shards into a dust pan. Maybe he could move her in more ways than one.

"You're a good boy," the old lady said, patting his arm. "Give him whatever he wants," she instructed on her way back to the kitchen. "On the house." The door swung shut.

Conversation resumed in the eating area.

Tricia plucked the shirt away from her skin. "What would you like?" she asked absently, eying the stain.

"Is that a trick question?" He stepped closer to avoid prying ears. "'Cause, darlin', I can think of a few things right now.

And if you keep playing with your bra and that wet shirt, I'm sure I'll think of more."

Her widened gaze met his. Then something changed, shifted, heated. She leaned in and whispered, "Oh, yeah? I'm moving into the apartment upstairs. My packed car is right outside if you'd like to make good on your offer. Then," she said, rising on tiptoe, her breath hot against his ear, "we'll see what we can come up with."

Something else was definitely coming up. He shoved his hands in suddenly tight pockets and nodded. "But I'll need a couple of those cinnamon rolls for energy. And I'll take a large coffee. To go."

Tricia jiggled the key in the door of the old living quarters, more than acutely aware of the heat of the man standing behind her.

The ancient tumblers finally clicked into place and the door swung open.

"Just put those anywhere," she said, taking one of the boxes from Nick. "I'll unpack later."

"I don't think so." He straightened and took a swig of his coffee then looked at her. "We have a dinner date, remember?"

"Oh. You don't have to really take me to dinner. I was just goofing around when I asked what I won."

"You have to eat. So do I. Why not do it together?" He glanced around the apartment. "It's bigger than it looks."

"What?" She tore her guilty gaze from the bulge in the front of his jeans.

"I said the apartment is bigger than I thought it'd be."

"Oh." She'd have known that if she hadn't been fixated on the size of other things. Things she needed to stop looking at before she got caught.

"My grandparents used to live here, before they had children," she explained, pushing a heavy carton with her foot in order to get the door closed. "It covers two stores—the tea room and the shop next door, which will be mine as soon as I get settled."

"Oh, yeah? What kind of shop?" He leaned against the jamb, arms crossed over his impressive chest.

Impressive only if you were interested in those sort of things, which she was definitely not. No sir. Not anymore.

He crossed one booted ankle over the other. Her gaze tracked the long expanse of denim . . . right back to the obvious bump behind his fly.

Okay, now *that* was impressive. Just a casual observation. It didn't mean she was even slightly interested. Anyone would have noticed.

"What?" What had he just asked? "Oh, um, intimate apparel. Custom-made, intimate apparel."

"Like Victoria's Secret?"

"Hmm? Kind of." Her lids felt heavy. Try as she might, she couldn't make her eyes obey her commands. No matter where she looked, her gaze always slipped back down *there*. Her pulse pounded. The effect he had on her was not normal.

Nick concentrated on not noticing the way the blonde was checking out his package. Damn, if she kept staring she'd really get an eyeful. Just smelling her sweet perfume and watching the sway of her jean clad butt as they'd climbed the stairs had him hard. If she didn't behave soon he'd embarrass both of them. It had been too long since his last sexual encounter. Way too long. He'd have her on the floor and naked in seconds, given the right encouragement.

"How much time do I get?" Her eyes met his.

"Excuse me?"

"Time. How much time do I have to get started on unpacking and make myself presentable before you come back to take me to dinner?"

Mind out of the gutter, Howard. "How about I help carry the rest of the stuff in and then come back around seven? While you unpack, you can decide where you want to go. I'll use that time to swing by the firehouse and get acquainted."

She nodded.

Damn, he didn't want to leave her.

"Well." He reached for the door. "I'll see you in a few hours."

"Right." She nodded. "See you then."

He turned to leave, stopped and turned back. "Tricia, I—"

"Yes?"

When he turned, she was standing right there, the coffee soaking into his T-shirt where the tips of her breasts pressed against his chest.

"I forgot something."

"What?" She looked up through her eyelashes, making his knees weak.

He pulled her close, ignoring the dampness soaking through his shirt. She didn't resist. He took that as a sign.

"I forgot to kiss you good-bye," he murmured, his mouth so close to hers he felt her breath on his lips.

"Oh. Okay," she said, standing on tiptoe and pulling him down until his mouth settled on hers.

Heat. He wasn't prepared for the incredible rush of heat that flashed through his body at first contact.

It was nuts. He gathered her closer, lifting her from the floor. It was insane. He turned, pinning her to the door, his hands pushing up under her soggy shirt.

Funny. He thought she'd fit his palms perfectly. Instead, her well-endowed bosom overflowed his hands. He experimentally squeezed her breasts, grinding his erection against her feminine counterpart.

Liquid filled his palms, shoving him from his erotic aspirations. Damn, was the woman lactating? It ran down his arms, saturating the front of his jeans.

Tricia gasped and struggled from his embrace.

Shocked, he let her go, still staring at the semi-congealed goop filling his hands and covering his person.

"What the hell is that?"

"I'd say about $68.50 worth of self-confidence." She grabbed a throw from the old sofa and wrapped it around her chest. "You just killed my bra."

3

"I what?" Nick looked so shocked, she would have laughed had she not been on the edge of hysteria.

Instead, she pulled the old afghan closer and pushed him out the door onto the little landing. "Never mind. Bye."

He stopped the closing of the door with his hand. "I'll be back. Seven."

She nodded, fighting back tears, then quietly closed the door.

Reaching under the throw, she maneuvered the bra until she had Her Highness off, then slung it across the room.

It hit the wall of the kitchen with a soft thud, then slid down, leaving a wet trail on the powder-blue wall.

What a waste of money. She dropped the afghan, unzipped her jeans and shoved them down and off. Her boots, socks and thong followed until she stood completely naked in the sunshine that streamed into the cozy living room. Maybe a shower would give her some energy.

The click of the door caught her attention.

Nick stood in the open doorway and swallowed, his gaze searing her from head to bare toes and back again.

She snatched the afghan from the floor and held it in front of her.

"Sorry," he said, biting back a smile and looking anything but. "I wanted to ask if I needed to dress up for dinner."

"Ah, no. Everything is pretty casual around here." She scanned his lean, jean-clad and oxford cloth shirted frame as if she didn't already have it memorized. "What you're wearing is fine, without the gel of course, just about anywhere we decide to go."

He nodded. "Okay. See you." Before the door closed, he stuck his head back in and said, "This time, you'd better lock the door behind me. If I come back in, I won't want to leave again."

Promises, promises. But she walked to the door and slid the bolt home anyway.

After Alex-the-aggressively-unfaithful had used and dumped her, she'd taken a vow of celibacy. Being home again, at the original scene of the crime so to speak, just made her more vulnerable. She could handle it. Ooh, bad choice of words. She was celibate. She wasn't going to handle anything.

She thought ahead to her dinner date, how sexy Nick was and the heated gleam in his eyes. Where were chastity belts when you needed them?

Nick tilted back in the metal chair of his new office and regarded the man leaning against the doorway. "What, exactly, are you telling me?"

Jack, his second in command, stepped in and lowered his booming voice a decibel or two. "I just thought you should know. All through school, she wasn't called Hurricane Lundsford for nothing. She just has a habit of, well, she attracts trouble." He chuckled and shook his head. "Hell, I give her credit for having the balls to come back, even after all these years. Small towns have memories like elephants."

"Sounds to me like she had too many critics in Harper's Grove. No wonder she bolted." He tried hard to not let his irritation show, but what right did Jack have to try to warn him away from the first woman he'd been even remotely attracted to in almost two years?

"That may be, but, aw, hell, do what you want." Jack raked his hand through his spiked blond hair. "You're gonna anyway. I thought you might stop thinking with your little head for a minute and realize it's not a good situation to have the town see you aligned with Hurricane Lundsford before you even get settled." He turned to leave.

"Jack?"

Jack paused, his hand on the door knob.

"Thanks, anyway," Nick said quietly. "I'll take it under advisement."

Jack nodded and let himself out.

Nick glanced at the industrial looking clock on the white wall. If he hurried, he'd have time to shave again and shower before he picked up Tricia.

He rubbed the stubble on his chin as he walked to the truck. He was only shaving again because it wasn't polite to go on a first date with five o'clock shadow.

The thought of Tricia's fair skin marred by razor burn had not a damn thing to do with it.

The scented lotion glided over her shower warm skin like liquid silk. Her body heat activated the cherry scent to waft over her, making her achy and restless.

She circled her areola, watching the dark skin pucker, budding her nipples into stiff peaks and bit back a groan.

Celibacy wasn't all it was cracked up to be. It was darn hard work.

Her lotion slicked hand skimmed down to the neatly trimmed

pubis and she couldn't help wondering if Nick would appreciate the little heart she'd painstakingly crafted.

Wait. Nick would never see it. She was celibate. She needed to remember that.

Her reflection in the wardrobe mirror of her bedroom snagged her attention and she studied her body with a scrutiny usually reserved for laboratory rats.

In hindsight, purchasing the Her Highness bra wasn't one of her brighter moves. She hefted her breasts and decided they weren't all that small and if she really wanted cleavage, she could always duct tape them together. Remembering the rash from the last time she did that, she winced and scratched. Then again, maybe not.

She turned and glanced critically at her rear end. Too much junk in the trunk. She thought of the way she'd caught Nick gazing at it and decided maybe she'd overcompensated when she bought the Her Highness in her effort to draw attention away from her hips and butt. It had seemed like a good idea at the time.

Heat flashed through her at the thought of Nick's hands on her breasts, his erection pressed firmly against her mound.

The last time she'd had sex was . . . way too long ago to count. That had to be the reason that just the thought of Nick made her wet and feeling empty.

Wait.

No one knew she was home, other than the few patrons of Cup Half Full. She could do pretty much what she wanted for at least a day or two.

She brushed her fingertips across the now swollen lips protruding from the close-cropped heart of sandy curls and gasped at the intimate feel.

Opening her eyes, she looked at her flushed reflection. Did she dare? Nick was practically a stranger.

All of her teenage boyfriends passed through her mind, a blur of humiliation.

A stranger might be a welcome change.

She could ride him all night, slake her lust, and no one would be the wiser. If she kept the lights off and lit enough candles to appear romantic, he might not even notice her less-than-perfect body.

Tomorrow she could begin her celibacy again.

Nick turned off the porn movie and finished shaving. He'd thought to watch the flick and whack off before his shower to take the edge off. He was as horny as his granddad's hound dogs. Weird. Just the thought of Tricia gave him an instant hard-on, yet watching the graphic movie had left him cold. What was it about the little blonde that had his dick twitching with eager anticipation?

He shrugged and stepped into a less-than-warm shower that caused a hitch in his breath and forced his mind to the evening ahead. Slow and easy. He'd take it slow and easy if it killed him.

Tricia lit another candle and coughed. They were more potently scented than she remembered. A glance at the clock on the microwave confirmed Nick would arrive in less than ten minutes.

She wiped her sweaty palms on the side of her terry robe and said a little prayer that she'd read the handsome firefighter correctly.

A knock sounded in the quiet apartment. Her heartbeat echoed in her ears.

"Who is it?" she called, even though she had a pretty good idea. It wouldn't do to open the door, primed for lust, and find anyone other than Nick. Like her grandmother.

"Nick," came the deep voiced answer.

"Just a sec!" She met her semipanicked gaze in the decorative mirror over the fireplace mantle, took a deep breath and tossed the terry robe into the closet. On wobbly legs, she walked to the door.

No retreat. "Take no prisoners," she whispered before opening the door.

Nick stood in the doorway, clutching the neck of the bottle of chardonnay in a death grip.

He was a dead man.

Tricia stood before him, the candlelight behind her playing a wicked game of peek-a-boo through one of the sheerest scraps of lingerie he'd ever had the privilege to encounter.

"Hi." She motioned him in. "I thought we could either have dinner here or have an appetizer here and eat later," she said, stepping back for him to enter.

So dead. "I brought some wine," he said inanely.

She took the bottle and set it on the side table next to the door. "Maybe a little later." She smoothed the gossamer fabric over her lush hips, then met his hungry gaze. "You asked, earlier, what I made." She put her arms out to her side and turned in a slow circle. "I thought I'd show you."

He may be a dead man, but one part of his anatomy was leaping to life at the sight. Her nipples were dark shadows beneath the elaborately embroidered red and hot pink hearts shielding them. When she turned, the sheer fabric swept against her hips in a sensuous rustle of silk. Beneath the sheerness, a red ribbon bisected a trophy ass if he'd ever seen one.

His eager cock pressed against the button fly of his jeans.

She rose on bare tiptoes to brush her lips over his, her pebbled nipples poking his chest through the layers of their respective clothing.

"This is from my Valentine Lovers Collection." Her voice was low, seductive, wrapping around his cock and squeezing from within. She ran a red polished fingernail along the embroidery until she came to the top of one nipple. "I call this pattern Secret Bliss." A crackling sound came from her chest before she flipped down the heart shape to reveal a pebbled nipple. "What do you think?" She flipped open the other little secret door.

He locked his knees to keep from falling at her feet in a pile of lust crazed hormones. Praying his voice wouldn't crack, he said, "Looks like a winner to me." He took a hesitant step closer. "But maybe we should do some product testing."

She closed the distance between them, looping her arms around his neck. "I couldn't agree more." She leaned back, her nipples jutting toward him. Begging him to take them.

It would be ungentlemanly to let a lady beg.

Tricia closed her eyes and clamped her thighs together to keep from rubbing against the man in her arms when he closed his hot mouth firmly over her nipple and suckled her.

Moisture saturated the crotch of the scanty thong.

He reached up to palm her other breast, squeezing rhythmically with his suckling.

One of them moaned. It may have been her. Thank goodness the guy was strong or else she'd have been on the floor. Her knees had taken on the consistency of overcooked spaghetti with the first strong draw of his mouth. When he added the tongue action, she all but swooned.

He gave a final lick to each well-tested nipple, his breath fanning the wet tips. "We need to check out the entire ensemble." His breath came in shallow pants, his eyes fever bright. "Where can we do more thorough testing?"

Hot damn. Her grandmother was right about the effectiveness of advertising after all.

She pointed to the couch. She'd have chosen the bedroom, but her bed was still a work in progress, piled high with clothing. Besides, with all the candlelight, the lighting was more flattering in the living room.

Just as she was thinking how romantic it would be if he swept her up in his arms and carried her to the couch, he came up with a much more interesting variation.

Behind her, he hugged her around her waist, his lips trailing kisses up and down the side of her neck, setting off tingles in places that hadn't tingled in a very long time.

One of his hot hands smoothed down her stomach then pushed on her pubic bone while he ground his hardness into her buttocks.

Before she could react or decide if she wanted more, he pushed both hands up her rib cage to cup her breasts.

Oh, yeah. She definitely liked this. To encourage him, she pushed back hard against his erection, eliciting a sound somewhere between a growl and a groan. It made her exposed nipples bead impossibly harder. She was sure her thong would literally drip if she tried to move.

He squeezed her breasts to the point of near pain, thrust his hips against her butt and lifted her from her feet to carry her to the couch.

Unconventional, maybe. Erotic . . . definitely.

He set her on her feet next to the couch and leaned around to lick her lips.

"Show me more," he whispered, his breath hot against her cheek.

Did she dare? Oh, who was she kidding? If she thought she felt wicked designing and making the prototype she wore, it was nothing compared to the way she felt at that moment.

"I plan on it." She turned and pushed him to sit on the couch, then stood straddling his knees. "This number is multipurpose." She ran her hands up his steel-like thighs to barely brush her thumbs against the hardness beneath his fly. "Designed to be used by one," she said, licking her flavored lip gloss, "or more lovers at a time."

"Do tell," he said, eyebrows arched.

She nodded, emboldened by the heat in his gaze that made her nipples tingle. "For instance," she explained, taking his hands and placing them on her exposed nipples, "you could play here." Her breath caught when he lightly pinched the hardened tips then brushed the pads of his thumbs over the points. "And, um . . ." She licked her lips. What the heck. "Someone else could play here." Before she lost her nerve, she placed one bare foot next to his thigh and canted her hips for him to better view the heart shaped opening in the crotch of her matching thong.

His eyes widened, along with his smile. "I don't think so, baby." Pressure on her nipples drew her closer.

He released one nipple and cupped her buttock to pull her up onto his lap until she was stretched along his length.

"I can multitask," he said, drawing her abandoned nipple into his hot mouth. At the next heartbeat, his fingers played with her slick folds, making them impossibly wetter before inserting one talented finger after the other.

The ribbon bow on her hip slipped, the thong falling away. His fingers left her for less than a second to drag off the wet fabric. On sensory overload, she could only whimper, unable to even move her hips in counterpoint to the renewed thrusting of his fingers.

Ripe sensation filled her until the dam burst. It was beyond the big O. Until that moment, she'd never experienced an all-over orgasm. Every pore gushed.

She gasped for air, her entire body one giant orgasmic contraction.

Sometime during her attempted recovery from her in-body experience, Nick had shed his pants. The feel of hot male flesh against her ribs barely registered before he lifted her from his blast furnace body.

Before she could form a protest—yeah, like that was going to happen—he brought her down on his more-than-impressive erection. The tip of his penis kissed her uterus. Again and again she slammed down on him until she was screaming her need.

She may have even passed out for a few seconds.

When her mind could put more than gasps and grunts into her thoughts, she tilted her head from his chest to tell him how spectacular he was only to be silenced with another rock-her-world kiss.

One of his fingers slid between them to draw lazy circles around her opening where his penis was still deeply embedded. His fingertip found her nub and began playing with it until it swelled with renewed lust.

She sighed.

Celibacy was so overrated.

4

The water had turned cold before they finished their shower. Lying on the bed, Tricia knew she most likely wore a sappy grin, but she couldn't stop smiling. She did some mental calculation and realized she'd had five orgasms. A new personal best. And the night was still young.

She moaned and moved restlessly against the sheet—they'd shoved her pile of garments aside for Nick to give her a massage. She should probably try to keep her butt tight while he was staring at it, but her muscles were recently converted to mush, thanks to Nick.

His oil-slicked hands ran up the insides of her legs, the pads of his thumbs petting her intimately.

He gave a playful slap on her bare bottom. "Turn over for me."

She grinned over her shoulder. "I've never had a massage like this."

He grinned back and waggled his eyebrows. "I should hope not." He nudged her hip with his naked thigh. "Turn over so I can see your mouthwatering breasts."

Uncertainty reared its ugly head. "I don't think that's a good idea. I'm—"

"Sexy as hell and all mine." He bent to kiss each knee apart. "For tonight, anyway."

What was she doing? She wasn't the type for casual sex. Heck, even uncasual, if she really thought about it. But . . . wow, there was just something about the man kneeling between her legs that made her forget all her flaws and uncertainties.

"Did you do this for me?" He traced the pubic heart with the tip of his fingers.

"Yes," she lied through panting breaths.

"Thank you." He placed a tender kiss in the middle of her artwork, then dragged his tongue all the way around the edge. Back where he started, he met her gaze and dipped his tongue into her slit to flick her clitoris. "So sweet," he said, his voice vibrating the sensitive bud.

He swirled his tongue around the rapidly engorging nubbin then sucked it deep into his mouth.

She arched off the mattress, her orgasmic screams echoing through the apartment.

Once again dressed in her Valentine Lover baby doll ensemble, she smiled at Nick. "I love it when you multi-task." She walked toward where he sat, naked, on her recliner, thrilling to the way his body responded to her.

"I aim to please."

Tricia climbed onto the recliner, one knee on each side of his lean hips, and brushed the head of his penis around the heart at her crotch, the embroidered edge branding the swollen head.

In response, he pulled her higher, dragging her along his throbbing cock until her ripe, cherry cola-colored nipple was level with his mouth.

Holding her high and away from his horny body, he touched

her puckered nipple through the opening with the tip of his tongue.

She moaned and tried to fill his mouth with her breast, but he held firm and continued flicking the tip with his tongue, torturing them both.

Holding her higher still, he grinned against the heart opening covering her sweet pussy and lapped at her already damp folds until he felt her muscles quiver.

He smiled against her nub and said, "I want you naked." He lowered her and stripped the sheer top from her delectable body, tossing it aside.

She grinned and slid down, her breasts blazing a trail down his chest, then lowered onto his cock.

They groaned and began moving.

Tricia stopped, her back stiffening.

He opened his eyes, her worried look putting him on alert. "What is it?"

"Do you smell something burning?" She raised to the tip of his shaft then screamed and jumped off his lap. "Nick! Fire!"

He'd smelled it the instant before her words were uttered, and jumped from the chair to beat at the flaming lingerie with the throw from the couch.

The throw immediately burst into flames that licked at the curtains.

In the distance, sirens sounded while Nick continued to battle the blaze, keeping it contained in one area.

Tricia hopped from foot to foot, screaming something about returning to the scene of the crime.

Her door burst in with a crash and three firemen ran in, extinguishers in hand. Within seconds, the flames were reduced to smoldering ashes.

Jack raised his mask and grinned. "Welcome home, Hurricane."

"Shut up, Jack!" She advanced on him, but Nick pulled her back and shielded her with his body.

Jack gave Nick a once-over and shook his head. "I'd ask what you were doing when the fire started, but I can make an educated guess."

Clenching his jaw, Nick attempted to cover his exposed privates with his hand while still shielding Tricia from the grinning hyenas.

The man Nick recognized as Bob said something into his transmitter then smirked. "Chief, when I said I was looking forward to seeing more of you, I gotta tell you, this isn't what I had in mind."

The third man stepped forward, the youngest of the bunch, Glenn. "Do either of you require medical attention?" he asked, his mouth twitching.

They assured them it wasn't necessary and the firefighters left, chuckling down the stairs.

Nick glanced around for his clothes and began putting them on. "I'd better go." He pulled up his jeans and walked to kiss her forehead. "Get some clothes on before you catch cold."

She caught his belt loop and pulled him back. "You still owe me dinner," she said in a small voice.

"Right." He pulled on his shirt and looked around for his shoes. "I'll have to take a raincheck. I've damaged your reputation enough for one night."

"I don't have a reputation to damage. Couldn't you tell?"

He walked out of the bedroom and wrapped her in the blanket he'd tugged from the bed. "No, all I saw were three goons practically gloating with the fresh ammunition they found to razz me tomorrow."

"I went to school with those goons."

"Yeah, they seemed happy to see you again." He pulled her to him for a thorough, but brief, kiss. "I'll swing by tomorrow to check on your progress with unpacking."

The door clicked shut.

She stood, surveying the fire damage, now mixed with the

white stuff covering most of her wall and living room floor, and pulled the blanket closer around her shoulders.

What started out as a harmless flirtation with the possibility of ending in sex had turned into a sexual gluttony that ended in her standard catastrophe.

She picked her way through the mess to the bathroom for a shower, singing, "Welcome back, your dreams were your ticket out . . . welcome back, welcome back, welcome back!"

The next morning, Tricia avoided eye contact with most of the regulars while she worked the counter at Cup Half Full. She just couldn't face the smirking faces and knowing grins so soon after her return.

She'd really messed up. Again. And, this time, she had no one to blame but herself.

Bus tray loaded, Tricia made her way to the kitchen. Her grandmother turned when she let the swinging door whoosh shut and put down her oven mitts.

"I was going to say good morning, sunshine, but all I see is clouds on your precious face." Gram kissed her cheek and pulled her into a hug. "What's up, buttercup?"

"I'm a failure." Tricia sniffed against the soft cotton of the older woman's shoulder. "It was a mistake to come back to Harper's Grove, Gram."

Her grandmother held her at arm's length. "Patricia Ann Lundsford! I don't want to hear talk like that! Why, everyone is thrilled to have you back. Harper's Grove just hasn't been the same without you."

"I believe that," Tricia said, digging for a tissue in the pocket of her baggy jumper. After wiping her nose, she forced a smile. "I thought I'd changed, Gram, grown up. But . . . last night just proved I'm still the loser I always was, always will be."

"Is this a private pity party or can anyone join in?" Gram regarded her with her hands on her hips. "Tricia, we all make mistakes. We're only human."

"You already heard, didn't you?"

Gram bit back a smile and nodded. "Don't worry about that. You just have to play the hand you're dealt and get on with your life. Not a day goes by that I don't miss your mama and granddaddy, but life goes on. I figure I owe it to them to live a happy and fulfilling life. So do you." She placed her hands on Tricia's shoulders and turned her toward the dining room. "Now get out there and push the cinnamon buns or we're going to have to come up with a way to camouflage them into the lunch menu."

Tricia had just finished refreshing coffee cups when the bell above the door jingled. Conversation, as usual, ceased. The air hung heavy surrounding her. She didn't have to look to know who just walked in.

Body heat pressed close to her back. "We need to talk," Nick's deep voice rumbled next to her ear. "Don't turn around. I feel like everyone is watching and listening to every word."

She put the pot back on the warmer, still turning away from the one man she wanted to see more than just about anyone. "That's because they are."

"Can you get away and meet me somewhere?"

She glanced at the old clock on the wall. "I can take a break for a few minutes now."

"Meet me out back."

She nodded and wondered who he thought they were fooling. Even if they hid behind the Dumpster, the whole town would know within minutes. It's just the way small towns were. And the more they tried to hide the worse it would be. Of course, someone from a big city like Houston wouldn't understand.

He was waiting beside the Dumpster when she walked out

the back door in her butt-ugly sack of a dress. He grabbed her around the waist and hauled her back against his eager body.

She gave a little shriek of surprise, then melted back against him. Lordy, he loved it when she became so pliant. Memories of last night flashed through his mind, bringing with them an instant hard-on.

He tweaked her breasts through the soft fabric, and wondered if she was wearing a bra. "Hi," he said, nuzzling her neck.

She sighed and nestled her tight little ass against his cock. "Hi, yourself. You do realize we're probably being watched, don't you?"

He grinned and turned her to face him, holding her close. "Yeah? Then let's give them something to talk about." He took her lips planning to give her a gentle kiss, but when she opened her mouth and touched his tongue with hers, all his plans headed south.

"Not here," she said in a breathy voice that tightened his gonads.

"Where?" He wasn't entirely sure he could walk with such a crippling hard-on.

"Let's go upstairs." She glanced nervously around, grabbed his hand and tugged him toward the stairs along the side of the old building. "But we have to hurry."

It was only through a tremendous strength of will that he refrained from running his hands under her skirt while he followed her up the seemingly endless steep stairs.

"I need a reward," he said, arms resting on the railing of the little landing at the top. His labored breathing had nothing to do with recent exertion. "Kiss me."

Tricia's glance swept the area. Evidently satisfied they were unobserved, she moved into his arms, her luscious curves aligning perfectly with his receptive body.

Teeth clicked when he jerked her tighter against him, his hands gathering the voluminous dress until he felt the soft smoothness of her butt. He ran his fingers along and up and down the thin strap of her thong, then wrapped the cord around his finger and tugged her up on her toes.

She whimpered and ground against his hardness, her tongue doing a passionate duel with his, her restless hands roaming all over his body, touching him everywhere.

In the distance, a truck motor rumbled, scarcely audible above the roar of blood in his ears. The louder sound of metal on metal sounded close to them. Very close.

A crackle filled the air, jerking them from their platform.

Before his lust crazed brain could decipher what he heard, they were airborne, bits of splintered wood floating around them in their free-fall.

Tricia broke the kiss with a scream. He clutched her to his chest and curled his body to protect her.

Rotting garbage broke their fall.

Relief lasted only a few seconds. They hovered precariously, held aloft by a giant metal claw, then fell into darkness.

Stinky darkness.

5

The garbage truck's powerful engine vibrated their personal cesspool. Tricia gagged and tried to stand up only to fall back against Nick.

Outside, voices raised and she thought she detected her grandmother's strident tones.

"Nick! Hold me up so I can see. I need to let them know where we are. Nick?"

She dropped to her knees and felt until she found him, lying atop a pile of particularly ripe garbage. She felt his face and found his eyes closed. Sweeping her hands down his chest, she felt for his wrist to check his pulse.

Instead, she found his crotch. Wow. She gave a little squeeze. He was still semierect. She knew she was getting distracted, but couldn't help mumbling, "Talk about staying power."

A hand grabbed her wrist in an iron grip. "Thanks."

She gave a squeak of surprise. "I thought you were unconscious!"

"Oh, yeah?" He rolled to his knees. "I was until you started playing with my balls." His teeth gleamed in the semidarkness. "Thanks."

"We don't have time for witty banter. We have to get out! We have to let someone know we're in here."

"Patricia Ann!" Her grandmother's voice could raise the dead. "Get out here right now, young lady!"

Nick leaned close and whispered, "I think they know."

The sunlight nearly blinded Tricia when Nick hefted her above the lip of the garbage truck. Voices told her most likely the entire restaurant had gathered to witness her latest mishap.

When her eyes adjusted, she saw her grandmother, standing in her ever-present hands-on-hips pose. She was not smiling.

Nick alighted first, then helped Tricia down, brushing ineffectually at the garbage littering her stained and wrinkled jumper.

"Are you all right?" Gram strode toward her, then stopped a good five feet away. "Woo-wee! You smell like a polecat! If you're up to it, I still need your help for the lunch crowd." She looked at her watch. "You have about an hour to clean up." Without a backward glance, she turned and walked back into the restaurant.

The crowd began breaking up. A man clapped Nick's shoulder. "Welcome to our world. For some reason, it always revolves around Hurricane." He looked over at Tricia. "Things have been mighty dull since you left. Welcome home."

Others mumbled much the same sentiments as they filed out of the alley.

"I'll walk you home." Nick took her elbow and steered her toward the exterior stairway.

She pulled away her arm. "I'm perfectly capable of climbing the stairs alone." Tears burned her eyes. She refused to let the small town gossips get to her again so soon.

"Yeah? Well, I'm not. The railing is rotted and I have a bitch of a headache. I need medication and something to eat. I suspect you can furnish me with both. And before you ask, yes, I have those things at my place, but yours is closer." He leaned close, eyes narrowed. "So don't even suggest it."

Biting her lip, she led him upstairs and wondered how many people watched their progress.

Inside her apartment, he grabbed her skirt when she attempted to walk to the little kitchen. "Wait."

She turned on him. "Why? I thought you were too hungry and/or hurting to make the five minute trip to your house." Humiliation still burned her cheeks, she didn't need the latest jerk in her life to start ordering her around.

"Strip." His quiet voice echoed in the room.

"You must've hit your head harder than we thought." She turned to resume her trek to the kitchenette. "You're delusional."

In response, he pulled her back again. The sound of ripping fabric filled the quiet apartment as her jumper and shirt were literally torn from her body.

"What are you doing?" Attempts to step away from his questing hands proved futile. Her thong was pushed down and pulled off her legs while he held her up off the hardwood floor.

Naked now, she stood before him, her hands covering her bare breasts and pubic area. Eyes wide, she watched him strip off his soiled clothing, his erection jutting and bobbing with his movements.

"Are you planning to force yourself on me?" she finally managed to choke out. How could she have been so wrong about a man? She glanced frantically around the little living room for a weapon.

He looked down at his personal tent pole and sighed, running a hand through his hair. "Don't pay any attention to that.

It seems to be its common condition around you. I wanted you naked because you stink. We both do. We need a shower." He held out his hand. "Don't get me wrong, I'd fuck you in a heartbeat, under normal circumstances." His shoulders slumped. He actually looked hurt. "But I'd never do anything you didn't want me to do. I thought you'd know that." He shrugged, avoiding eye contact. "I guess showering together is out of the question now. I'm sorry. I didn't mean to scare you." He turned toward the bathroom. "I'll call you when I'm out of the shower."

She stood for a few minutes after the water started. Was Gram right? Was she letting past experiences color her judgment and spoil her enjoyment of everything the future might hold?

Cool air ruffled the shower curtain before it was pulled aside. Tricia stepped into the claw foot tub with him and reached for the shampoo on the rack slung over the rod.

"Hi," she said in a quiet voice, as though they showered together every day.

She lathered and rinsed then lathered her hair again before she spoke. "I'm sorry about . . . what I said earlier." She rinsed her hair and looked up at him through spiked lashes. "I know you'd never hurt me."

It was hard to concentrate while watching water run in little streams from the tips of her nipples. One look in her eyes told him she spoke the truth. His heart expanded with the knowledge . . . along with other parts of his anatomy.

He brushed a kiss over her lips, tasting water and remnants of the soap she'd just used. Steam surrounded them, making a private oasis within the shower curtain. He drew a gentle line from her collar bone over the swell of her breast and around one nipple with the tip of his finger, smiling when the nipple puckered in response.

"I've never had sex in a shower," she said with a smile, stroking the tip of his cock.

"Isn't your grandmother expecting you soon?"

"We have a little time." She licked her lips.

His erection nodded its agreement.

"There's not much room in here to do it right."

"You seem like an inventive kind of guy." She drew her finger from his balls to the tip of his excited member and back down. "I trust you to find a way."

She trusted him. The fist in his chest eased. He grasped her waist and seated her on the back lip of the old tub.

She gasped. "It's cold."

"Not for long." He reached down and took her slender ankles in his hands and placed her feet on each side of the tub, then paused.

"What is it?" She tried to close her legs, but he held them spread wide for his viewing pleasure.

"Nothing. I was just figuring out how to do this," he lied. As new as their relationship was, it wouldn't do for her to know how much she affected him. He glanced down at his happy dick and amended that. She didn't need to know how much she affected him emotionally. It was pretty hard to hide the physical evidence.

He knelt between her legs, relieved to find the tub had a nonskid coating, and placed a tender kiss on her parted heart.

She rewarded him with a gasp and a shuddering sigh.

He edged closer, tugging her down a bit, the head of his cock so close to her wet heat, he could feel it wafting from her to surround him, beguile him.

One thrust took him home, buried to the hilt in her welcoming heat. He steadied her by placing one hand on her backside and one on her breast and took her remaining nipple deep into his mouth. With each thrust, he drew the pebbled nipple deeper into his mouth. Around his cock, her moisture made them slick and ran down his thighs. At his back, the hot water pounded a reciprocating rhythm, its warmth sluicing down to slide over his butt and caress his balls.

He increased the pace, now pounding into her slickness. Her heat surrounded him, creating a jungle beat of need to pulse through every nerve ending.

She wrapped her arms around his neck and held on, her breath coming in hot little puffs against the top of his ear.

One love bite on her breast pushed her over the edge, her scream echoing within the steamy enclosure, her tight pussy milking him of his orgasm.

With a shout, he shuddered his completion, grinding into her one last time.

They sat for a few seconds, water spraying his back, her face, while his heart rate settled into a more normal cadence.

He felt behind for the body wash and bathed her with all the foreign tenderness coursing through him.

Orgasm number two streaked through her while Nick so gently washed away the traces of their wild shower. She bit her lip to keep from crying out her pleasure and ordered her hips to refrain from bucking against his hand. Nick was being sweet and tender while she was being . . . well, sexually needy.

As they stepped from the shower, she discreetly dabbed her towel to hide her latest secret climax, face hot with guilt.

"Hey," Nick said, pulling her close to his warm, shower damp body and planting a kiss on her neck. "My headache is gone." He patted her butt and she worried it might jiggle beneath his palm. "Guess I just needed to get lucky, huh?"

"I guess." She grabbed a bath sheet and wrapped it securely around her flabby body. "I'll go make some sandwiches while you get dressed."

"I saw one of those stacking jobs in the kitchen." He followed close behind and scooped his clothes from the living room floor then held them at arm's length. "Would you mind if I threw these in the washer while we ate?"

"Good idea. The detergent's in the corner, fabric softener in the cabinet above."

He scooped her clothes up. "Great. Thanks. I'll throw yours in, too. They don't need any special stuff, do they?"

My, my all that sexy stuff and he does laundry, too. "Nope, they can be thrown right in with yours. Thanks."

Over peanut butter and strawberry jelly sandwiches, they got to know each other better. Tricia was delighted to find they had more in common than paint-peeling sex.

"I thought about coming over early this morning to volunteer to mop up the mess we made last night." He motioned to the scene of the fire. "But I see you already cleaned it up."

She nodded and took a swallow of cool milk. "Yeah, it's one of my nit-picky problems. I can't leave stuff like that around. Drives me crazy."

"Me, too!" He grinned around a mouthful of sandwich, and her heart constricted.

Another neat freak.

The shrink she saw after her mother and grandfather's deaths said her compulsive behavior was a control issue. She preferred to think of it as neatness.

How would Nick view it?

6

Nick watched Tricia tug at her towel, back stiff, as she walked to check on their laundry and wondered what he'd said to cause her coolness.

Warm jeans hit him in the face. His T-shirt followed. The warmth on his bare feet was probably due to his socks and boxers.

Yanking his freshly laundered clothes from his head, he glared at her. "What's wrong? Did I say or do something to piss you off?"

She sighed and tightened the damn towel. "No, of course, not. It was . . . fun. I just need to get down to Cup Half Full to help Gram." Clutching her clothing in front of her, she stared as though daring him to argue.

Nick Howard could never resist a dare.

"Fun?" He advanced until he'd backed her against the cupboard. "We had mind-blowing sex. Orgasmic sex. Universally revered sex. Fun is something you have at Disneyland."

He tugged until he loosened the towel enough to pull it from between their bodies, then ran his appreciative hands over every millimeter of her soft skin he could reach without letting her go.

She moaned, her head lolling to one side. He kissed a trail from her collar bone to the spot below her ear he'd discovered drove her wild. He sucked on it.

She gasped and shuddered in his arms, the hard tips of her breasts spearing his bare chest.

He moved his hands between them to roll her nipples between his thumbs and forefingers while he insinuated his knee between her thighs, pushing higher until he felt her dampness.

With a smile, he claimed her eager mouth, throwing every nuance from years of sexual experiences into a kiss she could carry with her until they were together again.

Her knees took on the consistency of microwaved Silly Putty. In fact, had she not been anchored by Nick's firm lips and his hands on her breasts, she was sure she'd float away on a cloud of sexual bliss.

With blind movements, she groped until she came to the edge of Nick's towel and gave it a yank. It fell from his luscious backside, but remained wedged between their bodies. She whimpered her frustration and he stepped back a fraction to allow her to pull the towel away. She wanted nothing to separate them. Skin to skin. Heart to heart.

Tab A to Slot B.

Her sexual aggression stumbled. Tab A had not worn a raincoat in the shower. Or last night.

"Wait," she said in a whisper then lost her train of thought when his hot mouth slid lower to latch onto her nipple.

His hand slipped down to cup her femininity. She groaned and widened her stance to accommodate whatever he wanted to do.

Shameless. She was shameless in her need for a sexual fix.

His fingers fluttered her labia and were rewarded by a fresh surge of moisture.

She moaned and hooked one leg around his to remain upright. The position opened her for his questing finger.

Ahh. What was she about to tell him? Something about a raincoat . . . shit! They needed condoms!

"Stop." She stepped back, breaking the lovely contact. "We can't. I don't have anything, do you?"

At his blank look, she said, "Condoms. Do you have any condoms?"

By the crestfallen look, she'd say the answer was no.

"I haven't been to a store for a while," he finally said in a strangled voice. His eyes met hers. "Oh, God. We didn't use any today. Or last night. Please tell me it's not your fertile time." He raked a hand through his hair then met her desperate gaze. "I'm so sorry. I'll get some before we go out tonight. I promise."

"I'm on the pill." Strange, she felt used and extremely sad that he obviously didn't want to have a baby with her.

Not that she'd want to have a baby with him or anyone else right now. But it should be her choice.

"And I don't remember us having a date tonight," she continued, to give him an out if he so desired. If he didn't want to have a baby with her, maybe he didn't want to have sex either. Or even date her, for that matter.

"We don't, I guess, technically, although I still owe you a dinner." He grabbed her wrist to prevent her from picking up her towel. "Don't. Not yet."

He closed the distance between them again and kissed her so deeply she wouldn't have been surprised to see her toes curl.

Within seconds, she'd melted into a puddle of need.

He grasped her waist and lifted her to the counter. Oddly, the marble cooled the skin of her buttocks yet heated her core, fueling her desire.

Carefully, he laid her back until she was stretched along the counter, petting and kissing her breasts, then lower until he reached his destination. He parted her lips, dragging his fingertip then his tongue along the plump inner lips while his finger probed her deeply, then deeper still.

He caught her nubbin with the edge of his teeth and worried it until her wetness covered his hand. Then he sucked the little kernel into his mouth, his suckling coordinating with the thrusts of his fingers.

Within seconds, she arched off the counter, its hardness biting into her spine, gasping her climax. He wiggled his fingers, still deeply embedded, and another wave of pleasure washed over her. He licked her clean and placed a gentle kiss on her swollen labia.

Weak, but still incredibly turned on, she watched him stride to the refrigerator, admiring the play of muscles on his tight butt. Shocked, she realized she wanted to touch him. All over. And, most shockingly of all, never let him go.

While she examined her recent revelation, he came back, shaking a can of whipping cream, a devilish smile on his handsome face.

He proceeded to fill her with the cold whipped cream and then suck it from her body, all the while laving her with his talented tongue.

Orgasms number three through five held her firmly in their grasp. Breathing was definitely impaired.

Bang, bang, bang! The old wooden door vibrated.

"Tricia! You in there?" Her grandmother's voice had her jackknifing to a sitting position on the counter. "You all right?"

"I'm fine," she called back, resisting only a little when Nick eased her back to the counter and spread her legs wider. "Aagh!" Cold water from the kitchen faucet sprayer bathed her recently well-loved and still sensitive petals.

"What? Tricia, should I get my key? Do you need help?"

Nick's sparkling eyes met hers. He slowly shook his head,

smoothing his hand over her, tantalizing her while he bathed her.

"No!" she called when she could drag enough oxygen into her lungs. "I'm fine, Gram, I just got out of the shower."

"What took so long? Oh, never mind. I need a break. Get down there as soon as you can." The sound of footsteps faded away.

Quiet once again filled the apartment, the only sound the tinkling waterfall of the kitchen sprayer and their labored breathing.

After Nick did a thorough job of drying her, with the occasional forays into areas that necessitated rebathing, she walked on wobbly legs to retrieve her jumper.

"It's torn." She turned accusing eyes on a very unrepentant looking Nick.

"It was ugly."

"That's your defense? It was ugly?"

"And it smelled. Really bad." At her continued stare, he admitted, "Okay, and I really, really wanted you naked."

She smiled. "I wanted to be naked with you, too."

He wiggled his eyebrows. "We're both naked now."

"What took you so long?" Gram untied her apron and grabbed her purse when Tricia walked into Cup Half Full half an hour later. "I was fixing to come up there and drag you out. We're almost out of sugar and eggs. I need to get some coffee, too. Where's my list?" She patted the pockets of her cardigan. "I'll be back in a little while."

"Wait!" Panic gripped Tricia. "What if someone orders something? Is anything made up?"

Her grandmother walked back, a tender smile on her face, and patted Tricia's cheek. "Don't worry, Sunshine. What happened last time was an accident. Besides," she said, her blue eyes twinkling, "Now you know one of the firemen, up close and personal. Maybe you'd get better service." She squeezed her granddaughter's shoulder. "You managed to make yourself scarce through the lunch crowd. There's plenty of iced tea, regular and fu-fu, and leftover cinnamon rolls. I don't care if you give them away. I'll cook when I get back."

Tricia had just finished wiping the counters when the phone rang. She made slow progress to the old black pay phone and lifted the heavy metal receiver.

"Cup Half Full."

"Your cups seemed a lot more than half full earlier," Nick's husky voice wrapped around her, warming her from the inside out.

What felt like a full body grin spread through her. "Hi, Nick."

"Are you busy?"

"Nope. I'm the only one here."

His growl came through the line. "You didn't put your panties back on, did you?"

Heat wafted through her. She glanced around and lowered her voice, even though there was no one to hear her. "No, but there's a definite draft."

He chuckled. "Darlin', I'd keep you warm if I was there." He paused. "Pull up your skirt for me."

"What?" She cast a quick glance around the deserted dining area and lowered her voice. "Why?"

"'Cause I'm so horny, I could steer my truck no-handed, if you get my drift. Humor me."

"What if someone sees me?"

"Aren't you behind the counter?"

"Yes . . ." He must've noticed where the phone was earlier.

"Okay. Push your skirt up to your hips. Close your eyes. Are they closed?"

"Yes," she whispered.

"Touch your pussy. Do you feel me? Feel how the little hairs tickle the pads of your fingers? Spread your lips and stroke your hot wetness for me. That's it. So soft and creamy. I want to be there, between your spread legs, sucking your clit, making you wet and trembling for me. Would you like that?"

"Y-yes," she managed to choke out, her hand learning the length and depth of her desire, the engorged nub dragging at her fingertips.

"Rub your clit, baby, hard." He chuckled when her breath hitched. "Oh, you're so good, so hot and wet and responsive. Pinch it for me." His breathing became harsh, his voice an octave lower. "That's me, I have you in my mouth, sucking, giving you love bites with the tip of my teeth."

Her breath caught, eliciting a moan while waves of pleasure washed over her.

"Do your tits ache for my mouth? Would you like me to suck you?"

"Y-y-es!"

"Dip your hand into the glass of ice on the counter. Take the ice and put it under your shirt on your aching nipples."

How did he know there was a glass on the counter by the phone?

Her fingers shook as she fumbled to unbutton the bodice of her jumper. The question didn't stop her from doing it. The ice immediately melted against her overheated skin, wetting the front of her T-shirt, dribbling onto her open jumper.

"Rub your pussy. Faster. That's me, with my cock buried deep within you, fucking you all night long. Oh, baby, that's right. A-ahh!"

She came at the same time, giant gushes of pleasure wetting her left hand while her right plucked at her nipples through the wet shirt, the phone wedged tightly against her shoulder.

Eyes clenched shut, she leaned against the counter, fingers petting while the pleasure vibrations ebbed and flowed in the afterglow, waiting for her breathing to regulate itself.

"Patricia Ann Lundsford! What in tarnation do you think you're doing?"

7

Nick flipped closed his cell phone, lowered the binoculars and looked at the mess in his lap. He hadn't whacked off in his car for years. Not alone, anyway. Thoughts of what just transpired had his cock vibrating with renewed interest.

Damn, tonight couldn't come fast enough. He looked down and smirked. He certainly had.

He tamped down the guilt of implying he'd been in his office and raised the binoculars, hoping for another glimpse of Tricia's world class ass.

He gave a surprised yelp and tossed the binoculars to the passenger seat when it looked as though the grandmother was glaring at him through the binoculars.

Tap, tap, tap.

He grabbed a napkin and swiped at the mess in his lap while he buzzed down the window.

"Having a car problem, sir?" A clean-shaven man close to his age, dressed in a starched tan uniform with the Harper's Grove police department insignia on it leaned against the window opening.

"No. I'm, ah, just looking around. I mean, I just moved here." He followed the officer's gaze to the telltale mess. "I don't usually . . . I mean . . ."

"License and proof of insurance, please, sir." He straightened, a hard impassive look on his face. "License, please. Now."

Nick listened, humiliation burning his ears, while the officer radioed his driver's license number in to check if he was a sexual predator.

Once his identity had been established, he thanked the officer, who assured him he was going to be watching him, and drove home.

Damn hormones. If things continued, he'd be blind and unemployed.

"Do you need to see a doctor, Tricia?"

Lord, she hated it when her own grandmother looked at her like that. Tricia swallowed her humiliation and shook her head while she righted her clothing.

"Nice girls don't go around without panties, flashing their woman parts for the world to see—"

"Gram! I wasn't flashing my woman parts. I was . . . masturbating!" She took perverse delight in her grandmother's shocked gasp. "Haven't you ever done that?"

She knew it was not likely, but she was tired and cranky and feeling generally bitchy.

Her grandmother's expression softened. "Well, your granddaddy, God rest his soul, has been gone a long time. If you don't prime the pump occasionally everything dries up, you know. I had you to raise. I couldn't take a lover and I had no desire for another husband."

Tricia put her hands over her ears. "Too much information, Gram!"

Gram grinned and pried one of Tricia's hands away. "Why

don't you invest in a good vibrator, sweetie? I have some catalogues—"

"Stop! I won't do it again, at least until I'm behind my own closed door. Okay? Could we drop this subject, please?"

"Why don't you stop trying to shock a poor old woman and go take a nap?"

"My machines are supposed to arrive today."

"So? You have the place cleaned and ready. I can let them in. It's the least I can do, since you'll be taking care of Cup Half Full while I'm gone."

Gone? Tricia did a mental head slap. She'd totally forgotten her grandmother's cruise. It was the reason she moved back a month earlier than planned.

"Ah, Gram, when were you leaving again?"

"Tomorrow morning, Patricia." Her grandmother shook her head and smiled. "I swear, you'd forget your head if it weren't attached."

"I didn't forget, I was just testing you. Old people tend to forget things." She grinned and sidestepped Gram's playful swat.

"Get on with you! I saw your young man a few minutes ago, sitting on the square in his truck. If I was forty years younger, I'd give you a run for your money." Gram fanned herself with her apron. "Mercy! That boy's a looker. If I was you, I'd forget vibrators with him around." She gave an exaggerated wink. "Nothing like the real thing."

Gram's words echoed in Tricia's mind while she trudged up the stairs.

The sound of hammering stopped at her ascent.

Nick stood, hammer in his hand, and wiped sweat from his forehead with the sleeve of his shirt. "I thought I'd work off some excess energy and fix the railing before someone gets hurt."

She grinned and unlocked her door. "Why don't you come in and take a break, have a drink?"

His gaze raked her from head to sandaled feet and back up. "I'm not sure that's such a great idea, after this morning."

From the way his heated gaze kept drifting over her body, he was definitely thinking about more than a drink. The idea of any male, but especially someone who looked like Nick, having the hots for her sent a spark of delight through her.

"Oh, come on. We're both thirsty. It's hot. We wouldn't want you to get dehydrated and fall into the Dumpster again."

He nodded and dropped his hammer into the toolbox at his feet then followed her inside.

After the bright sunshine, the little apartment was dark and cool.

She shivered and grabbed his sun warmed shirt to pull him close for a kiss.

"Hi," she said against his lips.

The kiss began as a sweet greeting, but quickly turned carnal. Teeth clicked, tongues dueled, hips ground.

Nick broke the kiss, clutching her against his heart. "Are you still not wearing panties?" His voice was raspy.

She shook her head and did a little shimmy against his hard body. "I'm not wearing *any* underwear." How much more of an invitation did the guy need? Did she dare do something blatant?

What the heck.

She strolled to the couch and sat down, hitching one leg over the rolled arm. Resisting the urge to squirm under his avid gaze, she inched the hem of the baggy jumper, enjoying the tactile pleasure of the chambray against her heated skin. Higher, higher until cool air soothed the spot between her legs that threatened to burst into flames.

She fanned the hem against her folds and found the sensation titillating, so she did it again. Nick's gaze followed every flutter.

With slow, deliberate movements she flicked open the button bodice. Next came the shirt until she'd bared her aching breasts down to her waist, fabric bunched around her hips to keep her nether regions open for his viewing pleasure.

"See?" she said, on the off-chance he hadn't noticed. "Nothing," she whispered, and licked her lips to keep from laughing at the stunned expression on his face. "Why do you ask?" If she didn't know, the bulge in the front of his jeans would be a great tip-off.

He took a step toward her, then another. "What time do you have to be back at work?" Crossing his arms over his chest, he pulled off his shirt without unbuttoning it and tossed it aside. The sight of his broad, bare chest, gleaming in the late afternoon sun streaming through the window, took her breath away.

"I'm finished for the day," she finally managed to say. Pretense at conversation stopped while she watched him toe off his boots and shuck his jeans. Beneath his white boxers, his intent was clear. His obvious reaction made her bold. "Why don't you go commando, too?"

"Because if I take these off, I know what will happen."

"So?" Spreading her bodice farther, she stroked the edges of her breasts, her gaze never leaving his.

His nostrils flared. "So I'll leave them on. For now."

He dropped to his knees and lifted her skirt a little higher, enjoying the view. His cock throbbed against the ever-tightening boxer fly.

The woman spread before him was a goddess. The living, breathing, embodiment of his every wet dream. How would he survive if he scared her away?

He watched her fondle her plump breasts, noticing her shallow breathing and flushed cheeks. A particularly torrid fantasy from college came back to him. Did he dare share it with her? Maybe the idea of role-playing would scare her off.

What the hell.

He raised her cold feet to rest on his pecs after kissing her toes. "Want to play a game?" Her legs were satiny smooth beneath his restless hands.

"Yes," she whispered.

He picked up the remote and the Nature Channel sprang to life on the flat screen above the library table.

They both watched the graceful leaps of the gazelle chasing its mate, and held their breath while viewing the two animals mating.

Wild animal sex. Nick bit back a sigh. How was he going to hold back or even pace himself with stuff like that?

"Pretend you're in a theater," he said, pointing at the TV. "Watch the movie." He pulled her skirt back down to her ankles but kept her legs spread. "Shh," he said when she looked like she wanted to protest.

Lifting her skirt, he stuck his head under and dragged his tongue up the inside of each leg before settling his mouth on her wetness.

Her muffled gasp filtered through the fabric, her hips bucking off the couch. Next to his ears, her muscles vibrated.

He ran his hands up and down her velvet soft inner thighs, spreading her wide for his hungry mouth.

Tricia's vision blurred, all her senses centered on the spot receiving such pleasure from Nick's mouth. Her heart banged against her ribs, her lungs wheezing to continue functioning. Was she having premature hot flashes? A heart attack? Was it possible to die from sheer bliss?

Gripping the upholstery in her fists to keep from floating to the ceiling, her breathing halted when the first flame of release flared to lick through her entire body.

Head thrown back, gasping for air, skin on fire, another

flame seared her when his mouth left her to be replaced by his cool fingers. Deep within, they stroked the fire hotter while his thumb rubbed her clitoris until it, too, joined the sensuous bonfire.

Before she could form a cohesive sentence or even string together two words, he reappeared from beneath her skirt to take one breast in his hand and draw the other deeply into the heat of his mouth.

Every cell in her body went on alert. Her back arched, pushing her breasts deeper into his hand and mouth. Under her skirt, her core sucked his fingers higher in an effort to appease the flames.

The heat flared as a flash fire of sensations swept through her.

Her hair may even have been smoking.

Bliss was such a tame word for what she'd just experienced.

Burn, baby, burn.

8

_____

Every muscle in Nick's body seized at the feel of the gorgeous woman coming apart in his arms. Her hot clit throbbed beneath his thumb while the blast furnace of her core sucked his fingers deeper into her lush, wet heat. Her velvet muscles clamped and unclamped, her come scalding his skin. He was burning up, on fire for the touch and taste of her.

Eyes closed, she drew a shuddering breath. Her internal muscles lessened their clamping, becoming soft and pliable.

Loathe to leave her heat, he slowly withdrew his fingers, stroking her along the way.

She opened slumberous eyes, their color now a brilliant green. "What's next?"

The second part of his fantasy.

"If I'd have seen you in a theater, when we were teenagers, I'd have walked up and asked if the seat was taken. You'd say no and I'd do this."

He swept her up and onto his lap as he claimed her seat, her back to his chest.

"Now, watch the movie." He looked down, fascinated by the contrast of his tanned hands against the creamy whiteness of her breasts. He flexed his hips, a spark of excitement shooting through him when she ground her sweet ass against his hardness.

Still actively fondling her breasts with one hand, his other one busily tugged her skirt up and out of the way. Shoving his boxer waistband down, he bit back a groan at the feel of his erect penis along the seam of her hot buttocks.

Tricia arched her back, pushing her breasts into his palms. He squeezed, glorying in her whimper and almost frenetic squirming against him.

Mine.

"Nick, please." Her dampness made his lap slippery.

"Watch the show," he whispered in her ear, reaching between them to fondle her ass, sliding his finger around to play with her wet lips, dipping into her slick folds, loving the little catches in her breath.

Tricia gasped, squirming on his lap, her wetness threatening to set him on fire.

He looked at the TV and groaned. Now it was two bears getting down and dirty. What was this, the Nature Fucking Channel?

Shoving her dress higher, he grasped her hips and impaled her on his cock.

They both sighed.

Tricia began first with a little hip movement that quickly gave way to full-out grinding. She grabbed his hands, pulling them up to cover her breasts.

He bucked against her, squeezing the soft pillows of flesh, a stupid grin on his face because he was finally living the fantasy. His balls tightened. He glanced at the TV. Damned if he'd let a bear out-fuck him.

He gave a final squeeze to her nipples and grasped her hips to bring her almost to the tip of his shaft, then slammed her down, grinding his hips against her ass.

She went wild, seeming to burst into flames in her passion.

She rode him hard, her hot pussy sucking him deep, releasing, then sucking again, her velvet muscles clutching him until they squeezed him dry.

Tricia, Nick, and the bears all roared their completion.

When his hearing came back and he was pretty sure he was no longer drooling, he hugged her tight to his heart.

Mine. But it was too soon to stake a claim. And it was for damn sure too soon to tell her he thought he may be falling in love.

She climbed off his lap, smoothing the skirt of that butt-ugly dress down to cover her hot body. And hotter piece of ass.

Maybe it wasn't really love. But he knew for damn sure hers was the best piece he'd ever had.

He pulled his boxers to cover his rapidly recovering cock and stepped into his jeans. "You do realize, now, we can never go to a movie."

She trailed a finger over his semierection, threatening to make the cotton burst into flames. "We could always sit in the back, where it's really dark."

He smiled and pulled her into his arms. "There are two problems with that idea. For one thing, I just realized I prefer to make love to you stark naked. That's frowned on, especially in small towns." Her giggle warmed him. "And second." He ran his hand under her skirt and plunged his finger into her wetness. Her muscles immediately clamped on, sucking him in. She groaned and moved against his hand. He petted her wet folds and tugged her skirt back down. "Second, you're a screamer."

He bent to lick her nipples then buttoned her dress. "Personally, I love it when I make you come so hard you scream. But, again, it might not be such a great thing in a movie theater."

"So you're telling me we can't go to dinner and a movie tonight?" She pouted, secretly thrilled to know she affected him so profoundly. "How about if I promise to be good?"

"Darlin', your goodness was never in question. It's my ability to keep my cock in my pants in that kind of situation. Hell, I'll be lucky not to throw you across the table and have you for my dinner. A movie would push me over the edge."

He walked to the door and paused. "I should probably tell you, I wasn't at the firehouse today when I called you." He shrugged. "I know it's a small town and word gets around. I wanted you to hear it from me."

"Hear what from you?" A chill swept the heat from her skin.

"I was, well, sort of watching you get off while we talked on the phone. With binoculars. And before you get all embarrassed or mad, I want you to know I did, too."

"Did what?"

"Got off." He looked sheepish. "I can't remember the last time I whacked off, especially in a car in broad daylight. If it's any consolation, I got caught and the guy thought I might be a sexual predator. Can you believe it?"

Quiet.

"Let me get this straight," she said, walking closer. "You masturbated in your truck while you watched me through binoculars. And you got caught . . . by whom?"

He shrugged. "I don't remember his name. Some cop."

Tricia rolled her eyes. "I'm related to most of the policemen in town and half the highway patrol. This is going to spread through town like wild fire!"

"How would what I did be connected to you?"

"Where were you?"

"In my truck, on the square . . . across the street from you."
Color left his face. "Damn, I'm sorry, I—"

"Nick, I think we need not to see each other for a while.
This has all happened too fast for me." She touched his arm. "I
think we both needed something and the chemistry was like
spontaneous combustion. But it can't burn that hot and last."

"But—"

"I'm tired of being the brunt of jokes. Been there, done that.
And, great as it was, I'm not cut out to be someone's sex toy."

"I never thought of you like that." He stopped her from
closing the door when he stepped into the hall. "Can we at least
date and see what happens?"

She knew what would happen. Hot sex. Her heart was already in danger of a meltdown.

"I don't think that's a good idea. Not now, anyway."

"I'll call you."

Famous last words. She nodded and closed the door.

Through her tears, the TV came into focus. Two more animals were going at it. She picked up the remote.

"Oh, get a room!" Click.

9

"Done any Dumpster diving lately?" Jack stood at the coffee-maker, grinning, the next morning when Nick walked in. He tossed the stirrer stick into the trash. "I tried to warn you about Hurricane Lundsford."

Nick whirled at his office door. "Damn it, Jack, stop calling her that!"

Jack shrugged and picked up a doughnut. "It's what we've always called her."

"Well, maybe it's time you all grew up and let her do the same."

Jack's blond brows rose. "Does someone have a crush on the Hurricane?"

"Don't be an ass."

"I could make a smarmy remark about ass, but I'll refrain." Jack stepped close and lowered his voice. "Tricia Lundsford is nothing but trouble. There's a reason she had the rep she had in town. You and I have to work together. Maybe I'm trying to watch your back."

"And maybe you're not. I know you put in for this job. What I don't understand is what you've got against Tricia."

"Okay." Jack glanced down the hall in each direction before speaking. "I'm only going to tell you this once. She's a cunt. In high school, she fucked just about every member of the football and basketball teams. Even had a few baseball players. Chews men up and spits them out. You don't believe it, I can give you my friend Alex's number. He'll tell you."

"And why would I believe anything your friend has to say?"

"He was her last Harper's Grove victim."

Tricia wiped a trickle of sweat from her forehead with the edge of her apron and glared at the pitiful excuse for cinnamon rolls. It was the last batch Gram had made and frozen, a week ago, before she left. All Tricia had to do was let them rise and bake them. They rose. Sort of. She baked. They looked great when she first slid them out of the oven. Now they were more deflated than her Her Highness bra.

The bell above the door jingled.

Great. Yet another soon-to-be-dissatisfied customer.

With a last glance at the sickly buns, she trudged through the swinging door.

"Hi," Nick's soft voice wrapped around her heart and squeezed.

Tears sprang to her eyes. He was so gorgeous, tall and strong. At the moment, she'd give anything to feel his arms around her. Blinking furiously, she sniffed and said, "Hi. Want a cinnamon roll?"

He looked around the deserted tea room. "Did I miss the breakfast rush?" He sniffed. "I don't smell cinnamon rolls."

"I baked them last night." *When I couldn't sleep because I missed you.* "I figured I'd get a jump start on the day."

He nodded. "How'd that work for you?"

She pointed to the platter of deflated rolls on the counter. "And there're more where that came from. Unfortunately."

"I'm sure they taste great." Nick settled on a stool at the counter. "Gimme a cup of decaf, too, please."

"Decaf? When did you start drinking decaf?"

"Since I stopped seeing you. I haven't slept worth a damn." He glanced around. "I miss you, Tricia."

"I miss you, too." She shined the already clean counter. "But nothing has changed. We live in a small town." Her watery green gaze met his. "Here, there is no such thing as casual sex." She shrugged. "Well, not in my case, anyway."

He thought about that remark and found it didn't bother him. Everyone had a past. What mattered was what they did with the future.

Nick tapped his roll on the edge of the plate. "How long did you cook these things?"

In answer, she dumped the entire tray of rolls into the trash. "I'll try again tomorrow."

He threw money on the counter. "I'll be back then to check them out." He waggled his eyebrows. "I love your buns."

The bell tinkled merrily. She watched him cross the street and step up into his truck.

"I love your buns, too," she whispered.

Tricia yawned and took a sip of reheated coffee while she surveyed her handiwork. She hoped the cinnamon buns tasted better than they looked.

"Oven should be hot by now," she murmured, placing her hand in front of the oven door then flat on the cold interior. She coughed. Was that gas she smelled? "Pilot must be out." That would explain why, despite turning on the oven, it was still cold.

Leaving footprints in the flour covering every surface, she

retrieved a box of matches and struck one in front of the oven to get a better view.

Boom!

The alarm sounded in the little firehouse. Voices raised. The horn calling for volunteers filled the air with its drone.

Hearing the word "Hurricane," his ears perked up. He grabbed his coat and helmet and ran for the truck, arriving in time to see it turning the corner on the square.

Heart in his throat, he ran for his truck, laying a patch of rubber and fishtailing to the corner.

"Oh, God, no," he breathed a prayer, squealing to a stop in front of Cup Half Full beside the fire truck.

Racing to the kitchen, he found Glenn giving a dazed looking Tricia oxygen. Flour coated the room like a fresh snowfall.

He dropped to his knees, pushing Glenn aside. "Tricia, can you hear me? Are you okay?" He gathered her close, ignoring the snickers of his men behind him.

Green eyes opened. After a second, she smiled, causing him to almost weep with relief.

Tricia glanced around. "Am I dead?"

"No, but you'll wish you were when your granny gets back," Bob chortled from somewhere in the room.

"We've checked everything out," he said to Nick. "No gas leak. Most likely operator error." He clapped Nick's shoulder. "See you back at the station."

"Do you need to see a doctor or go to the hospital?" Nick helped her to her feet, his arm feeling too right around her.

"No." She brushed a layer of flour from her linen skirt. "I'm fine." She glanced around at the destruction. "I wish I could say the same for Cup Half Full."

"I'll help you clean it up. Tell me what to do first."

Kiss me. But, of course, she couldn't say that.

An hour later, Nick helped her up the stairs and into her apartment, ignoring her protests.

"Nick, really, I'm fine. I—"

He crushed her to him when she turned, his mouth devouring hers.

She should be strong. Resist the urges he inspired. But he was so sexy, smelled so good, and she'd missed him so much.

Her back met the wall with a thud, rattling the dishes in the built-in china cabinet, while they tore at each other's clothing.

As soon as they were naked, he entered her with one powerful thrust, slamming her against the wall with each flex of his well-honed hips.

Her orgasm burst into flames to devour what little self-preservation she had left. Screaming his name, she climaxed again and again. She may have even spoken in tongues, out of her mind with pleasure.

He stepped back, allowing her feet to touch the floor again, and pulled up his jeans.

Picking up her skirt with shaking hands, she covered her nudity.

"I'm sorry," he said in a low voice, "I meant to stay away. Then the alarm sounded and all I could think about was finding you, making sure you were all right. I should have stopped there. I'm sorry," he repeated and stepped out the door, closing it with a final click.

Body still tingling with aftershocks, she slid the bolt home.

"Well . . . wasn't that special?"

Nick drove slowly around the square, squinting in the midmorning sun in an attempt to see into Tricia's shop, Intimate Stranger. He'd heard about her stock. Seemed to be all the town talked about these days. He could understand why. Hell, he'd seen a sample, up close and personal. It was forever burned in his mind.

On his second pass, Tricia came out the door, followed by a plume of black smoke.

Throwing his truck in park, he jumped out and ran to her. In the distance, sirens sounded.

"Are you all right?" His anxious hands skimmed her body. Had she lost weight?

"I'm fine." She coughed. "I was sewing. The machine started power surging and smelling funny. I noticed I'd forgotten to unplug the steamer." *Cough.* "I got up to go do that and just as I got there, it burst into flames. I tried the fire extinguisher, but it didn't work."

The hook and ladder rounded the corner and came to a stop.

Jack jumped off and strolled over while the other three men went inside. "Anyone else inside?"

"No." She glared at him. "And I'm fine, thanks for asking."

Jack opened his mouth, then shook his head and walked into the shop.

"I don't want you staying in the apartment until I can get the wiring checked in the whole building," Nick told her.

"Well, that's not a problem, since I have no desire to be fried in my sleep. I'll go stay at Gram's."

"You could stay with me." He spoke so low, she barely heard him.

Her heart did a little happy dance before she remembered why it wasn't a good idea. "Thanks, but that's not an option."

Wondering if he should cut his losses and leave town, Nick made the turn in his jog that would take him back to the little house he rented. He hadn't seen or spoken to Tricia in over two weeks. Maybe it was time to read the writing on the wall, he thought, and make a new start somewhere else. Harper's Grove felt like home already, but he didn't know if his heart could take the possibility of running into Tricia on a regular basis, knowing he couldn't have her.

He stopped midjog as reality slammed into him.

He loved Tricia.

He resumed his run. Big deal, so he loved her. Fat lot of good it did him when she wouldn't even go out with him.

He turned left and rounded the town square, passed Patterson's Hardware, Henley Mens Apparel and the J.C. Penney Catalog store, turned again and slowed his pace past the newly remodeled Intimate Stranger and Cup Half Full.

According to the grapevine, Gram was back from her cruise and Tricia was once more in residence above the two stores. All this was heard second hand, since Tricia was not talking to him these days. Or any day for that matter.

Time to implement his grand gesture so he and Tricia could get on with their lives.

Tricia held a white bakery bag in her teeth and jiggled the lock on her shop. Stepping inside, she stopped in her tracks at the sight of several workers.

"Excuse me," she called over the sound of power tools. "Excuse me! What are you doing?"

An older man put down his nail gun and walked over to her, removing his protective earmuffs. "You must be Tricia Lundsford." He pulled a wad of papers from his back pocket. "I got orders to install a fire alarm and sprinkler system."

"I can't afford that!"

He stuck the papers back in his pocket. "Not necessary. Bought and paid for. We'll get out of your way directly."

She strode to the connecting door and into Cup Half Full. "Gram!"

Her grandmother stuck her head through the open kitchen door. "Yes, sunshine?"

"I appreciate the thought, but I can't let you pay for it."

"Pay for what, dear?"

"That." She gestured to her shop and the noise vibrating the walls. "The sprinkler and fire detector system."

"I thought you did that. They installed mine earlier."

The bell tinkled above the dwindling sound of tools. Nick walked in.

"Look, sunshine, he brought you flowers!"

Nick approached as though he feared castration, holding the red roses in front of him like a shield. "Hi. I brought these in case you were mad about the systems." He leaned closer. "You're not mad, are you?"

She glared at Gram and pulled Nick to a side booth. When they'd slid into opposite sides, she set the roses on the table between them. "Nick, I don't want you to spend money on me. I'm perfectly capable of taking care of myself."

"What if I want to spend money on you?" He plucked at the green tissue covering the rose stems. "I need to know you're safe." He slid out of the booth. "Humor me." He walked out the door, the bell jumping on its brass spring.

"I think he loves you." Gram picked up the flowers and took them to the counter where a vase of water waited.

"No, he just feels sorry for me. He's being nice."

"Hmm." Her grandmother nodded, fussing with arranging the flowers. "Did you see that button?" She pointed to a red disk the size of a saucer on the side wall of the dining area. "It's linked directly to the fire station. There's one in your shop, too, as well as automatic sprinklers. They don't seem like pity purchases to me."

"I need to get to work, Gram. Why don't you keep the roses in here? I don't really have a place for them."

"Plenty of room in your apartment. Tricia?" she called when Tricia had almost made her escape. "Maybe you should think about buying a cat or two."

"A cat. Why would I get a cat?"

"To keep you warm at night."

After her nightly shower, Tricia smoothed on her scented lotion and pondered Gram's cat theory.

"It's official," she told her reflection in the dressing table mirror, "you are really a loser."

The elaborate fire detector and sprinkler systems flashed through her mind. She'd thought Nick was different. He obviously had the same opinion of her as the rest of the town. Why was she surprised?

"Laugh all you want." Nick grinned against the receiver and waited for Dave's laughter to subside on the other end of the line. "I'm telling you it's true."

"And you're serious about marrying her? Did you hit your head?" Dave dissolved into more laughter.

"It's not funny. And I'm serious about you being my best man." Assuming, of course, Tricia accepted his proposal. His stomach knotted at the prospect of her refusing.

"When's the wedding?" Dave asked when he finally recovered.

"I haven't exactly popped the question yet."

"I don't believe it! You're afraid! Old love 'em and leave 'em Nick is scared. I never thought I'd see the day. Hey! You could always kidnap her and force her to marry you at gunpoint."

"Don't laugh, it's crossed my mind."

"Seriously, man," Dave's voice sobered. "I'm happy for you. I know it's what you really want and I'd be honored to be your best man."

"Thanks." He hung up and nodded at Bob in the doorway. "Just the man I wanted to see."

*   *   *

Nick adjusted the bow tie on his rented tuxedo and gave the signal to raise the ladder. Cool air bathed his face. He patted his pocket and held the roses in a death grip.

On the ground below, his men stood in silence, watching, waiting. It had taken some doing, but he'd finally convinced them of the seriousness of his feelings for Tricia. Now they were all there, waiting to witness whatever was about to happen.

He tapped on Tricia's darkened window. A light came on in another room. Crap. He overshot her bedroom window. He tapped again.

Through the opening in the curtains, he saw her tying the belt of her robe while she walked to the window.

Her eyes widened when she saw him. "Go away." Her voice was muffled by the glass, but it was pretty succinct.

"Open the window. Please."

She stood for so long, he thought she might walk away. But she finally reached out and flipped the latch, dragging the old wood-framed window up a few inches.

"What do you think you're doing Nick?" She spoke through the three or four inch opening.

"Proving my love."

"Love?" She pushed open the window until she stood in the opening. Tonight she wore some kind of silky thing that shimmered in the light from the streetlamp.

Damn, he wanted to touch her. Everywhere. Forever.

Her stiff posture, hands on hips, drew him back to the conversation. "Yes. Why do you think I've been doing the things I've done? I helped you move, I fixed the railing. I brought you flowers." He shoved the roses at her. "Twice."

She backed up a step. "So that's supposed to prove what? Love? Commitment? Help me out here, Nick, because all I've seen is a guy who wants to hump me at every given opportunity—don't get me wrong, it was great, but it doesn't spell commitment." She snatched the roses from him and tossed them to the street. "And flowers are the oldest trick in the book."

"Oh, yeah? What about the smoke detectors and the fire alarms? Nothing says commitment like a good fire deterrent system." Let her deny that. He fumbled with the ring in his pocket, grabbing her arm when she began closing the window. "Wait! Tricia Lundsford, will you marry me?"

Finally, she blinked.

"Please." He held out the engagement ring he'd taken literally days to pick out.

Tears sparkled her eyes when she looked at him.

"Hell, no."

10

Nick glumly regarded his bruised fingertips then gingerly picked up his cup of coffee. He should have known better. He'd put Tricia on the spot. Women hated that.

He heaved a sigh and leaned back in his recliner. And he'd made it a hundred times worse by doing it in front of his men.

He had to give the guys credit, though, for not hooting with laughter when Tricia added injury to insult by slamming the window on his fingers after she refused his proposal. In fact, they were almost sympathetic. Almost.

Now what? Giving up was not an option. Maybe he should try talking to her grandmother. He thought of the expression on her face when they'd climbed out of the garbage truck, then later, after the masturbation fiasco. Maybe not.

"Patricia Ann! That's the fourth plate you dropped today." Her grandmother shoved a broom toward her. "Please be more careful. I can't afford to replace all the dishes!"

Tricia stared across the square, hoping for a glimpse of Nick.

Gram sighed and set the broom and dust pan aside. She walked up behind Tricia and placed her arm on the younger woman's shoulders. "Why don't you call him, honey?"

"And say what?"

"How about that you're miserable without him, you love him and hell, yes, you'll marry him if the offer's still open."

"You heard about the proposal."

Gram grinned. "Sure did. The whole town's been buzzing about it for days. If you weren't so caught up in your misery, you'd have heard." She untied her apron. "I need to run. I have a hot date!"

"Oh?"

"Yep. Doc Burnside, you remember him, don't you? The vet? Anyway, I'd appreciate it if you'd close for me tonight. It will be the last time for a while. Rose will be back tomorrow."

"Sure. It's not like I have anything else to do."

Gram kissed her cheek and left.

Tricia thought about her grandmother's advice while she loaded the dishwasher, wiped the counters and swept and mopped the floor.

What possessed her to throw away a perfectly good man like Nick Howard? He was perfect. Everything she'd ever wanted. So what if he thought she needed a keeper? As long as he was volunteering for the position, she could live with that.

She'd call him when she got home, she decided, stashing the mop and bucket in the storage room closet.

Ding.

Darn. She must've forgotten to lock the front door.

"Sorry, we're closed," she yelled, walking toward the front door, hoping to lock it before anyone else came in.

"I know," Nick's deep voice brought her up short. "Gram told me it was okay to come on in."

Good old Gram. Next time she saw the tricky old lady, she'd give her a big hug and kiss.

But right now she had other plans. Nick was here and she made an immediate decision not to let him out until they were engaged.

"If you'd rather not talk to me—"

She walked toward him.

He took a step back.

She grabbed a handful of his starched shirt and pulled him to her. "I have an apology to make, then we're going to have hot make-up sex. Quite possibly all night long. Is that clear?"

He grinned down, putting his arms around her. "Yes, ma'am."

"I'm sorry I slammed your fingers in the window the other night." She took each hand and kissed the tips of the fingers, then placed his hands on her breasts.

"I like the way you apologize." His thumbs rubbed her nipples. "Beats the hell out of a card." He brushed a kiss across her lips. "Much more personal."

"Shut up and kiss me. Please."

The kiss skyrocketed out of control the second their lips touched. Chairs scraped against the tile floor, tables were knocked over. They couldn't get close enough.

She struggled with his zipper, then shoved his jeans to his ankles and tugged his boxers down to his knees. His erection bobbed its agreement before she took it into her mouth and sucked, running her tongue up and down and around the shaft, a dart of pleasure streaking through her at his guttural sounds.

His hands were equally busy, divesting her of her shirt and

bra in record time, then pulling her to her feet to rub her breasts against his now bare chest.

They groaned.

Both their hands shook while attempting to get her out of her jeans.

Tricia swore under her breath. "What a time I picked to wear underwear."

"We can fix that." He shucked her jeans and panties in one movement. "That's better." He patted her moist curls. "I've missed you so much."

She hopped into his arms, her legs around his waist. His erection probed her.

Gazes locked.

"Marry me," she whispered.

He thrust into her, his mouth fused to hers, his tongue imitating their lower bodies.

She broke the carnal kiss long enough to demand, "Harder! Faster!"

He stumbled and fell against her, pushing her naked back against the wall.

She sighed into his mouth. Much better.

Rain began to gently shower them. She was sure they were making steam.

Wait. They were still inside.

"Nick. Nick, why are the sprinklers on?"

In response, he bent to take her nipple into his hot mouth and suckle. Heat streaked to her womb and all points in between.

She tightened her legs and met him thrust for thrust. Flames of passion licked her, taking her higher and higher until she reached flashpoint.

Nick bumped her against the wall, thrusting faster and harder. The tip of his penis bumped her uterus, setting off more fireworks deep within her. He roared his completion about the same time she felt the flare of her third ogasm.

Clutching her tight to his wet chest, he began laughing, the sound setting off vibrations deep within where they were still intimately joined.

She laughed, too, and hugged him, her arms locked around his neck, her legs still around his waist. A knot of happiness filled her chest.

Through the pounding of her heart, applause sounded.

They turned to find a circle of firemen by the front door.

Nick crawled into her bed and licked the tips of her nipples. "Wake up, future Mrs. Howard." He held up a white bakery bag. "I brought doughnuts."

Future Mrs. Howard. Wow. She loved the sound of that. She glanced guiltily at the bakery bag. "I love you, but I should probably pass on the doughnuts if I expect to fit into my wedding gown."

Nick made a rude noise. "You're perfect." He set the bag aside and grabbed a handful of her right buttock and her left breast. "See? You fit my hands perfectly. Now eat the damn doughnut."

"But my dress—"

"I'm not marrying your dress or dress size. I'm marrying you. I love you just the way you are. And if you gain weight someday, I'll just have more of you to love. As for the dress . . . I prefer you naked anyway. Oh, speaking of naked"—he tossed the newspaper on the bed—"check out our engagement photo on the front page."

She licked powdered sugar from her fingers and picked up the paper, then almost choked on her last bite of doughnut.

Plastered across the front page was the headline: ENGAGED! Below it was a full color picture of them, Nick with his pants and boxers at his feet and a sappy grin on his wet face and her with her bare butt facing the camera, legs wrapped around her brand new fiancée.

"We can save it for our grandkids," she said with a grin. "Now, isn't that special?"

Fighting Fire

Alyssa Brooks

1

"That doesn't look safe." A deep, smooth voice issued from behind her. "Get down. I'll get whatever you want."

Shivers chased her spine at the sound of the order. Though Carmen couldn't quite place it, a sexy note in the deep tone rang a strangely familiar bell. Masculine, with a hint of a country accent, she recognized the man.

Holding on tight to the rickety shelf, she tried her best to ignore the voice at her feet as she reached for the blasted file on the top ledge. The boards under her feet shook and creaked, hardly able to stand the hundred and twenty pound punishment. Just when she'd almost grabbed the old yellowing folder, two strong hands grabbed her around the waist. They burned through her clothes, their touch soft yet demanding. Intimate. A ripple of anticipation coursed through her, wanting his touch, much as she didn't. She wriggled, trying to shake off his grip.

"Let me go."

"I told you." Though she tried to hang on, he pulled her from the shelf as if she weighed nothing and set her on her feet.

"Brent Sommers!" Carmen cried as she stared at a ghost

from her past, a once fellow Rocky Falls High student. Not just any old classmate, but *him*.

Despite herself, she couldn't stop staring. No doubt, he was as handsome as the last day she'd seen him. Even then, no matter how much she didn't like him, she couldn't help having a secret little crush on him.

But now, good gracious, now he'd grown into a man. The boyishness to his golden stature had vanished, any softness filling out with the hard cut of earned muscles. His shoulders were broader, his tanned skin slightly weathered. Blond whiskers shadowed his jaw.

Her eyes scanned over his uniform. A crisp white shirt, with a small silver badge pinned on the left breast. A name badge, and some sort of small, gold medal decorated it. A navy tie and slacks finished the ensemble, making him appear neat, clean, in charge.

H-o-t.

She'd always been a sucker for a man in uniform. Always.

Her eyes swept his length again, enjoying every inch of him as she tried to figure out which branch of service he was from. What he wanted from her. In the deep recesses of her mind, she wished he'd come for her.

"I told you to get down." He stared at her with his deep emerald eyes. Eyes she could never forget, not even after she'd left Rocky Falls all those years ago. They were so green, not bright green but a darker hue, like the color of pine and trimmed with a gold that made them sparkle with life.

Damn it, why was she melting into a pile of mush? So the guy was attractive. So what? He'd always been. He was also the one who used to call her Pinky and give her wedgies. Besides, she didn't come home to find romance. She'd come home to find freedom from it. "I don't know who you think you are, coming in here as if you can boss me around. But you can't. If I want to fall to my death, I damned well will, thank you."

"Okay." His tone mocked her.

"You can leave now," she almost shouted. One thing she didn't take kindly to was someone—anyone—telling her what to do. No one had done so since Doug, and no one ever would again.

"Afraid not. We have business."

"Business?"

"I'm here for your inspection."

"What inspection is that?"

"Carmen, I'm the fire chief. Now let's get this finished with so I can shut you down and get on with my day."

"Excuse me?" A streak of anger ripped through her. "You're not shutting me down. In fact, you're not even inspecting The Lucky Hart today. I scheduled nothing with you. You can't just drop in here on a dime."

"As a matter of fact, this building was due for inspection well over a month ago. You never called, nor did you answer the letter I sent. I can inspect it right now, or I can shut it down right now. But you aren't opening tonight without my okay."

"I've been in town for weeks now, getting this place in order. You can't just come in here the day I'm opening and threaten me. If an inspection was due, I should have been notified. I wasn't."

"You were. Check your mail."

Carmen threw the folder on the front desk, and her hands flew to her hips. For a moment she almost yanked them away, remembering how Doug used to make fun of her when she did it. Years of being mocked by him hadn't erased what he'd seen as annoying tendencies, it only trained her to be constantly on guard. She held her hands in place, determined. Doug had Lisa now. And she had her hands on hips, where they would stay all she liked.

"No."

"Have it your way. Let me know when you are ready for in-

spection. Until then, you have been officially shut down."
Brent turned and headed toward the door. "I'll post the notice
now."

"Wait." Carmen gritted her teeth as a wash of insecurity
boiled in her stomach, and made her sick. What if he could really
do that? Maybe she should just let him look at the place. What
could it hurt?

After all, why wouldn't the inspection pass?

Her uncle had run The Lucky Hart for years, and though
the building was over a century old, he'd kept it in good working order until he got sick. Maybe the lapse in time had allowed
the inspection to expire, maybe she'd been so busy she'd
missed Brent's notice, but really, she saw no reason for her to be
shut down.

"This way," she offered tightly. Through swinging doors
that once had been the original entrance, she led him into the
main hall. It really wasn't large, but about twenty-five feet
square with a large stage in the front composed from the original oak. Now aged, it was rustic yet still sturdy and adorned by
a velvet curtain that had been hung there sometime in the twen-
ties. The entertainment performed there to the tinkle of an antique piano, mostly girls in old-fashioned costumes showing
off their legs. Though occasionally they'd bring in a band or a
funny act, the men's interest lay in the ladies. Funny to think
how, though their clothes never came off, some high kicks and
demure smiles could still make a crowd of men go wild.

A bar made of plank wood sat on the right, complete with
spittoons and tobacco rags hanging from its front. Jars of pick-
led onions and pigs feet sat along it, and many antique liquor
bottles and dishware decorated its surroundings. Under the bar
the actual drinks could be found, but they were kept stashed
for the purpose of appearance. Several tables surrounded it, all
new but crafted to appear older. A deck of cards and a box of
poker chips sat atop each table as not only entertainment but

also as a souvenir for the tourists that came in. The rest of the dirt floor was left open, and the men could buy a dance with a lady for a dollar just like in the olden days. Though the punch in the card was only good for dancing now—no upstairs hanky-panky as everyone knew had gone on in the past.

Brent took the stairs to the stage, looking around. "Let's see the back."

He bent to examine some wires at the base of the stage, and through his trim blue pants his tight, chiseled rear strained. The kind of ass you would see on an action hero, or in a *Playgirl* magazine. She imagined herself reaching to take a squeeze and . . .

A vision of him in yellow pants, red suspenders, and a fire helmet flooded her mind. Instantly, her pussy clenched. Damn. How she wanted him over her, stripping away her clothes as she hung onto those red bands and begged him to extinguish her fire.

A heat rose to her cheeks, embarrassed by the rush of desire traveling south in her. Her pussy heated with desire, dampening. She fought to push the lust away.

Where had that come from? Good grief. Sure, she'd always had a thing for firemen. She even had a calendar in her office. But you'd think she could control herself.

"How long will this take? I'm very busy."

He ignored her, continuing to analyze every detail with his hard gaze. Carmen fumed as he brushed through the red velvet curtain into the stage area.

The Lucky Hart had belonged to her family for over a hundred years. It was old. She wanted to carry on the family tradition. She needed to. If he didn't pass her . . .

Maybe she should be nicer to him.

She watched him browse through the dressing area, where racks of costumes hung near vanities. Black lace and red satin surrounded them, along with silk and fishnets, gaudy feathers and fur.

She decided to make an attempt at friendly conversation. Maybe then she could distract herself from that firm rear.

"I thought you had some big football scholarship?"

Brent whirled around violently, his big black boot catching on an electrical cord. The next thing she knew, they were both plummeting to the ground.

He lay atop her, his face only an inch from hers. The fullness of his lips hovered right above hers, as his deep green eyes gazed into hers with a look of both shock and anger.

"I thought you'd gotten married."

His words brought a sharp pain to her chest. Yeah, she'd gotten married—the worst mistake of her life. It certainly wasn't an issue she wanted to discuss with him. Besides, all she wanted was him off of her, right now. His hard body felt a little too good pressed against hers, the build of his pecs hard against the softness of her own breasts. "Things change. Are you going to get off me now?"

"No."

Her insides fluttered. "No?"

"Bad knee."

No? Good heavens, the simple smell of him became too much. Spicy, woodsy, mingled with a little sweat. The scent of a man. Already her nipples hardened. My God, what if he could feel them? Her shirt was so thin . . .

"Oh, for heaven's sake. I'll roll you off of me."

She gave him a shove, a little too hard for her own good. Rather than pushing him away, she ended up rolling atop of him. His strong arms wrapped around her. Her blouse hung open, revealing the curve of her breasts to him.

"Now, I like this," he murmured with a chuckle, his hands moving to her hair. His fingers grazed across her tender scalp, sending tingles along her spine.

She should really get off him. But she couldn't. Damn it, she wanted him and bad. The next thing she knew, his mouth had possession of hers.

She'd always had a secret little crush on him.

He'd always had a secret little crush on her.

Slowly, he fingered the mass of silky brown hair cascading around him in waves. Every inch of her body pressed close to his. Too close. The sweet scent of her attacked his every sense, the soft tones of vanilla making him ravenous with need. Damn it, he should push her away. Get the hell out of here.

But he couldn't. Something stopped him short and made him kiss her deeper, something that he'd secretly wanted to do for a very long time. He traced his finger along her spine as he explored her mouth, enjoying the taste of her sweet lips. If only he'd been a little more of a man in high school. God, he could still remember her like it was yesterday. Pinky, he'd called her. The way she'd kept with the styles had been close to laughable. Teased hair. Neon clothing. Leggings. Skintight, ripped up jeans.

Damn, she'd been hot.

But guys like him didn't go with girls like her. They went with girls like Suzy, cheerleaders who dumped you the second you lost your football scholarship.

But hey, what girl wouldn't have done that? They all wanted the same thing. A free ride.

This needed to stop. Brent pulled his mouth away, but as if it were magnetized, Carmen's stuck to his. Their lips fought each other, fury in the hard kiss. Devouring her, Brent crushed her mouth with his need. Flicks and swirls of her tongue dared him to do more. To do the unthinkable. To take her.

The sweet, unimaginable flavor of her enveloped him. Nothing had ever tasted more delicious or smelled more intoxicating. He let his hands wander across her body, feeling all of her. Despite the fact that she was lean, she curved in all the right places.

The smoothness of her deeply tanned skin reminded him of caramel, the softness of her long brown hair was like fine silk in his fingers. But her eyes, huge and brown, framed by long dark lashes, and so . . . so . . . there were no words to describe them.

God help him, she was beautiful. Irresistible.

Ripping apart the buttons on her blouse, he found her pert little nipples and took one in his mouth. He rubbed the hardened bud with his tongue, then massaged it in between his fingers. Her breasts fit perfectly in his hands. He cupped them, enjoying their weight. Then he moved onto her other nipple, giving it the same treatment. Carmen moaned and arched.

How he wanted more of her. All of her.

All of her?

Damn it, what was he thinking? This was a mistake. A huge one. And he needed to stop now, before it went to far.

He needed to do his job. Not her. Determined to end it, he grasped her waist, and rolled her off him. "That's enough."

Carmen reached for the buttons on her blouse. "You're right."

"I'm sorry that happened." Brent stood slowly, favoring his knee. Though it sometimes went out on him, not many people were aware of it. In fact, besides his father and his best friend, Carmen was the first person to whom he'd ever admitted the problem. The town had no idea he'd never quite recovered from his football injury, and they didn't need to. The pain was always short-lived, and quite manageable. He could still do his job just fine. No, better than fine.

"So . . . did I pass the inspection?" Slight laughter traced her voice, as if she found something humorous about the situation.

So that was it. He couldn't believe it. He pushed her away. "A make out session with you changes nothing. I have more pride than that. Apparently you don't."

"You jerk! I never meant it that way, and how dare you insinuate that I'd allow you to touch me just to pass your petty inspection! You fell on me! You came on to me!" Fire enraged her voice. "Besides, I'd have no reason to. There's nothing wrong with this building and you know it."

"I beg to differ. Codes have changed recently." Really, he was surprised Carmen had fared as well as she had with this inspection. The place was a firetrap; at least some updates had been done, but not nearly enough.

Colorado laws had been revised after two club tragedies had hit the national news. In both cases, sufficient exits would have saved many lives.

Shaking her head, Carmen rolled her eyes and swung her hand toward the door. "Just finish the inspection and get lost."

She said it as if he could help it. Carmen hadn't passed inspection, and that he couldn't change. How could he?

From his pocket he yanked free the notebook of inspection slips, filling it out. "I'll post the notice on the door. The Lucky Hart has not met fire codes. You're not to open. You're not to entertain customers of any sort."

With that he walked away.

2

Insufficient exits. Expired fire extinguishers. No fire escape plan within customers' eyesight.

"Damn it." Carmen jerked her eyes from the posted notice to her reflection in the recently cleaned glass door. Sometimes she wondered who the woman staring back at her was. Oh, on the outside she still looked the same, though perhaps a little mussed, hair astray, without a drop of makeup. But not the Carmen Harte who'd left Rocky Falls all those years ago.

That Carmen always looked her best. And that Carmen would have put Brent in his place.

Not almost slept with him.

God! How could she have just fallen into his arms? To think *he'd* had to stop things. Not only did she feel like the world's biggest fool because of what had happened, but much to her own embarrassment, she couldn't stop thinking about it.

About him.

The touch of his rough, calloused hands caressing her soft skin, making her crawl with fiery want. His expert lips on hers, jolting tingles along her spine as his tongue roamed her mouth, making her wish he'd been exploring other areas.

After he'd left, she'd needed to change her panties. And if she didn't stop thinking of him, of those rippling, thick muscles and evergreen eyes, she'd have to do so again.

Blast the man.

Once again, she read his majesty's royal decree. In a nutshell, she couldn't open tonight. It wasn't fair. How could her life be so screwed up, yet only continue to get worse? This couldn't be happening.

Hands on hips, she shook her head. *No.* No, it wasn't going to happen. She wouldn't let it. She was woman. Hear her roar!

A tiny giggle escaped her. But as silly as the thought was, she was dead serious. She refused to be the pathetic fool the glass door reflected. Slowly, she peeled off Brent's notice and headed inside.

"Hey, Sam," she greeted her bartender-assistant in a sing-song voice.

With a look of shock, Sam lifted her face from her hands and wrinkled her blond eyebrows. They made for a sharp contrast against the girl's brilliant blue eyes, outlined in black, and over-dyed red hair. Carmen wanted to shake her head. If only she were more natural, she'd be breathtaking. Women would die for that figure and porcelain doll face.

"You're surprisingly cheery." Disbelief coated Sam's words. "Did a miracle happen while you were staring at that sign?"

Carmen chuckled. "You'd be surprised what half an hour of staring can accomplish. I have a plan."

"I hope it involves opening tonight. My rent's due tomorrow." There was no mistaking the worry in her voice. "I was already late a couple of times after your uncle died. The landlord is on his last string with me."

Determination crawled through Carmen's veins as she headed

toward the bar. "Why don't you go grab the phone book from my office? We have some calls to make."

"Sure." Sam bounced from the bar stool with a flourish.

"Oh, and don't forget about that door." Carmen called after her. She was lucky. Brent hadn't noticed that. No one would ever expect the seemingly normal door to be so treacherous, but it had been locking people in and out for ten years now. Why her uncle hadn't ever gotten it fixed was beyond her, but it ranked tops on her list. "And grab a pen and paper."

Plopping in a chair, Carmen ran a hand through her hair. No way Carmen was just closing at his order. She would fight that man tooth and nail before she let him shut her down.

Tonight she *would* open, and legally at that. She'd just have to fix what he'd said was wrong before she opened the doors. He could come and post some more notices after that, but tonight she would be the winner.

If Carmen thought she'd get away with this, she had another thing coming. Flabbergasted didn't begin to describe Brent's reaction when he'd driven past The Lucky Hart, and discovered it open. What was going on in her head? Now he'd have to fine her.

Brent worked his way through the thick crowd, trying to locate her. He didn't see her anywhere. Sudden applause roared through the room, drawing his attention to the stage. The velvet curtains drew open slowly, the piano's jingle carrying through the air.

Carmen. Dressed in an old-fashioned, ruby-colored satin teddy, trimmed with black lace, fishnets to her thighs. A long feathery boa wrapped around her sleek neck, her hair swept into an elegant twist of brunette silk.

The applause quieted as she came forward, and the piano picked up the pace. Her body moved with its beat, shaking and twirling. The boa flowed around her body. Two girls backed her, though somehow they appeared fuzzy blurs to Brent. All he saw was Carmen, her legs kicking high, so long and slim and tan. The tight cut to her old-fashioned outfit, accentuating the smallness of her waist compared to her hips. And her tits. Dear God. Black lace pushed them into a voluptuous swell, and they teetered on the brink of falling right out.

With each of her sultry movements, Brent hardened against his jeans and strained for release. He couldn't move, couldn't think. Ragged breaths escaped him, and if the heat had him perspiring before, he sweated like a stuck pig now.

Once again, applause roared through the room as the jingle ended. Carmen took a bow, her smile brilliant. "Welcome, gentlemen. Thank you." A saucy little laugh purred from her throat. "You boys are too kind. Well, I just wanted to give all of you a proper welcome. As you know, I am Henry's niece and I will be taking over The Lucky Hart. The prices will remain the same, and the rules as well. Bad behavior isn't tolerated here, gentlemen. Remember your limits because drunkenness, fighting, and obscenities will get you thrown out. And above all, respect the ladies. We all want to have fun, right? So no one ruin the good times and I won't end yours." The crowd remained quiet, and respectful.

Carmen glowed. She looked so damn beautiful Brent wanted to race on the stage and throw her over his shoulder. Thirty men were standing here, watching her, all wanting her as he did. For some reason, he didn't like it. Not one bit. He gripped his fists tightly and willed his feet into place as he waited for her to finish. "Many thanks for your attention tonight. I just have one other thing to say and then we'll turn the music on again. I would like to extend my appreciation to those who helped me get this place open tonight. You know who you are. We couldn't have done it without you. Many thanks."

She waved as she took the stairs on the left of the stage. The piano jingled through the room once again and the talking picked up. But Brent stood paralyzed, staring at her as she mingled through the crowd. Finally she caught his eye, and her gaze hit him like throwing stars.

The woman had some nerve standing there, in the midst of men, in only a teddy, directing a nasty glare toward him. How he wanted to shake the smirk right off her, then wrap a robe around her and tie it tight.

The hardness tightening his lower regions melted away as red-hot anger pulsed through him, reminding him of why he was here in the first place. He couldn't believe she'd opened the club despite him. Her stubbornness could cost people their lives if something bad happened.

Suddenly his feet could move again, and move they did. With long heavy strides he charged across the room to her.

"Brent. What a surprise." Her smile turned fake as she held her wine glass as if to toast her success, and raised her eyebrows in mockery. "Well, do enjoy."

She started away but he gripped her by the arm, leaning to murmur in her ear. "We need to talk. Let's go."

"Really, this isn't the time."

"Now. Or we can do it in front of everyone if you'd rather."

Her huge chocolate eyes frosted, and narrowed into two dark slits. For several seconds she stared at him, anger radiating from her. Then her expression melted into false friendliness. "Why don't we talk in my office?"

"Fine."

"Fine." Her phony smile grew wider, until it pushed her cheeks to a point where he wondered if her face didn't hurt. "Follow me."

Every second he spent behind her was excruciating. Try as he might, he could focus on nothing but her perfect little rear end swaying back and forth, and those damned long legs. The black high heels she wore did her calves justice, accentuating their curves as they lifted her perky ass.

Cheese and crackers!

Despite the fact that he tried to look anywhere and everywhere else, his cock twitched and started to harden. Gnashing his teeth, he followed her into her office and slammed the door behind him.

"Don't you have any shame at all? I can't believe you, Carmen." His voice boomed off the walls. "How can you walk around in that outfit? And that dancing, good grief."

"Not that it's any of your damned business, Brent," she hissed.

Several moments passed by silently as he fumed, too angry for words. Carmen stood, arms crossed, her back to him.

"And by the way, there is nothing indecent about this outfit. Most bathing suits show more than this. And that's bathing suits, not bikinis. My God, look at these tap pants, Brent. They're cut nearly halfway down my thighs for heaven's sake. Some women wear skirts more revealing than this." She plopped in her chair. "Grow up."

True, her outfit was old-fashioned. But still. "You didn't have to dance like that."

"Like what? So I kicked my legs a little. You know, I am a single woman attempting to run a man's establishment. I needed them to know I was on the same level as them. I needed their attention. For them to like me . . . listen to me. And it worked. They heard every word I said, didn't they? And you know what? I don't owe you any explanation. If this is what you wanted to speak with me about, you should just get lost." With a wave of her hand, she directed him to the door. Then her face fell, her jaw nearly dropping to the ground. "My God, you shut the door."

"So?"

She stamped her foot, obviously at her wit's end. "So? So it's broken, that's what. It's always locked. We're stuck in here."

"Well hell, that's not very safe."

3

Two hours of pure hell. The shouting, screaming and banging hadn't helped a bit. No one heard them, and no one would. Carmen slouched in her office chair, and ran her hands through her hair. Time to face the facts. "Well, Mr. Know-It-All, I hope you're happy. We're stuck in here until morning. No one is going to come, much less hear us. Thanks to you, we're stuck."

Brent slammed a large, knotted fist against the heavy oak desk. "Thanks to me? You're the little idiot who could've fixed the door a long time ago but didn't. And who doesn't have a phone in her office? And need I mention, I wouldn't even be here, except for the fact that you violated an order not to open." He pointed a thick finger at her.

It took everything she had not to try and yank it off. "I told you, mice chewed the line. The repair man is coming tomorrow. Good grief, I can't stand men like you. Bossy jerks."

Just like Doug, who thought just because he stood a half-foot taller than her, he'd the right to push her around. And look down on her. Even now she could see the disapproval in Brent's frowning jade eyes, judging her.

"That order—"

"Oh, an *order*, is that what that was? See, 'cause I thought it was a notice. Forgive me, your highness. Let me bow and kiss your feet." Slamming her hands against the desk, she whirled her wheeled chair around so she didn't have to watch his expression. His eyes were easy to read, entirely too expressive, and at times damned heart wrenching. She just didn't want to see them condemn her for one second more. "Oh, and by the way, all the silly grievances on your *order* were fixed."

"Give me a break, Carmen. Don't expect me to believe you managed that in a day. And even if you did, you still needed to have the place re-inspected." The hard edge to his voice boomed off the walls that trapped them.

She whirled around to face him. "And don't you expect me to lose money when I don't have to." Carmen raised her voice level to match his. He needed to realize she wouldn't be pushed around. "Two more exits have been opened. Jake Warner volunteered to cut them out today. Curtains cover them now, but they are clearly marked with bright red exit signs. He'll be installing the doors tomorrow. The actual exit signs will be here day after tomorrow. I had them priority shipped. As for the fire extinguishers, Tom Harding, who owns the hardware store, was happy to donate several, seeing how excited he was to come here tonight. And I drew three, not one, fire escape plans—very large, and very legible. They've been posted."

So there. Folding her arms, she sat back in the chair and dared him with her eyes.

A little muscle in his jaw twitched and he looked so damn angry it was almost sexy. Flashes of their previous kiss invaded her mind. His lips were so soft, yet so demanding. Never had a man possessed her with such fervor. What would it be like for him to kiss her now, while his blood boiled? Would he completely ravage her, like a wild beast, untamed and out of control?

"Bull. You can't expect me to believe you got all that done, and to code." Brent practically jumped from his chair and paced.

Carmen couldn't even respond. She was too busy fighting the electrical tingles nipping at her breasts, the cream ruining her new silk thong. Hating her betraying thoughts.

What was wrong with her? Even now, after all she'd been through with Doug, she hadn't learned. A tiny piece inside of her yearned to be dominated—even ached for a man to control her out-of-control urges.

Another one of her naughty, unfulfilled fantasies. It went right along with the firefighter one. Both wonderful to dream, but fulfilling them didn't come so easily.

Carmen propped her head on her hand, her elbow resting on the desk, and wondered what to do or say next. With the way he made her feel, she'd just as soon spend the night in silence with her back turned. Yet something tempted her to talk to him, to continue the argument, to win.

A silence had fallen between them, so thick one could whip out a knife and cut through the air. Time passed slower than molasses dripped, every second seemingly longer than the one before it.

Good grief, how would she ever get through the night trapped in this tiny box of an office with him? He was like a caged animal, prowling back and forth between the desk and the door. Sometime this afternoon his dress uniform had turned to formfitting Levi's, and a black skintight T-shirt. Every muscle in his thighs and rear flexed as he paced, and despite herself, she stared. Her eyes became ping pong balls, darting to and fro between his strutting, sculpted lower half, and his rippling muscles across his shoulders. Even unflexed, his arms bulged with strength.

God, she needed to turn her attention elsewhere. *Anywhere.* "This is silly, Brent. We can't spend the whole night this way. Let's at least try to be civil."

He just grunted.

"Oh, come on. Sit down. You're making me nervous." And hot. Very damned hot.

Amazingly, the disgruntled bear plopped into the chair across from her, his shoulders still perfectly squared. "You're right. We're adults. Let's get along."

They were adults, weren't they?

Carmen couldn't help it. He was so close to her, just a leap across the desk. A rush of naughty thoughts boggled her mind. She'd had about enough of the tension. She wanted this man. A lot.

Damn it, she couldn't hold back any longer. Her body took control of the situation, shoving sense and reason aside. Like an animal attacking its prey, she pounced across the desk, lunging for his mouth.

Brent pulled her to him as she crashed upon him with a kiss. She wiggled into his lap, straddling him. His already hardened cock pressed between her legs. Tonight, she would have it.

Carmen was in a rush, but he wasn't. He'd wanted her so badly all day. He wanted to savor every second. Stroking his tongue along her lips and tongue, he suctioned them. She moaned, curving her back. Little by little he released them, parting her mouth to allow him in. He explored every corner of her. Along her teeth, her gums, her cheeks, he caressed her with his tongue. She tasted so sweet. Like candy. He couldn't get enough. His body stiffened with desperate need. Ever so slowly, he caressed her with his fingertips, running them across the square of her jaw and down her neck as he continued his appraisal of her mouth. Carmen responded all too eagerly. Her kisses were so hungry, so desperate, her passion undeniable.

He wouldn't refuse her now, could he? No way.

Reaching around to her sleek, graceful back, Brent ran a finger south along the exposed groove of her spine until he found the fasteners holding together her costume. The bodice was laced, tied with a tight bow at the top. But the damned thing was knotted. He tugged and tugged, but to no avail.

Then he grabbed the penknife from his pocket. The ribbon was coming free, one way or the other. With one long swipe, he cut her free. The bodice fell forward and he cast it aside then pulled her breasts in his face. They were perfect, full, but not large. A mouthful.

He explored with his tongue, slowly tracing the outline of her nipples, then flicking them. The buds turned into rock hard pebbles, which he took in his mouth, and suckled gently.

Carmen arched and yanked his head closer. "More, oh God. Please."

More? Oh, he could give her that. Despite that fact that he'd grown as hard as steel, the thumping in his cock almost unbearable, he wanted to fool around. And Carmen, she was obviously the playful type. Some liked to rush in, seeking fast gratification. But he liked to explore, to enjoy maximum buildup before he exploded. And he intended to pleasure every inch of Carmen.

He took her left nipple between his teeth, and rolled it, tracing his teeth lightly across the sensitive bud, all the while flicking it with his tongue. Then he pulled, and ever so slowly released it. It popped free, and once again he caught it, suckling as if to draw milk from it. He wasn't gentle in the least. He was hungry, and it showed.

With his penknife once again, he sliced away the bottom of her costume and the black lace panties she wore under it. Cocoa brown hair covered her womanhood. He pressed his fingers in the mound, all the while enjoying the taste of her tits in his mouth.

Carmen rose, allowing him to find her spot. Fire lit her body, her mind a blur with desire. She could think of nothing but him, his appraisal, and the new way her senses reacted. No one had ever touched her so thoroughly, so intimately. And certainly, she could expect a lot more to come.

Tingles raced along her spine, and heat seared at her breasts. Her nipples were so hard they hurt, the best pain she'd ever experienced.

His fingers explored her nether regions, stroking her, teasing her. He took her clit between two fingers and rubbed, followed by gentle caressing. His attentions were hard and demanding, soft and loving. Clenching with need, she lifted her hips a tad more, an invitation for him to enter her with his fingers. He did, slowly and deliberately exploring her until he hit her G-spot. She half screamed, half moaned at the touch. He followed her lead, diving into her with two more fingers to unmercifully tease that tender area.

Heaven help her, she could hardly stand it. Her body was ready to come, but she held it in, not wanting to ruin it. It was too soon to end it, though she didn't know how she could possibly continue. Her body shook with bliss, ready to overflow at any second.

"Mercy," she cried as he released her nipple and took her clit between the fingers of his other hand. "I can't . . ."

"Come." Husky, and deep, his voice left no room for argument. "Come for me and I'll give you more."

More? How was that even possible?

4

Did he actually think he could make her come twice? Well, if he could, she'd certainly like to see it. And enjoy it. But no man had ever driven her to that point.

She didn't want to ruin this moment. She wanted his magical pleasuring to go on. For a long, long time. Despite herself, his deft fingers couldn't be denied. He was going to make her explode like a damned bomb. Ripples of intense bliss shocked through her, lifting her to heights of ecstasy. For several moments she teetered at the edge. Her pussy convulsed. Then she lost it. The rapturous tension inside her shattered into a million tiny pieces, and left her breathless.

Brent didn't skip a beat. As she panted beneath him, he lifted her into his arms as if she were naught but a feather. Depositing her onto the desk, he swiped it cleaned and spread her before him. Her rear end rested on the edge, and he propped her feet on his shoulders.

His lips found her slit, sucking it gently then attacking it with his tongue. Up and down, back and forth, his mouth licked and appraised her lavishly. He worked in tiny circles, occasionally diving into her, but driving her completely mad. Another wave of ecstasy shook her body, making her quiver as she once again teetered on the edge. As if he sensed it, he sucked at her, gently nibbling her clit between his teeth. Carmen screamed like a madwoman, so overwrought with passion she couldn't contain herself.

Maybe someone would hear her that time. But she hoped the hell not.

Brent hadn't lied. He had a hell of a lot more to give. The blond deity stripped away his clothing, revealing his hardened body. The sight of him only increased her desire twofold. His muscles rippled as if he'd been chiseled from stone, his built pecs and six-pack stomach were enough to make her gulp. Then he slid off his jeans, his long thick cock tenting his boxers.

Carmen shot up and ripped away the barrier between herself and the prize. When she found it, she swallowed the meaty rod, relishing in its size as it slid down her throat. She licked and sucked, enjoying every inch of his length with her tongue and her teeth.

Brent stiffened and moaned. "Oh, God, no more." He pushed away and moved atop her. Kneading each of her buttocks in his hands, he slid deep into her. All of him filled her.

Carmen moaned aloud. "Oh, yes. Oh, yes."

"You like that, baby?"

"You have no idea how badly.... ah ... I've wanted you since I set eyes on you in that uniform."

He barked a laugh. "Now I know what to wear around you."

The rhythm of his hips increased as she met his demands, rocking in a passionate frenzy. From deep within her a heat filled Carmen, burning her alive with carnal needs. His thrusts drove her to the brink, and she exploded from within.

Brent pushed himself even deeper, and convulsions shook his body. His warm seed spilled inside of her, filling her with him. And then he collapsed, resting his head against her chest, obviously exhausted from the deep breath he drew.

Several moments passed before he drew himself off her, the realization of what they'd done sinking in. He was here to shut her down. Instead, the bar partied on while he was in here, fucking her.

He'd allowed her to get to him. To make him slip, and he'd made no small mistake. People's safety was compromised. He didn't take his job lightly.

A woman who could possess him like this was trouble to be around. He'd do best to remember that.

As soon as he stood, Carmen skittered to her feet and grabbed for her underwear, her hands and arms covering her breasts.

How had they gone from bliss to this awkward tenseness floating around them like a poisonous gas?

Maybe he should say something. Clear the air.

But she did it for him. "That was a mistake."

He stared at her as she slipped on her panties, a little sickened by the way those words spoken aloud, by *her*, made him feel. An unexpected knot formed in his chest and worked its way to his throat. So tight, so unbearable he wanted to throw something.

"You got that right. Let's pretend it didn't happen." He uttered words he realized he truly didn't feel.

Even now, he wanted Carmen again.

Her back turned to him, her shoulders shrugged. And even though he'd just taken his fill of her, the simple sight of her sleek back made him swallow hard. The tiny groove that ran between her muscles along her spine, the daintiness of her shoulders, the escaped strands of her hair falling carelessly around her neck. Lord, help him. Why didn't she have herself covered by now? You'd think she'd put something on. "Aren't you going to put on a shirt? Or do you plan to stand there all day with your arms crossed?"

"I can't," she snapped. "You took a knife to my top. At least you have clothes."

Oh.

Well, hell. That hadn't occurred to him, any more than the fact that his cock was still exposed. "Just stay put. I'll throw you my T-shirt. Then you can toss me my boxers and jeans."

Ripping it off as fast as he could, he threw her the T-shirt. Never had he felt more naked than he did as he turned around and awaited his Levis, his whole backside exposed to her. "Hurry up."

He heard her turn, but no jeans came. What was she doing? Staring at him?

An eternity passed. He should demand his pants, or anything to get her moving. But a rock caught in his throat again, and he couldn't breathe much less speak. The thought of her looking at him, enjoying him, turned him on like nothing else. It was almost enough to make him not want to put his jeans on again.

Finally, the thump of his clothes landed beside him. Without hesitation he threw them on, but he still couldn't turn around. He owned too great a bulge in his pants.

"You okay?" Carmen questioned.

"Yes," he managed to grit between his teeth.

It seemed like forever passed before his little man decided to give it a rest. But finally he could turn around again, and he did, only to regret it. She stood innocently, his huge T-shirt swallowing her up. He'd thought to cover her, but that was even worse. Because it was *his* T-shirt on her, making her look so damned adorable. And sexy.

Then she loosened her hair. Already sweet little tendrils fell loose and graced her neck, framing her face. The rest of her silky mass followed as she dropped it free from the twist that held it, then slowly, ever so seductively, combed her fingers through the cocoa mane.

Cocoa. How suitable. Carmen was chocolate and vanilla. Two opposite flavors twisted into one and both too tasty for any man to ever get his fill.

Fucking her only made everything worse. Much, *much* worse.

The tiger returned to his pacing.

Brent was driving her crazy. Things had gone from bad to worse. It was horrid enough she was locked in this tiny room with him. But now she had to wear his T-shirt. It reeked of him, a woodsy scent, traced with a spicy musk and just a hint of their recent physical exertion.

But even worse, he *wasn't* wearing the T-shirt. And try as she might, she couldn't avoid the sight of those tight, knotted muscles spread across his shoulders. Or the way his triceps bulged. Or the strong build of his pecs. His bare upper body was everywhere she looked.

And if she'd wanted him before, she was dying now. Having had him only made things worse. Now she knew what he had to offer. Knew he was the best she'd ever experienced.

Never before had any man fucked her like he'd done, and though she knew there must be, she couldn't think of a single reason why they shouldn't be doing it again.

She didn't even dare so much as to speak—she didn't trust herself to.

She went against her own advice, and stared at the clock. Watching every second, every minute, every hour. Sam wouldn't be in until eight. Heaven help her until then.

When she got out of here, she swore she'd never so much as set eyes on Brent Sommers again. She hadn't come back to Rocky Falls to find romance. It was the last thing she wanted at this point in her life. She'd loved once and lost. She wouldn't do it again.

* * *

Sam was late. Carmen plopped her head on the desk, so miserable she could cry.

Again.

Flashes of the repercussions of last night's episodes flooded her mind, torturing her with the prospect. She certainly didn't need that to happen again. No thank you.

Fatigue almost yanked her to the floor as she stood and crossed her arms. Neither of them had slept last night. Oh, she'd tried. But after what'd happened, and with him right *there*—so close, so sexy, so available—well, it simply hadn't been possible.

What she wouldn't do for a strong cup of coffee and a hot shower. "Move, please," she ordered Brent, exhaustion making her voice hollow. With a weary look of annoyance, he moved from his spot where he leaned against the door and went to sit in her chair.

Minutes meandered by as she pressed her ear against the door and hoped for Sam's arrival. The clock's ticking only seemed to get slower and slower. God! Would she ever get out of here? Why was she being punished like this?

Finally, when she was ready to give up and slump to the floor in defeat, she heard the familiar clack of Sam's heels. She started pounding with all her might against the door. "Sam! Sam! In here!"

Brent flew from the chair to join her, actually lifting her to place her aside. His display of strength reminded her once again to look at those damned muscles exhibited from his lack of attire. The bang of his fist against the metal door echoed through the room, but his hollering nearly shook the building.

She was so tired. You'd think she'd have lost interest by now. But everything about his actions teased her, just as they had all damned night.

She couldn't wait another second to get out of here.

Thankfully her prayers were answered. The door swung open, almost smacking Brent in the face as he leapt clear. Sam stepped in, looking half asleep and as artificial as ever. As if the black eyeliner wasn't enough, she'd added charcoal eye shadow, and tacky stick-on star decals. Her hair had obviously been dyed again last night, leaving it coarse, and frizzy.

Carmen had never been more happy to set eyes on anyone. "Thank God," she muttered as Sam wrinkled her blond eyebrows in puzzlement.

"Should I ask?" she chuckled, her voice clearly hinting. "Or this a private matter?"

"Don't ask," Brent grumbled, stalking from the room. About halfway down the hallway she heard him pause, then he hollered, "Be ready this afternoon, Carmen. If this building isn't ready for inspection then you're shut down permanently. And get rid of that damned door."

They both jumped at the sound of the front door slamming. Sam turned to her, a deep frown creasing the thick makeup on her pretty face. "Can he do that?" Her voice was as tiny as a mouse.

A pang of deep despair pierced Carmen's heart, not only for herself but also for Sam, and everyone else involved. A lot of people would be hurt if Brent closed the place.

"I think so." Carmen hated the ugly truth, but there it was. "But not if I can help it. Find me some strong coffee and a screwdriver. I'm going upstairs to get dressed, then we're making this place so damned fire safe we'll win an award."

Even after a nap and three strong cups of coffee, fatigue still pulled at Carmen. It seemed the day would never end.

At least they'd finished with the repairs, so Brent's impending visit could go quick and painlessly. The new doors had been hung, while her office door was removed and replaced. Everything else was in good order. Brent couldn't shut her down now. Thank God.

After today, she shouldn't have to see him again until next year. Now that was a blessing. She didn't need a repeat of last night. But resisting it would be impossible if she were near him. Damn. Whatever it was about him, she'd had enough of it.

Or, not enough, Carmen thought with a shake of her head.

She leaned in her chair, and released a deep sigh. Soon her problems would be gone.

Sudden heavy footsteps stomped into her train of thought. A tremor ran through her. It was definitely a man's walk coming toward the office. She hopped from her seat. She didn't need Brent in *here* again.

"Hey, Brent. Coming." She chewed her last bite of her sandwich, and headed to the door. At the last minute, for some odd reason, she got the urge to give herself a straightening. Ridiculous. But she decided to anyway. "Be right with you."

The footsteps didn't stop. She forfeited trying to smooth her hair, gave her skirt one last yank, and rushed from the room.

No sooner than she rounded the threshold, she ran smack into his chest. She squealed, the blow knocking her backward. Brent's arms caught her, drawing her to her feet.

"Sorry about that."

Their eyes locked, passion igniting around them. She'd promised herself she wouldn't do this again. She didn't need this in her life right now.

Yet . . .

His lips were too tempting, too full and kissable. His expression implored her, her sex wetting with memories of the night before.

She could not look away.

She did not want to.

He swallowed, a look of fight in his eyes. Yet, raw desire

must've won the battle, because rather all of a sudden, his mouth crashed upon hers. He swept her into a needy kiss, his tongue invading her. It swooped along hers, caressing the inner recesses of her mouth.

She kissed him back with all her heart, aware she shouldn't. That she'd promised herself she wouldn't.

She didn't care.

Forbidding herself from him only made the kiss all the more wicked and wonderful. She dampened, her pussy growing juicy and hungry for him. His hand traveled to her left breast, cupping it. He rubbed his thumb across her hard nipple then pinched. Together, they stumbled into the office, their lips locked, their hands petting.

They headed toward the desk. In their furious rush, Carmen's foot caught and she tripped. Stumbling to the floor, she landed on her rump. Hard.

"Ow!" she squealed, though more hurt by the fact they were now both rudely knocked into reality.

He offered her his hand, and she took it. Pulling herself to her feet, she yanked at her skirt and tried to compose herself.

"You had no right to do that." Annoyance bubbled in her, though more at herself than him. "I told you, I don't need—"

Damn.

She didn't know why she yelled at him when she carried half the blame. Easier, she supposed.

She shook her head. She needed to make herself clear, but she didn't have a right to put it all on him. "Look, I'm—"

"No, I'm sorry." Brent cut her off. The tone of his voice surprised her, soft and patient. "I just can't keep my damn hands off you. But I will, from now on. I promise."

"No," Carmen shook her head. "I'm just as guilty. Look, let's just get on with the inspection. But, this shouldn't happen again—we can't allow it. I returned to Rocky Falls to run this place, not get involved. So no more . . . episodes."

"Understood."

Rubbing the blond whiskers shadowing his jaw, he fidgeted as he stood. The rugged yet endearing action made her lower regions tingle. She found herself summing him up once again, everything from the way the dark jeans fit against his skin to the undone buttons at the collar of his flannel. Despite herself, she wondered at his chest, undressing him in her mind. Everything in her wanted him. Wanted another last night. Needed it.

Tightness coiled in her lower regions. Her nipples hardened against the lace of her bra. Could he see them? Was he even looking?

Why did she wish he were?

She noticed the bead of sweat running down the side of his face. It wasn't hot in here, not enough for that.

No, he wanted her, too, just as badly as she wanted him.

Hell, if they both really wanted to they could, right now . . .

And why not?

Hadn't she already discussed this with herself? Enough already!

Brent turned from her, yanking his eyes from hers, and squaring his shoulders. "How about I just run through this inspection and get lost?"

"Sounds good to me," she sighed, disappointed yet thankful.

She led him toward the bar, not missing the way he eyed the office door as they exited. As they walked into the bar, she tried to reason with herself.

Another romp with him wasn't what she needed. Wanted maybe, but needed—no. The sooner this was done, the better. Besides, she felt like crap. Though Brent appeared to have taken a shower and caught some sleep, she hadn't. No doubt she looked like pure hell. "I'm pretty tired."

Flipping out his little notebook, he nodded. "Yeah. Me, too. Long night last night."

Long didn't even begin to describe it. Besides, she could think of better words. Like tantalizing. Heavenly. Erotic.

Shaking, she left him to sit at the bar. She scooted on a stool, feeling as if she were losing her mind. For him.

"Sweetie, ya okay?"

Carmen looked to her left to see Sam, finally returned from lunch. Thank God.

Carmen ran a hand through her hair. "Sam, I need you to look after things."

Sam plopped onto a bar stool next to her, her movements as exaggerated as her style. "Okay, sure. Everything all right?"

"No. Yes. I don't know. Brent's here, doing the inspection. But I'm just too tired."

"What if he fails us?"

"Then he fails us. But he has no reason to. Look, Sam, I'll hardly roll over and take it. But let's face it, there's no chance of me convincing him to do anything but what he wants. If there's any more trouble, I'll just go around him. Don't worry, Sam. Just take care of things."

But for now, she had to escape. And change her underwear.

Stepping into the bathroom, Carmen flipped on the heat then turned on the water. It poured from the faucet, steaming hot. Perfect. All she needed now was bubbles. She found the bottle under the sink, and dumped a very generous amount into the water. Suds frothed, filling the room with the scent of vanilla sugar cookies. Inhaling deeply, she stripped away her clothes, and stepped in.

"Ahhh." Heaven wrapped around her as she leaned back and rested her head against the bath pillow.

Before she had a moment to enjoy it, her cloud nine was grossly invaded. Thoughts of Brent raided her mind, and as hard as she tried to push them away, she couldn't. Her relaxation time disappeared as her body tensed at the thought of him. At what he could do to her, and the places he could take her.

She wanted to go there again, very, very much. Never had she experienced such pleasure. All she could think of was his hands on her, in her, rough and calloused but ever so soft. The way he coaxed her body, teasing her unmercifully before he took for himself.

Her nipples hardened. Her lower body tightened. She clenched against the desire boiling within her. Was Brent really so different, so great? He was just a man, which she hardly needed in her life. Maybe she just needed sexual release. Maybe it wasn't him at all. Maybe it was her. After all, it had been so long since she'd been properly sated. Actually, had she ever been? Not until last night. No one had ever pleased her body like Brent did.

Slowly, she let her hand drift south. Men did it all the time. So did a lot of women. Why shouldn't she? She sunk deep into the water, fondling her breast as she touched herself. Thoughts of Brent danced in her mind, from his muscles to his tight buns. Mimicking the way he'd touched her, she escaped into a fantasy of him, where he touched her, loved her. Not herself.

Forever she searched herself for her release. A heat built within her, filling her, and even tipping over the edge into bliss. But it wasn't the same. No great explosion. The world didn't shatter.

Leaning back, Carmen rested her head against her hand. She was tired, and just plain sick of simply reaching the point of lukewarm release. It never really satisfied her. Not like last night, when she'd touched the stars. It had been like flying away on a magic carpet ride.

But she could never find that in her own hands, or in any other man's. Somehow, deep down she knew it to be true. Call it a woman's intuition. Call it anything you want. But she couldn't doubt the facts. Only he'd been able to turn her inside out with ecstasy. And if she ever wanted to experience that again, she needed him. Brent Sommers was the one, the only one, who could ever complete her happiness.

Heaven help her.

5

Weeks passed by, ever so slowly, each day spent on her toes. Never knowing when or where, but having to face the fact that Brent was everywhere. At the grocery store, the hardware store, even the library on one occasion. Almost every time she left home she ran into him. Just today, she'd gone for lunch at the corner diner, only to be conveniently seated at the table next to him.

Life just wouldn't fall into place. When she'd returned to Rocky Falls, she'd imagined a peaceful life. Quiet and secure with no worries, and least of all no men problems. So much for that.

At least Brent had finally passed her on the inspection. She'd been able to stay open, though she'd spent all week worrying about having the actual doors and signs installed.

Carmen grabbed her keys with a jingle, and stuffed the over-filled ring into her crammed purse. Swinging the straw bag on her shoulder, she headed for the door. What she needed was a break from it all.

Brilliant rays of sunshine greeted her as she stepped out the door. Squinting her eyes, she dug through her bag and found a pair of dark sunglasses. Already her skin warmed under the heat beating on her. The perfect day for what she had planned. She'd been a teenager the last time she went to the falls, and swam in her favorite hole. Hopping on her bike, she pedaled lightheartedly and hummed to herself as she headed out of town.

Brent couldn't believe his eyes. Frozen where he stood, he watched Carmen slowly peel away a tiny striped tank top. Underneath she wore nothing. No bra. No bathing suit top. His mouth watered as he traced his eyes along the length of her graceful back, the delicateness of her shoulders, the smooth deep caramel coloring of her skin. Like a tasty morsel of the most delectable yet forbidden of candies, he craved her.

He hardened against his blue jeans. God help him, he should get lost. But the sight of her shirking off her cutoffs, revealing a tiny black thong paralyzed him. What he wouldn't give to trace the path of that tiny thread of coverage, slicing between her perfectly rounded rear with his fingers. Exploring. Slowly, she bent and removed the panties as well, casting them aside as she stretched in her full glory. Beams of light filtered from between tree limbs, and cast shadows against her body, making her look ethereal as she stood upon his rock next to the cascading falls. Diving gracefully, she splashed into the clear, pristine water.

Taking another step back, Brent's mind pleaded with his feet to leave. This was just like that time in high school, when he'd caught her here. Except this time he would never be able to sit behind a bush and watch. Now he was a man. A man with needs.

He stood there, his cock as hard as steel, watching as she bathed under the falls. The water ran over her slicked hair, dripping down her face and breasts as she reveled in it. She looked like a woman enjoying great pleasure, so natural, and so sexy.

Before he could think things through, his clothes were flying off and he raced to the water's edge. Carmen's beautiful cocoa eyes caught his. The initial shock in them faded into desire as he splashed into the water and swam to her. All he knew was that he wanted her, needed her. Ravenously. Greedily. Savagely. And he'd be denied her no more.

His presence caught her by surprise, but as soon as she saw him, great warmth filled her. Though she'd denied it even to herself, she'd been pining for this very moment. A chance when they couldn't relinquish to reason or reject what they really felt in exchange for rationale. A time when passion could cast aside doubts, ruling both their actions.

Brent swam to her in powerful strokes, his muscles glistening under beads of water as their strength rippled with might. She glided from under the falls and into his waiting arms. Brent's arms wrapped tight around her, pulling their naked bodies together. Her breasts squashed against his rock hard chest, and teasing electric shocks ran through her nipples. They tightened into buds ready for his kissing.

His mouth claimed hers, taking it into a fiery embrace. His lips and tongue were impatient, searching, and teasing her as if he'd been starved. She responded with equal fervor and a battle ensued.

His manhood danced between her legs, the water making the rock hard rod float. It brushed against her, teasing her with its presence. Slowly, she drifted one hand along the length of his body, tracing her nails lightly against his chest. She continued to fight him with her tongue. It was a war he would win and one she'd surrender to. Her attentions were being distracted to elsewhere.

She grasped his cock with her fingers, caressing the long shaft in her hands. It responded with a twitch as Brent groaned low and deep. He sounded savage, like a beast ready to claim his mate.

He pulled her closer, wrapping her legs around him. His demanding hands gripped her fanny and spread her sex open. She held his shaft in a firm grip and used it like a tool against her nether lips. Another desperate growl rumbled from him. Even in the cool water, her body lit on fire. She traced the length of her pussy, then massaged his sex against her clit. The power of control made her greedy.

"No more," Brent commanded. Of course, he was right. She couldn't stand anymore toying much less expect him to. Now was the time. She relinquished her hold, grabbing his powerful shoulders for support. He dived into her with a deep, forceful plunge. Her nails dug into his back as pleasure shocked her body and she released a wild cry.

Holding her hips in an unyielding seize, he drove into her with no patience. Demanded her body to meet his. She matched his hard, fast thrusts.

"I want to see you. I want to memorize your beautiful body while I fuck you," he murmured and pulled her backward by the shoulders. She floated in the water, her legs still wrapped around him. Licking his lips, he held her by the waist and drove into her once again. "Perfect."

Water swished around her as he took her, making her feel as primal and as basic as her incredible surroundings. The hot ecstasy building in her mounted, now at the edge of explosion. His pace slowed and he dived into her with little circles that pushed her to the edge. Screaming out, she convulsed.

Distantly, she became aware of Brent's own orgasm as he shook within her, animalistic sounds grunting from him. When he finished, he pulled her from the water, and held her tightly in his arms.

Slowly, the pleasure-filled high faded, and reality settled in around them. Carmen waited, knowing he'd likely pull away once again, as she should do. Glorious fulfillment encompassed her. Quickly she decided she wouldn't. Not this time. She'd found something, someone, who could take her where she'd always dreamt of going. Her heaven was in his arms. She was tired of running from it.

Brent's hold on her released and she swam away, contemplating her decision. Was she crazy? Perhaps. But better mad than unhappy.

Brent splashed closely behind her as they crossed the pool and climbed on the large, jutting rock.

Squeezing out her hair, Carmen turned from him as she spoke. "I'm not sorry that happened." When he still made no response, she continued. "Like you once said, we're both adults."

"I'm not sure about a relationship between us. We're just not . . ."

"Compatible? Oh, please . . . and a relationship? Is that what you think I want?"

Leave it to a man. When she was thinking fun, he thought in more permanent terms. It should be vice versa, him thinking of her as nothing but a play toy. But here he was, mucking up their fun for fear of complication.

"Brent I have no use for a man in my life except in one area. I don't want you. I want your body. The same as you want mine. If you didn't, you wouldn't have come after me today."

"True." A wicked grin curled on his face as he caught on to what she suggested. "What exactly are you proposing?"

"Some fun." Shrugging, she licked her lips. "A lot of fun.

Nothing more. Nothing less. Whenever we want, for as long as we want. Nothing complicated, certainly no relationship."

Realization washed over his face as he ran his thick fingers through slicked blond hair. A devilish look entered his green eyes. "Bend over then."

"What?"

"You heard me." His voice flat, each of his few spoken words carried a certain challenge.

One she'd be all too anxious to meet.

Maybe he thought she wouldn't. Thought if he pushed her too far she'd relinquish this crazy idea. But little did he realize she wanted to go too far and then some. She'd denied herself the pleasures of this world for far too long. Now she wanted to experience them all, and through him.

Her body tingled in anticipation as she obeyed his command. Never had she felt more exposed, or so deliciously naughty at the prospect. She braced her hands against the cold, wet gradual slope, her fanny posed high in the air. She expected him to drive into her, but that didn't happen. He knelt between her legs, caressing their length with his fingers. Electrical shocks tingled through her at the touch. She clenched in anticipation.

He spread apart her pussy lips with his fingers, his touch gentle yet sensual. Holding them spread, he licked her as if she were a lollipop or an ice cream cone. He tasted her from front to back. Thoroughly. Never had anyone ever explored her so. The new touch made her ignite in a fresh way. She clenched her hands, bracing herself, though positive she'd crumple into a pile at any moment.

Brent's mouth taunted her, sucking and nibbling. Moving back and forth. He alternated with circles, some tiny and forceful, others large and playful. His tongue dove inside of her, flicking. Her body constricted under his attention, building to a point she could hardly bear. "Brent, please."

"Oh, but you taste so good." Sucking on her clit, his fingers explored her, and her nether lips quivered. Her whole body shook, tremors of ecstasy quaking through her.

He stood and drove himself into her, holding tight to her hips as he plunged. He did not pull out, but worked himself in circles, his cock as far inside of her as possible. His consistent depth rubbed at her G-spot, giving her no rest from the orgasm that recently shook her body. An almost unbearable force built in her. Pleasure so intense, so fierce, she couldn't bear it. She wanted to beg him to cease, to grant her mercy. But she knew he'd give none. And as much as she wanted it, she didn't.

Brent reached around, attacking her pussy with his fingers as he fucked her. His big, thick thumb rubbed at her clit unmercifully, making Carmen pant and cry out. She meant to order a cease to this torture, but instead she howled, "More, more."

At his hard, final thrust she shattered. Both her body and her mind experienced heaven as it shook with final release. They both collapsed on top of the rock into each other's arms.

Brent surprised her by laughing, his chuckles like that of a teenage boy, light and happy. As if he hadn't a single care in the world. His humor was contagious and she joined him. She giggled until it hurt.

"That was great, Brent," she murmured and moved closer to him. He made no response, except to pull her into his arms and cuddle her against his chest. "By the way, thanks for passing me."

He grunted. "Yeah, you owe me big for that."

"Oh, no, you don't!"

He laughed. "I know. I just thought I might get a blow job out of you."

"Ass." She gave him a playful shove. "You'll probably get one anyway."

He made no response, except to pull her into his arms and cuddle her against his chest. Everything between them quieted, a calm settling in.

There wasn't any telling how long they lay together, the whooshing sound of the falls blended with the sweet melody of birds—a peaceful lullaby to them. Occasionally, the crunch of a nearby deer or skittering squirrel intermingled with nature's song. Beams of sun peered through the trees, warming their naked bodies.

Such peace surrounded them she dared not move. At this very moment she felt better than she could ever remember in her whole life. Tranquil. Content. Complete.

A shame it could not last forever. In time, the chirping of crickets warned of nightfall. Soon she'd have to get home. If only she could convince herself to budge.

Brent made the first move. He stood, stretching his lithe naked body and then he dove into the water. No good-bye, no kiss until next time. Could it be that he'd already tired of her? Of their plan?

Feeling like a desperate fool, Carmen called after him. "Next Monday, Brent. Same time, same place."

For several moments he gave no response as he swam toward his clothing, but then he paused and turned to her. "That was nothing, Carmen. You're playing with fire. I hope you're ready."

"Oh, yeah?"

Anticipation at the promise raced through her. She watched him swim to the tiny rocky beach, and bend to gather his clothes. The muscles in his powerful legs pulled, tightening into ripples of strength. His rear retained its rock solid shape. She decided it was indeed the cutest thing about him.

Through and through, Brent was as good looking as they could come. No wonder she wanted him so much.

If only she could get him in those damned suspenders.

Once again, Carmen licked her tongue along her teeth, her hands unconsciously falling to her hips. God help her, she couldn't wait until next Monday.

Jeans on, Brent walked away, stopping only once to shout a final warning. "Next time I won't be nearly as nice."

6

Thank goodness. His truck was parked under the old twisted oak tree next to the path leading to the falls. A strange relief flooded through her, releasing the tension that had built in her all week. With each passing day, she'd been more and more sure he wouldn't come. That he didn't really want to do this. And though she swore to herself she didn't care, it had kept her on tippy toes all week.

Riding her bike on the trail until it became too bumpy and rocky to continue, she ditched it against a baby pine. She continued on foot, gingerly making her way through the sticker bushes that grew in over the years. Maybe Brent would trim them.

Ouch! One stuck her, drawing a droplet of ruby-red blood from her forefinger. She bit back a curse on the tip of her tongue and continued as quietly as possible. She didn't want him alerted to her presence. Not yet at least. Let him be surprised, like she'd been the last time.

The falls could be heard before being seen, the sound of gushing water against rocks, a soft roar. Soon the woods opened to the clearing, where a rocky landscape surrounded the pool of water at the bottom of the cataract.

Her quiet was well rewarded. Unaware of her, Brent swam in the water's depths. Wetness sleeked his blond hair from his face, accenting her view of his strong features. Even from a distance his eyes glowed with green depth. His lips teased her with notions of what they could do. He moved under the falls. The cascading water poured over him as he stretched. The movement tightened every muscle in his glistening chest, pulling taut his pectorals and six-pack stomach. If only he would turn around . . . complete the show.

But she couldn't wait until then. Seeing him only made her impatient. A week of pent up passion bubbled in her. She wasted no time tearing off her clothes and diving into the pristine pool. Though she wanted desperately to rush into his arms, she didn't swim to him. If he desired her, he could catch her.

"Nanny, nanny, boo boo," she taunted. "If you want it, come and get it."

Brent took the bait and gave chase as she half swam, half ran from him. By any means, she was no match for him, especially not when laughter spoilt her ability to flee.

Brent pursued her with a look of pure determination. And won. He caught her in a tight embrace, crushing his lips upon hers. Demanding, the kiss smashed her with a desperate passion.

One thing was clear. Brent meant business. She laid her head in the water, all too happy to enjoy his eagerness, even the slight pinch of pain that came from such an intense, furious appraisal. His roughness lit a deep fire in her, one that secretly burned for domination.

Leaving her breathless, he released her. "I'm in no mood for games."

"Too bad for one of us, huh?" she teased, pushing away from him in the water.

"Don't toy with me, hellcat." False warning rang in his voice. "Or what? What will you do about it?" She continued to float in the water, moving farther and farther from his grasp.

He disappeared under its depths, catching her by surprise as he appeared under her. In one swift movement he threw her over his shoulder and headed toward their rock. "I'll teach you a lesson you'll never forget, that's what I'll do about it."

One of his hands cupped her rear, and held her in place. When she wiggled in response to him, determined to act the bad girl, he squeezed hard. His thumb pressed hard into her, pushing into an area never entered before. The touch was new to Carmen, as was the intense feeling that flooded her lower stomach. He laid her on the rock and she scooted away by natural inclination.

"Don't you move another inch," he growled as he pulled himself from the water.

Of course, Carmen deliberately ignored him. His hand flashed out, gripping her by the ankle. "Keep toying with me."

"Just try and stop me," she purred.

Stop her he did. His fingers grasped her nipples, pinching them tightly as he pushed her against the slab of cold granite. He attacked her pussy, spreading her lips and working her clit with his fingers. Pulling at it slightly, he used his other hand to caress her pussy. Moaning, she arched her hips for more.

And more he gave, though she never expected it. His finger pressed into her anus. With his other hand, he inserted three fingers into her pussy. She screamed at the touch, shocked by the intense pleasure of it.

His fingers gave her no mercy. They worked hard to drive her to a point of insanity. They slid in and out, playing with her. Sometimes he went deep. Other times he simply teased her. The torture made her moan and writhe as shocks of intensity coursed through her. Her breasts burned with heat, her lower body tingling.

He withdrew his fingers, and pulled her hips to him. He drove into her with his rock hard cock. Her body gushed with pleasure, nearly spilling over as he, once again, inserted his finger into her anus. She held strong, determined to enjoy this moment to the max.

He was greedy as he rammed into her body with no mercy. She met his thrusts with her own, slamming herself against him harder and harder. The sound of skin meeting skin smacked through the air amongst her cries.

"Are you ready for me?" he half asked, half moaned.

"I'm going to come soon. Too soon," she panted. "Oh, God, yes. Give it to me."

"Good." With that, his movements ceased and he had her by the hips once again, pushing her around. "On all fours."

His order filled her with a naughty anticipation. She told herself to refuse to obey. Let him make her. That would be more fun.

Her dominant lover quickly caught on to her game. Grabbing her tightly, he pushed her into place and slapped her rear with his open hand. She jumped at the sting, and naturally moved away. He grabbed hold of her, locking his hands tightly around her hips. He pulled her ass against his manhood. It poked and prodded slightly before he gently pushed into her and thrust. It hurt for a moment, but faded as he reached around and explored her pussy with his fingers.

Gradually he worked himself deeper into her, all the while fucking her with his fingers. Her pussy clenched against him, her body threatening to give in to ecstasy at any time.

Deft fingers worked her clit in hard, tiny circles. The pressure overcame her, sending her off the edge. Her back arched as she cried out, shaking as she grasped at the rock's cold surface for anything, something, to steady herself with.

"Oh, oh," she panted, begging for what she did not know. Everything went white for a moment. She swam in a sweet oblivion. Rode on her magic carpet.

Brent's own violent climax brought her from her fog. He shook as he grabbed at her hips, and flooded her with his seed.

Brent stood and dived into the water, abandoning her to the rock. Rolling, she sat up, breathless. She watched as Brent let the cascades flow over him.

The way he looked under the water was too good to pass on.

Standing, she stretched and slid into the water. It's coolness wrapped around her as she stroked toward him. Diving under, she popped up right in front of him.

She swiped the water from her eyes, flashing him a smile.

He grunted a surprised laugh, and grabbed her. "Come here."

He drew her against his chest, holding her tight. She relished the warmth, the way her bare chest pressed against his muscles. The water churned and bubbled around them, creating sensations against her skin.

She wrapped her arms around him, letting her finger trail across his spine. "You seem tense today. Serious."

"It's been a long week."

"A bad one?"

"Well, that depends on how you look at it." He tangled his hands in her hair, kissing her along her neck. "In everything I did, every moment, every second, all I thought of was you. Today. I'm afraid meeting on Mondays isn't enough."

"Oh?" She raised her brows. "Hmmm . . ."

He floated, pulling her toward the dripping rocky wall. From a small ledge, he grabbed a bar of green soap.

"You come prepared."

His eyes frisked her. "More than you know."

How could it be possible, after the climax she'd just experienced, for her body to light on fire again so quickly? It beguiled her. Just the thought of him washing her seduced her. . . .

She wanted that soap to clean every inch of her body. Every inch.

"Mmm, what can that mean?"

He ran the soap across her breasts, circling her hardened areolas. Burning desire lit her lower regions, her clit throbbing. Slowly he slid the bar south, leaving a soapy trail behind.

The suds slid down her belly, and around to her back once again. He massaged her as he cleansed it, gradually working farther and farther south. He slipped between her rear, over her anus, to her throbbing, hungry pussy. She moaned and arched, so hot for him she could no longer relax and enjoy it.

"Mondays aren't enough," she moaned. "Not nearly enough."

His mouth suckled her clean skin, working down to her collarbone. "Then we forget the rules?"

"No. Mondays are a must. But whenever else, whatever else, hey, we're adults, right?"

"Right . . ."

His hardened cock danced between her legs, and she pressed against it. How she wanted him in her. "You know, I still haven't had you in uniform. . . . I want a fireman to put out my fire."

"Tomorrow," he promised, lifting her. "Tomorrow."

Cradling her in his arms, he carried her to the water's edge. "I'm hungry. How about you?"

"Starved. What's to eat?"

"You." Depositing her on their rock, he climbed from the water and stood before her, gloriously naked and dripping wet. His weathered skin, just slightly tan, glistened. The shine accented shadows across his muscled body and she longed to run her hands through the tiny curly blond hairs across his chest.

She gulped, half from the sight of him and half from his answer. What could he mean? Anticipation of the worst kind washed through her, making her skin tingle in excitement as he reached into the basket.

First he pulled out a blanket and spread it with the simple flick of his wrist. "Lie down."

Licking her lips, she obeyed, all too anxious to see what

other treasures the basket held. Out came a can of whipped cream, followed by strawberries and a jar of cherries. Chocolate syrup. A banana.

And last, but not least, an expensive bottle of white wine, along with two glasses. Popping the cork, he filled only one then drank it in one full swoop.

"Thirsty?" he asked, as he refilled the glass and brought it to her lips. He tipped it into her mouth and the sweetly bitter liquid flowed over her tongue. Trails of it ran from the corner of her mouth, and down her neck as Brent chased to catch them with his tongue. When he'd licked away the spillage, he tilted the glass and poured a liquid path between her breasts, over each nipple and into her belly button. Slowly he suckled and drank it away as well.

Peeling the banana, he took the tip of it and ran it along her mouth sensually. In the spirit of things, she attacked the banana with her tongue as he pushed it into her mouth. Eagerly, she gave head to the fruit, all too aware of what the display did to Brent as well as herself. His long thick cock jutted forward, standing ready for its own attention. Biting off the banana, she swallowed and went for him.

But Brent pulled away, taking the remainder of the banana with him. She gasped as he positioned himself between her legs and used the fruit on her nether lips the same way he had on her mouth. First, he softly teased her with it and then he pressed it just inside of her. He only inserted it far enough into her to make her pulse for more. Wanton needs made her whole lower region unbearably hot and tight for him.

Next, he opened the cream, first squirting it around her nipples, then down her belly and lastly covering her sex. The coolness of it tortured her, making her sizzle with desire. He topped each whipped cream mountain upon her breasts with a cherry, as well as on her lower region. Then he poured chocolate syrup over her, swirling the syrup all across her body.

He'd finished his artwork, but the true torment had not even begun. Yet, Carmen was so alive for him she could hardly bear it. It took everything in her to lie still and wait for more. She tingled so intensely from her thighs to her breasts it felt more like electrical currents shocking her body.

"Time to eat," Brent announced as he gathered several strawberries. Feeding her one, he used it to tease her lips as he allowed her tiny bites. The remaining strawberries he used to dip in the dessert covering her body, just barely brushing her skin with the red fruit.

When he'd eaten every last one, he went for the banana. He bit it down, nearly to where he'd inserted it. With tantalizing licks and strokes of the tongue, he consumed her and the remaining dessert. He ate his meal slowly, enjoying each taste and the fact that she was writhing under him. Her hips arched against his appraisal as she cried and begged for both more and for him to cease.

All she needed was a nudge and she'd fall over the edge. As if he sensed the fact, Brent went for the remaining banana, slowly pulling it from her with his teeth. The sensation pushed her to the limit and she went flying to cloud nine in a blinding swirl of ecstasy.

7

A smile as wide as her happiness spread across her face as she hummed and finished the last of the bookkeeping. Time only made business flourish, and with the influx of tourists in the area for the up and coming end of summer events in town, she'd done great this week.

Clicking off the computer, she stood and stretched. Life couldn't be better right now, though this winter she might be singing another tune. There wouldn't be as much business, and there certainly wouldn't be any more swimming at the falls.

She supposed they'd just have to find another private spot, because no way would she give up their meetings. This past month she'd had the best sex of her life. But not only that, she enjoyed Brent's company. After their lovemaking sessions, they'd developed a habit of talking. Never about themselves, or anything important. Just chitchatting. The time they spent together was so intense, and yet so casual.

A look at the clock made her realize it was only lunchtime, and she'd finished what she needed to accomplish for the day. A rarity, and one she'd just have to take advantage of.

The firefighter calendar hanging on her corkboard caught her eyes. Licking her lips, she stared at the three hot men leaning against the fire truck. Wearing only tight jeans, one held a yellow hat, another a big hose, and another an axe. All of them rippled with muscles and sexuality.

If only she had three of Brent.

Her lower regions heated, desire grabbing her psyche. She realized Brent was working today, but that made it all the more tempting. They'd been so *busy*. She'd yet to see him in his territory.

Would stopping by be okay? Surely no one would mind, especially not if she brought lunch.

Grabbing her purse, she headed out the door, jumped in her car, and sped off. Her body itched for satisfaction, making her drive a little faster than she should.

Surely Brent could take off a little time.

Her lips curved in a wicked smile as she pictured him in her mind, wondering what he might be wearing. After all, she was headed over to the fire hall with a little hope of catching him in those yellow pants and red suspenders.

He'd better be.

Pulling into Dana's Fast and Fresh Chicken, she drove to the first window and placed her order. "One bucket of extra crispy chicken, two orders of potato wedges, and an extra-large Coke please."

"Nine eighty-eight. Pull around please."

She pulled to the next window, and waited, opening her wallet. She paid, waited for their lunch, and then sped off. Within a few minutes she pulled into the station. One fire truck was parked around the rear, two guys washing it with large brushes.

Not Brent though.

Shoot, she'd have to look for him. A nervous bubble tingled in her stomach as she approached the men. She hoped she wasn't bothering anyone by coming here.

The closer she got, the more she noticed the men. The way their T-shirts and blue jeans clung to them, wet from the water they squirted from the hose. The way their muscles flexed as they washed. She didn't even look at their faces. She didn't want to. Their bodies were h-o-t.

Yet, despite her attraction, she experienced no rush. No tingle down her spine or warming. They weren't Brent.

Right then and there she realized she was falling for him. And she didn't mind a bit. Her reasons for not wanting a relationship had dissolved, overpowered by the compatibility. Physically, emotionally, they clicked.

She nodded a smile, and held the chicken in front of her as a peace offering. "Hi. I'm looking for Brent. Is he here?"

"Depends." The taller one flashed her a smile. "Is that chicken for us?"

She laughed. "I'm Carmen, by the way, and yes, it can be. If you get me Brent."

"All right, Carmen. Fair warning from Mack—Brent is a terrible cook. Remember that before you decide to marry him." He chuckled, his eyes sparkling with fun. "You'll have to feed us all when it's his shift to cook. Let's go, Tom."

Tom dropped the hose and snatched the bucket from her. Mack grabbed one piece of chicken, then another.

She gave a light laugh as they bickered about a chicken leg and headed off. "I'll keep that in mind."

They disappeared through the door next to the bay, and seconds later the buzz of the door slowly shutting filled the air.

Brent pulled on a pair of yellow turn out pants over his jeans then put on a fire helmet. Reaching for a pair of red suspenders, he clipped them to his pants. Though many people thought it, firefighters didn't always wear red suspenders. But he'd bought them especially for Carmen. They were part of her fantasy, and he wanted to give her that.

He'd arrived from training some cadets this morning and had just finished showering when Tom had announced she was here. He could believe it. His shift was over. Her timing was perfect.

How many times had she mentioned her firefighter fantasy? Quite a few . . .

He'd been meaning to indulge her for some time. Now, he would.

Finished dressing, he took wide strides outside. She leaned against the fire truck, her brown hair cascading around her shoulders. The hardened buds of her nipples jutted, visible under the light blouse she wore.

Damn, he wished he had a camera. She looked sexier than ever. Lately she'd had a glow, an aura about her. He hoped it was because she was enjoying herself as much as him. His cock twitched, ready to come to life.

"Hi." She raised her brows, flashing him a smile. "Wow."

"Hey."

He leaned against the truck, placing his hand above her head. "What's up, sugar?"

He tangled her hair around his finger, relishing its silky feel.

She looked at him with huge, needy brown eyes. "I'm on fire, baby. I need a fireman to put out my fire."

He couldn't help but laugh as he lifted her. "I better hurry then. Wouldn't want you to burn."

He threw open the rear door to the fire truck, lifting her into it. She scooted back, lying on the slim bench. She propped up a leg, and her skirt hung open, allowing him a view of her silky black underwear.

Damn.

His cock stiffened, a surge of lust searing through him. He needed to have her. Now. He didn't give a crap if they were in public, in a company fire truck at that. The naughtiness of it thrilled him.

Climbing inside, he slammed the door shut.

Wet desire dripped between her legs. She couldn't believe it. Her little fantasy was reality, and even better. They were going to do it in a fire truck?

Yes!

She began to unbutton her shirt as he climbed over her. Propping himself with one knee, he brought his mouth to the exposed skin on her chest. He suckled and kissed at her as she opened for him. His lips trailed along the edge of her bra. He slipped his tongue under the silky fabric, darting for her nipple. He brushed the hardened bud, driving her crazy. She needed more.

She slipped the straps off her shoulders, scooting the bra to her waist. His mouth claimed her left breast, licking around her areola. She arched, flooded by desire.

He trailed his kisses south, to the rim of her skirt. The edge of his helmet caressed her skin, sending excited tingles through her.

His hands slid up her skirt, pulling down her panties. He tossed them aside, rubbing along her thighs. His fingers explored her lower regions, toying with her clit. The nub pulsed, pleasure radiating through her. She arched her hips for him, inviting more. With two fingers he plunged inside her, then three, then four.

She cried out, bucking against him as he moved back and forth. She wanted more than this!

"Brent, please!" she moaned, pushing her hips against his hand. "More."

He chuckled. "Say it."

"Say what?"

"You know . . ."

She could only think of one thing fitting. "Oh, Brent, put out my fire. Please!"

A pleased look crossed his face as he slid his hand free. Unbuttoning the thick, mustard-colored pants, he freed his cock and positioned himself between her legs. She grabbed onto the suspenders, drawing him to her. With one hard thrust, he buried himself inside her.

He fucked her so fast and hard she swore he was shaking the fire engine. She screamed, meeting his demands. Ecstasy wrapped around her, threatening to burst at any moment.

He plunged deep within her, hitting her G-spot. Moaning, she tightened her lower muscles around him. He slowed, continued to hit the special area.

She exploded into an orgasm, coming in a series of quick convulsions around his cock. He moaned, diving deep and jerked, spilling himself inside her.

Collapsing on top of her, he shook his head and laughed. "I can't believe we did this."

"You're a wild one, fireman."

"Me? You're insatiable."

"Only when it comes to you, Brent. Only when it comes to you."

He nodded, pausing. He lifted himself off her, kneeling beside her. He frowned, seriousness contorting his face. "I've been thinking. About us."

"Us?"

She stilled. He'd said it so soberly. Was he going to end it?

She didn't want to end it. If anything, she wanted more.

With each passing day that feeling in her had grown, despite how hard she had tried to reason it away. Now, no amount of rationale could change her mind.

Today she'd realized it full force. She was ready for another relationship. She wanted Brent in her life.

She waited for his answer, but the wail of a siren cut through the air.

His eyes jumped. "Shit." He leapt to his feet, buttoning his pants. "Get out of here. Fast."

Her heart skipped a beat then leapt into a race. She rushed to obey him, flinging down her skirt, yet her mind held back. Confusion boggled Carmen.

Had they been caught? What was he going to say?

"What . . . ?"

He cut her off before she could finish.

"There's a fire, Carmen!" Urgency flared in his tone. "Hurry up."

Shoot! Again the need to rush burst through her. She worked the buttons on her blouse, her fingers fumbling. He did not wait for her as he flung open the door, bounding out it.

A wave of men's laughter burst through the air, mingled with the loud howl of the warning siren. A moment later, it silenced, replaced by clapping. Hooting.

She looked up, finding a crowd of six or so men shrieking in hilarity.

They'd been caught.

Carmen clamped her shirt closed with her fist, embarrassment heating her. She didn't know what to say. To do. Never had she been stuck in such a situation before.

If Brent was going to break up with her before, he'd really do it now.

Brent rubbed his jaw as if he'd been hit.

"There's no fire, huh?" Deep and gruff, his voice coated with humored annoyance.

"No," one of the firemen answered. "Except in that truck."

More sniggers followed, continued by, "Nice suspenders!"

Carmen prayed that meant it was all being taken in good humor. She'd hate to see him in trouble because of her fantasy.

"Shit." Brent shook his head. "You guys . . ."

Suddenly, he whirled around, jumped in the truck, and slammed the door shut.

"Forget them." He shook his head. "They've had their fun; hell, they'll have it for the next two weeks—if I'm lucky. But, there's something I want to say to you."

Carmen chuckled, listening to the sound of their ragging outside. "Easier said than done."

"About what I was saying . . ." He ran a hand along his jaw, and imploring her with his eyes to listen.

Nervousness bubbled in her. "Yes?"

"I want us to start getting to know each other."

Relief rushed through her, washing away the tension. "Are you kidding me?"

"No." He frowned, looking doubtful himself. "I just thought maybe . . ."

His voice trailed off, leaving her with the obvious knowledge that he was afraid she'd say no. He really did want this.

He wasn't just talking about sex anymore. He really wanted to be *with* her. A bubble welled inside of her, filling her with both excitement and happiness.

"Oh, yes. Hell, yes," she answered.

A smile beamed on his face. He bent, and pulled her close to him. She nuzzled in his chest and enjoyed his warmth. Wrapped in his embrace, she realized she'd belonged there all along. If only she'd known years ago, her prince charming had laid within the same man who'd called her Pinky and given her wedgies. Sometimes life just isn't what you expect, and the man of your dreams is the last person you'd imagine.

He wrapped his fingers in her hair, drawing her close to him. Together, they relished in the new closeness between them.

He kissed her forehead. "What do you say we start tonight? The carnival is in town, we could go, then afterward . . ."

She lifted a brow. "You'll wear your suspenders?"

"The suspenders *and* the hat."

"It's a deal," she promised with a quick kiss.

Brent leaned in, sweeping her into a sweet kiss. His lips touched hers with passion. Slowly, he slipped his tongue along hers. She matched his appraisal, increasing the kiss from nice to naughty. Fire blazed its way through her body, one he'd need to put out. Good thing he was a professional.

Turn the page for a look at
P.J. Mellor's sizzling new book,
GIVE ME MORE,
coming soon from Aphrodisia!

1

Eric gave a roar of completion and collapsed on her. Within seconds, her oxygen deprived lungs began to protest. His chest hair tickled her nose.

Allowing him to come home with her again was a mistake on so many levels. She wedged both hands against his clammy, Aramis scented skin and shoved.

He grunted and drooled on her neck.

"Eric," Maggie Hamilton said against his clavicle, resisting the temptation to close her teeth around the offending bone. "Get off!"

His chuckle rumbled his chest and set her teeth on edge. "Just did, Babe."

Pig. "Eric, I can't breathe. Move!" What possessed her to let him come home with her? She shoved again and he rolled off to lay, spread eagle, next to her. She glanced at the poster of the cruise ship, docked at an exotic island port, tacked to her wall for inspiration, then over at Eric's Mr. Happy, which looked decidedly droopy. "It's time for you to leave."

"Aw, Babe, don't say that." He turned on his side, one heavy arm crushing her ribs in an effort to draw her closer.

Plop! Mr. Happy slapped against her thigh like a dead snake. She eased away from the offending member.

"Really, you should leave." She pointed the toes of one foot toward the floor, gripping the edge of the mattress for leverage.

Eric grumbled something and rolled off to stand on the other side of the bed. He scratched his butt and shuffled toward the bathroom.

"And shut the door, this time, please." That was definitely something she did not want to view.

She swung to her feet and pulled on her floral silk robe, then frowned at her reflection in the wardrobe mirror. Too sexy-mussed.

With a quick look at the still-closed door, she rummaged in the dresser. She'd just pulled on her oversized University of Michigan sweatshirt, tugging it to her knees, when Eric walked out.

He wasn't all that bad looking, if you liked the dumb jock persona. Tall and heavily muscled, his dark hair spiked and clothing rumpled, there were many women who might find him attractive. She looked at his heavy lidded eyes and suppressed a shudder. Attractive only if you went for the Neanderthal look.

She didn't. Not anymore. Yet, after swearing she'd never allow Eric into her home, let alone her bed, again, here he was. She had to start being more assertive.

"So, what time should I be here tomorrow to take you to the dock?" He scratched his belly through the gaping fly of his jeans. At least she hoped it was his belly. "Babe," he said, walking toward her, "I'm telling you, I think a singles cruise is a really bogus idea."

She took a step back, then side-stepped toward the open bedroom door. "Well, I don't. And you don't have to take me. I made other arrangements."

"But, Babe, who's gonna kiss you good-bye?" He spread his arms, palms up in supplication.

Not you. Anyone but you. Of course, she couldn't say that. Her mother had taught her to never be rude. "Karyl said she'd take me." She ushered him toward the door.

In a flash, he turned and closed his arms around her. He smelled of aftershave, beer and sex. On him, not a winning combination.

Barreling her arms to break his embrace, she stepped back and reached to open the door. "I'll see you in a few weeks."

"Babe! How long is this damn cruise?"

Not nearly long enough. But she couldn't say that either. "I'm not really sure," she lied. "I'll call you when I get back." *Yeah, why don't you hold your breath on that one.*

His beard-stubbled face leaned close to her, intent clear in his bloodshot, mud brown eyes.

A quick side-step took her out of target range. She pushed him out the door and closed it.

He pounded on the solid imitation wood. "Babe!" *Bang, bang.* "Open the door!" *Bang, bang, bang.* "Aren't you even gonna to kiss me good-bye?"

"No!" she yelled, sliding the chain home.

"But, Babe!" His voice carried through the door.

She strode to the bathroom and stripped, then stood under the tepid spray, waiting for the hot water.

"Babe," she growled in a mocking voice, grabbing the shampoo and squirting a liberal amount into her palm.

She lathered her short hair with a vengeance, determined to wash away every trace of Eric. Shampoo foam ran everywhere. It oozed down her face, slithered over her shoulders, slid over her hips and sluiced down both legs to tickle her toes. Way too much shampoo.

"I'm never going to get this rinsed out." She rinsed until her arms ached. Her hair still felt slick to her questing fingers.

"Babe," she growled again, twisting the controls off and jerking a towel from the duct-taped towel bar.

Then reality hit her. . . . Eric didn't remember her name.

After stripping the sheets and starting the washer, she remade the bed and fell in. Exhausted, she should've been instantly in dreamland. But no. Instead, she tossed and turned. Her back began aching. Did she remember to run the dishwasher?

With a sigh, she tossed the covers back and stomped into the tiny kitchen. Her dishwasher had two cycles—on and off. While it appeared to be off, steam oozing from the top told her she'd turned it on.

Back in bed, comfort and, therefore, sleep eluded her. Maybe she should invest in a new mattress when she came home. Did she remember to pack her red dress?

Feet again met carpet, neatly side-stepping the brick Eric had used months ago to "temporarily" fix the leg of her bed.

Grunting with effort, she dragged her heavy suitcase over and plopped it onto the bed. There it was. The red dress was right on top.

The sound of her suitcase zipper closing filled the silent apartment. She dragged it back to the closet.

"I wonder if I can fit in an extra bikini? It shouldn't take up too much space."

On tip-toe, she felt along the top shelf of her closet. No bikini, but she found a box she didn't remember having up there.

Pulling it down, she walked closer to the light.

She gasped, then glanced guiltily around.

"No one's here, dummy." She stroked a finger down the amazingly realistic plastic. Then gave the bulbous tip a little squeeze. Wow. It even felt semi-real.

Mystery Lover Model 4099. A present from Karyl, for her

birthday last year, the vibrator had caused raucous laughter and comments from her friends when she'd opened it.

She'd never even tried it out.

She glanced around, then checked the locks on her door, just to make sure.

Walking slowly back to her bed, she untied her robe, her gaze never leaving the gleaming phallus where it lay nestled in purple velvet, surrounded by an impressive assortment of flavored body gels.

"Let's try raspberry." She opened the tiny pot and dipped the tip of her little finger in, then sucked off the sweet concoction. Not bad.

Dipping her index finger this time, she slathered the gel all around the top of the vibrator, then swirled her tongue around it until every speck of gel disappeared.

Next, she finger painted the entire length of the plastic shaft, squeezing her legs together to calm the sudden restlessness she felt.

Dropping her robe, she climbed up on her bed to lie on her back, the vibrator held high above her.

"Open the hanger," she said on a giggle, remembering childhood games. "V-v-room." She guided her private missile in a gliding circle, then to her open mouth, taking as much in as she could without gagging.

After a while, the ache between her legs became harder to ignore.

The wet tip of the vibrator cooled her skin where she dragged it between her bare breasts, down her abdomen until she reached the point that wept her need.

A few circles around her clitoris had her moving on the sheets, wadded against her back.

No point in letting the gel go to waste.

She held the vibrator between her thighs and reached for another little pot. Strawberry.

She coated the entire shaft, swirling her tongue and fingertip around the top, imagining herself on her singles cruise, a hot island breeze bathing her bare skin while she licked and sucked one of the many lovers who existed solely for her sexual gratification.

It wasn't enough. How did she turn the dumb thing on? It was allegedly the top of the line of vibrators—Karyl spared no expense when it came to embarrassing her.

The phone rang. Maggie screamed, automatically squeezing the vibrator.

Slick with gel, it shot from her fist like it was coming out of a rocket launcher and scored a direct hit on her grandmother's china lamp, plunging the room into darkness.

The phone rang again.

With a last look at the remains of her lamp, she reached for the cordless phone on the floor.

"What took so long?" Karyl's voice echoed from the speaker. "Oh, don't tell me you actually took pity on that throwback and let him spend the night!"

"No, of course not." Maggie glanced around the room as though her friend could actually see the contrary evidence—which was no doubt on her bathroom floor somewhere. Eric never could seem to hit the trash can.

Karyl let out an exaggerated relieved sigh. "Thank You, Lord. So . . . what are you doing? I know you're all packed. Mags? You sound like you're breathing hard. What's going on?"

"What makes you think anything's going on?" She gave a feeble laugh.

"Because I've known you since kindergarten and I know when you're hiding something. Now . . . what?"

"Vibrator," Maggie managed to mumble.

"What? Is there something wrong with your refrigerator? I can't hear you. Are you talking into the wrong end of the phone again?"

"I said," she almost shouted, "I was just fooling around with the vibrator you gave me."

"You were?"

"Don't sound so pleased. I can't even figure out how to turn the dumb thing on." She gave a bark of laughter. "Story of my life." She walked to pick the *dumb thing* up and returned to sit on the side of the mattress.

"Mags, it's state-of-the-art. There isn't a switch."

"But how do you—"

"See the little fake testicles at the base?"

Maggie's eyes widened. "I wouldn't exactly call them little." She ran her palm over them in an idle caress, tracing the flowing script of the gold ML at the base with her fingertip.

Karyl laughed. "Whatever. When you're using it, you, um, sort of grip the balls and squeeze them together. The tighter you squeeze, the stronger the vibration."

Maggie gave an experimental squeeze. The vibrator emanated a low buzzing sound, vibrating the hand holding the shaft. "Oh!" She gave a shriek of laughter and dropped it to the floor.

"I'll let you experiment for a while," Karyl said, a smile in her voice. "I'll be there tomorrow morning by no later than eight. You already printed up your boarding pass and everything you need, didn't you?"

"Yes, I—"

"Great! See you tomorrow." Karyl hung up.

Maggie depressed the off button and laid the phone on the nightstand, then picked up the vibrator.

It wouldn't hurt to try it. After all, it had been a gift. It would be rude to never use it.

The rounded tip teased her opening. She looked down and wondered how it would ever fit.

The gel was cool against her labia, but quickly warmed as it came in contact with her internal heat. She stretched to accommodate the girth of the vibrator.

To her surprise, it slid in to the hilt quite smoothly. Maybe the gel helped. She tightened internal muscles. ML—or Mel, as she nicknamed it—slid back out to her waiting hand. Bereft, she glided Mel back in. In. Out. In. Out.

Close. She was so close.

Panting, she reached a shaking hand down and squeezed the rubber testicles.

And screamed when the foreign object within seemed to take on a life of its own.

When she was able to relax a bit, the vibration worked its magic, setting off tingles deep within. Her muscles began to vibrate. Internal lubrication made Mel slippery. She squeezed the testicles in her fist, unable to gasp more than shallow pants of air. Her heart thundered, pounding as though it would rip from her chest.

Her next scream had nothing to do with surprise as wave after wave of pleasure washed over her, drowning her in sensation.

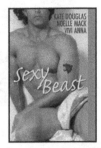 

CPSIA information can be obtained
at www.ICGtesting.com
Printed in the USA
LVHW051155260423
745298LV00003B/319